Marines began pouring
another, unsure where to g
Witzko spotted Kasug
wide, and his face drained

"It's . . . it's klicks, sir," Kasuga blurted out. "*Klicks* are boiling out of the ground back there!"

In praise of Roland Green's works

On *Tale of the Comet*

"It's always a chancy proposition mixing SF and fantasy in one package, and Roland Green has done just that in this adventure story . . . an entertaining, thoughtfully conceived blend of the genres."

—*Science Fiction Chronicle*

On *The Wayward Knights*

"Green . . . provides a . . . unified story about an aging knight who is called upon for one final effort accompanied by a group of his one-time followers. His tone is more serious, his adversaries more credible and the plotting is tight and well constructed."

—*Science Fiction Chronicle*

THE HARBINGER TRILOGY

DIANE DUANE

VOLUME ONE:

STARRISE AT CORRIVALE

VOLUME TWO:

STORM AT ELDALA

(March 1999)

VOLUME THREE:

NIGHTFALL AT ALGEMRON

(October 1999)

STARFALL

EDITED BY MARTIN H. GREENBERG

(April 1999)

ZERO POINT

RICHARD BAKER

(June 1999)

THE SILENCE BETWEEN THE STARS

DENISE VITOLA

(August 1999)

ON THE VERGE

roland green

Eliot Ness had his Untouchables. This book is dedicated to my Indispensables:

Brian Thomsen, for bringing me into the TSR flock in the beginning.

Margaret Weis and Tracy Hickman, for their splendid DRAGONLANCE® universe in which I cut my teeth.

Bill Slavicsek and Phil Athans, for the literary midwifing of the STAR*DRIVE® universe.

Bill Slavicsek, Richard Baker, and David Eckelberry for fine game designing. Thanks for all the ships and the weren.

Mark Sehestedt, for conscientious line editing above and beyond the call of duty.

Mary Kirchoff, for admirable patience with my disgraceful delays, and for tearing out her own hair instead of mine.

Peter Archer, for making payments move like cheetahs instead of sloths.

Neal Barrett, Jr., for a helping hand, a word processor, and storytelling talent at a vital moment.

There must be other Indispensables who are at the moment also Invisibles, but I am grateful to you also.

ON THE VERGE

Distributed to the book trade in the United States by Random House, Inc. and in Canada by Random House of Canada, Ltd.

Distributed to the hobby, toy, and comic trade in the United States and Canada by regional distributors.

Distributed worldwide by Wizards of the Coast, Inc. and regional distributors.

Cover Art by Brom
First Printing: December 1998
Library of Congress Catalog Card Number: 97-062385

9 8 7 6 5 4 3 2 1

ISBN: 0-7869-1191-3

2814XXX1501

U.S., CANADA,
ASIA, PACIFIC, & LATIN AMERICA
Wizards of the Coast, Inc.
P.O. Box 707
Renton, WA 98057-0707
+1-800-324-6496

EUROPEAN HEADQUARTERS
Wizards of the Coast, Belgium
P.B. 34
2300 Turnhout
Belgium
+32-14-44-30-44

Visit our web-site at **www.tsr.com**

Chapter One

September 21, 2501

"TENNN—*SHUN*! Attention on deck!"

The words echoed through the great hall. In answer, thirty-three pairs of spit-polished boots came together as one. The harsh light of a yellow sun pierced the thick window above, turning the dark uniforms a brilliant cobalt blue.

The men and women gathered there took a collective breath and held it as a tall, deeply tanned officer walked through the HQ portal and stepped to the front of the room with three majors and a captain at his heels. All eyes looked straight ahead, not an inch to the left or the right. Still, no one missed the man's slight but discernable limp, the sharp, peregrine nose, or the tinge of gray in his hair. For these men and women were Concord Marines, and marines were required to see straight, sideways, up, down, and backward if required. These particular marines could do better than that, for they were the officers and non-coms of the Third Battalion, 26th Regiment. They were the best, the leaders of the best—for that, too, was a requirement of *all* Concord Marines.

Respect and tradition accounted for the silence in the hall, but there was curiosity there, too. Lieutenant

Colonel Wilm Seymoyr was brand new to Bluefall, and more important than that, new to combat as well. Every marine on the watery planet knew this was his first field command after twenty years of staff and teaching posts. Why was he here, they wondered, out on the thin galactic edge, out in the untamed regions of the Verge? There were as many guesses as marines—but no one imagined he was unfit for duty. This was the last place you'd want to send a loser. Even the best of the best could die quickly out here.

Seymoyr stopped and spread his legs slightly in a snappy parade rest but didn't invite the others to do the same. Okay, Lieutenant Witzko thought to himself, anybody get a clue from that?

Seymoyr nodded at a major. Thick metal shutters slid across the hall's windows, plunging the room into darkness before the interior lights flashed to life.

"Good evening, ladies and gentlemen," Seymoyr began. "In the interest of getting you all back to your regular duties, I'll be as brief as possible. I can confirm the rumors you've no doubt been discussing for some time. It's true. We're going into action. We're shipping out."

No one spoke or moved, but Damion Witzko could almost feel the tension, smell the sharp scent of anticipation in the air as Seymoyr's words echoed silently through the group.

A flickering holodisplay danced before them in the air. Stars rushed by at speeds too quick to follow with the naked eye before finally settling on the image of single system. Four planets and their moons circled a pale yellow G5 star. One of the planets, labeled "Spes," glowed a luminescent green, signifying that it was an inhabited world. A moon, labeled "Arist," flickered in the same green as it circled a gas giant farther out in the system. Neither the pale sun nor any of the other planets in the system were labeled. Still, Witzko and every marine in the room knew the system at once: Hammer's Star. They're sending us to Hammer's Star!

Witzko felt his heart skip a beat. Directly behind him, Master Sergeant Irina Lavon released an almost silent breath. For the duty-bound Irina, Damion thought, this was a violent burst of emotion.

Hammer's Star was the most remote Concord outpost in the Verge, and the most notorious. Spes, the innermost world of the system, had once been the site of a Borealin colony named Silver Bell. When the Long Silence of the Verge had ended only five years before, the first message from the rim was a wake-up call to everyone who heard it.

"I don't have to tell any marine about Hammer's Star," Seymoyr went on. "You know what happened there, and you know what it means. You also have a damned good idea why we're going back. If anybody needs a reminder, listen to it again."

Seymoyr pressed a sequence on the keypad before him, and as the hall's audio system hissed to life, a voice, cracked and broken with fear, filled the darkened room.

Borealis colony Silver Bell in Hammer's Star, calling any FreeSpace Alliance vessel . . . We are under heavy attack by . . . Repeat, the colony is under heavy attack by unknown forces. Send help. Repeat, send help. It's May 3, 2489. We need help, damn it! Please—

Nobody needed a reminder, certainly no marine. The message was seven years old when it arrived. By the time help got there, nothing remained of Silver Bell but a decimated crater on the surface of Spes. There were no survivors, and the attackers had left no sign of who or what they might be. Not until seven months ago when Concord forces had been struck by external ships near the asteroid Rakke, had any clue been found about the identity of Silver Bell's destroyers.

The few survivors of the Battle of Rakke had dubbed the aliens "klicks" after the unnerving clicking sounds they made. Since then, more klick outposts had been overrun, but no one doubted there were plenty of the creatures still out there.

"Effective at 0630 tomorrow," Seymoyr continued, "this battalion forms two separate battle groups. One is going directly to Spes by the most immediate available transport. The second group will embark later aboard the *Fortinbras* class transport, *Stormbird*. We'll be operating as part of a combined task force in the Revik Asteroid Belt. Concord Intelligence has reports of unfriendlies attacking merchant ships there. We sent in a scouting vessel two weeks ago, but they never came back. We don't know what we're looking at here, marines. We're going in quick, and we're going in heavy. We don't intend to be knocked around this time."

The colonel paused and let his gaze sweep across the group. "You can handle it. That's why you're here."

He turned and walked back toward the portal with two of his aides. Major Sill put the group at ease by getting directly to business: running holos of unit assignments, manpower, weapons—the hundreds of details that were a part of shipping out.

It was the same, Witzko thought, for moving across the street or a hundred light years of space. It was the way it had always been, clear back to old times on the Solar Union worlds. When a marine left town, he took everything he owned. Where he'd been was no matter. Where he was *going* was now home.

* * * * *

First Lieutenant Witzko stood out of the sun in the shadow of the five-story structure that housed the HQ, training rooms, and supply depot of Bluefall's Concord Marines. The building rested on a grassy hill that sloped gently down to the sea. To the south, Witzko could see kilometers of construction sites, half-completed structures, and improvised landing pads. The never-ending work stirred an ever-present cloud of dust into the air. The dust in turn mixed with the intense humidity of the planet's atmosphere, creating a salty grit that wreaked havoc on electronics and machinery.

Just to keep the base combat-ready kept the desalinization facilities going night and day. Witzko was certain there were as many robots and construction vehicles on the Diandes Island base as there were marines. There was everything on the planet humans needed to stay alive—as long as it dropped in from somewhere else. Land took up a bare two percent of the planet's surface. The rest was an endless stretch of water.

Witzko remembered his first month on the planet, the comfort of the 0.89 gravity, the rich, intoxicating atmosphere, the beautiful beaches, and the dazzling blue of the sea.

He also remembered his second month. Sand and salt turned to aggravating grit, the sun became a relentless, overheated star, and the "dazzling" blue of the sea became the most boring color he'd ever seen. When he'd first arrived, he wondered why off-duty marines spent all their spare time in the small expanse of green forest on the hill above the base. What was the matter with these people? The greatest beaches in the galaxy were at hand, and they crowded together in the *trees*?

Now, six months later, he didn't ask the question anymore. Instead, he watched with sad amusement as newcomers—"aquamarines" as the old timers called them—ran like fish out of water to splash about in the sea. It wouldn't take long. They'd begin to scratch and complain, and then they'd head for the trees, surprised to find everyone else already there.

Now it was only a matter of hours before several hundred of the island's marines would be back in deep space, complaining about conditions there while fondly remembering the comforts and pleasures of Bluefall.

I'll be first in line, Witzko thought, drinking Salty Spongers and recalling the "good old days" by the sea.

An orbital shuttle lifted off from the south, raising a cloud of grit and sending a wrenching wave of sound across the island. Witzko glanced up, watched it a moment, and then shifted his gaze to the more interesting sight of Master Sergeant Irina Lavon coming toward him from the building.

Watching Irina was a favorite pastime of every male marine, from private up to general. Irina knew it but didn't seem to care. She had important things to do. The only danger in watching her was getting caught. Let her turn around once and see the wrong look in your eye, and you'd wish you had never been born, never even thought about joining the Concord Marines. Military or personal affront, Irina's fury was something to behold, and you never wanted to experience it twice.

She handled each sin according to rank. Privates wilted on the spot. Non-commissioned officers apologized at once. Master sergeants didn't call officers on the carpet, of course, but Irina had a way of letting them know they'd made her list. Records would go astray. Vital equipment would disappear. Once—or so the story went—a certain major found himself unaccountably transferred light years away, to someplace called Wet Dog IV. No one could find the place on any chart, but that didn't mean it wasn't there.

The thing about Irina Lavon was she didn't *look* like trouble. Even in an age when males didn't look upon females entirely as sex objects and usually gave them the respect they deserved, Irina's appearance tended to cloud the male mind. Irina was tall, lean, and fair-haired. She had azure eyes, a too-wide mouth, and a slightly turned-up nose. It was easy to forget she also had an outstanding combat record, was an expert in dispatching the Galactic Concord's enemies with her hands, feet, and a number of weapons, and had a broad range of administrative and technical skills. Everyone knew she would very likely be sergeant major of the Concord Marines one day, if she didn't burn herself out, offend too many officers, or wind up with a disgruntled private's grenade beneath her bed.

"Have you seen these damned things? You see what kind of—of . . . You see what they're handing me?" Irina crushed a handful of printouts in her fists, careful not to *quite* shake them in an officer's face.

"I have not, Master Sergeant," Witzko said, "but something tells me that I'm about to find out."

Witzko knew his sergeant's moods, and the one she

was wearing now he called "Rage, Frustration, Barely Under Control."

"It's the bloody T.O.& E., the so-called phony-baloney Table of Organization and Equipment for our upcoming hop, *sir.* A truly marvelous document some half-witted officer in HQ—no offense intended, sir—has patched together from his dreams and intends for us bring into the real world of Concord Marines. I have been given the honor, sir, of being named Senior NCO and Acting Sergeant Major of this little picnic to the stars, and there is no bloody way I can possibly bring this stinking mess together in a *month*, much less by Oh-Six-Thirty in the A.M., sir!"

"I can certainly understand your concern, Master Sergeant," Witzko said, the voice of calm and reason. "These things can be a little difficult sometimes, especially on such short notice. Let me take a look at what you've got there."

Irina handed him the flimsies without question. Though Lavon had the reputation for loathing officers, Witzko seemed to have put through to her that he knew where the lines were drawn and would not interfere with her authority as Master Sergeant. You couldn't say that about every officer in the Concord Marines—especially the lieutenants. Most of the other lieutenants on the island were scared to death of her, and Irina encouraged that fear as much as she could.

Witzko shuffled through the papers, frowned now and then, and punched in figures on his data slate. Irina was right, of course. He'd guessed that from the start. Some incompetent officer had hurriedly shuffled some numbers together, hacked them into a T.O.& E. that would never work short of outright magic, and then passed it down the line—confident, Witzko was sure, that the NCOs would somehow work it out and leave him alone.

This, of course, was precisely what would be done. That was the way, Witzko knew, that it had *always* been done. The NCOs would get together, shuffle the deck again, and somehow make it come out right. This meant they would borrow or steal what they really needed for such an expedition and pay no attention to what the papers said they ought to have.

Master Sergeant Lavon knew the answer as well as Witzko did. She was unofficially showing her officer the muck up she had to deal with and getting his non-permission to non-perform the work she had to do. Witzko was ultimately responsible for her acts, and Lavon, as a proper NCO, was telling him that although her mighty first lieutenant was certainly on the hook, she would get the job done, and everything would work out in the end.

"It looks fine to me," Witzko said. "Let me know when you're done, and I'll sign off and get us on the way."

"Very good, sir." Irina Lavon snapped to attention, showing him a razor-edge salute. Witzko returned the courtesy, and Irina started off.

"Hold it please, Master Sergeant."

The voice from behind them caught her mid-stride. Irina froze and came to attention again, Witzko only an instant behind.

A hard knot formed in Witzko's gut. He cursed himself for the familiar reaction, one he'd tried desperately to control yet couldn't put aside.

Captain Woodlaw Savant stepped into the shade, facing the two.

"At ease, Lieutenant, Master Sergeant. Is everything under control? Any way I can be of help?"

"No, sir," Witzko answered. "Thank you, sir."

"Good, that's fine." Savant, hands behind his broad back, nodded to himself as if everything he saw left him deeply satisfied. Anyone who knew him was aware that this wasn't so. The perpetual smile was the result of a battle scar that left his mouth curled in a death's-head grin. Savant had the hard, stocky physique of a heavyweight boxer, a square, balding head, and a predator's eyes. Add those features to a tiny hooked nose and a permanent, ghastly smile, and Savant earned his name of The Owl. This was no allusion to the "wise old owl," not for Captain Savant. Those who named him that meant a bird that stalks its prey at night, a creature you'd never want to find at your back.

"And the T.O. & E., any problems there, Lieutenant? We have a most vital mission to perform. I hope you're deeply aware of that."

"Yes, sir. No problems, sir."

"I see. Very fine. Lieutenant, is Master Sergeant Lavon performing her duties in a satisfactory manner?"

Damion Witzko was taken aback by the question and tried not to show it. "Yes, sir. Sergeant Lavon is most proficient, sir."

"Oh?" Savant raised a heavy brow. "If that's so, Lieutenant, why do you have to show her what to do? Why do you find it necessary to do the job she was *trained* to do?"

"Sir . . ." Witzko risked a quick glance at Savant, then snapped his eyes to the front. "I don't understand the question, sir. To my knowledge, I have not in any way—"

"Damn you, Lieutenant! Don't play the dummy with me! I'll have your hide for it if you do!"

Savant stuck his face a few centimeters from Witzko's, his face flushed with rage. Witzko stood his ground, every muscle rigid, eyes straight ahead. He knew what Savant wanted, and he wouldn't give him that, not if he wanted a career, if he wanted to remain a Concord Marine.

"I watched you, Lieutenant Witzko, from over there. The master sergeant came to you complaining about her job. I didn't have to hear you; I could see what both of you said. It was clear she couldn't handle the problem. Anyone could see that. So you took out your slate and worked it out *for* her. What a nice thing to do, Witzko. Do you hold all your NCOs' hands, or just the attractive ones?"

That almost did it. Before he caught himself, Witzko turned to look at the captain, and his gaze was the one that only a few enemies had seen in the instant before they stopped seeing anything. Savant had nearly pulled Witzko over the line, and from the startled widening of the captain's eyes, he knew it. They faced each other for the span of three heartbeats, then Witzko regained control and returned to attention.

"Sir—" Irina began, jumping in quickly, acutely aware of what was happening here.

"At ease, Sergeant." Savant held up a restraining hand. "I was addressing this officer; I was not addressing you."

Irina took a breath and let it out slowly. She could smell the captain's breath and feel his eyes upon her.

"I think what we have here," Savant said, "is a rather loosely run platoon, one that has grown fat and lazy under your command, Lieutenant. It is quite clear there is fraternization between officers and NCOs, and I suspect this unhealthy environment has filtered down into the ranks as well. This is most alarming to me, especially on the eve of an important and possibly perilous mission. By all I hold sacred as a Concord Marine, I will *not* have a *lazy* platoon in my company, Witzko. I assuredly will not. You will have your platoon form up at once on Training Course D. Full field packs, Class One battle gear." Savant slapped his hand against his side. "If there is indolence in this platoon, and I know damned well there is, I will sweat it out of you. I will turn every one of you into real marines again!"

Captain Savant glared, turned on his heels, and stalked across the broad plaza.

Witzko let out a breath. "Master Sergeant," he said, "you will form up the men as ordered, full field packs, Class One battle gear. I'll see you on the grounds at fourteen hundred hours."

"Sir," Irina said, without looking at him, "begging your pardon, sir, but you can't kill him. That wouldn't be a good idea. You'd get us all in a lot of trouble, sir."

Without giving Witzko time to answer, she snapped another salute and stalked off. After a dozen steps, she began double-timing her way back to the enlisted barracks. From the receding shadows of the high building, Damion Witzko watched her cross the broad plaza. He was thankful—not for the first time—that the infamous Irina Lavon was a loyal and supportive NCO. She was, truly, an absolute marvel. Even under the heavy burden the insufferable Captain Savant had placed upon the platoon, Witzko was certain Irina would somehow juggle all her troubles at once and see them through. She was a—

Witzko blinked and realized with a start that he'd kept his gaze upon the illustrious sergeant until she was completely out of sight. He felt the color rise to his cheeks, glanced quickly about, and was doubly thankful that no one had seen him do that.

Now, besides the impossible task of organizing and properly equipping the entire Third Battalion, 26th Regiment of Concord Marines overnight—preparing them for drivespace and possible combat—Witzko had the additional duty of telling his platoon that they were not finished for the day but were just getting started.

Chapter Two

September 28, 2501

Kuhudag sniffed the icy wind coming down from the Gumad Mountains. Even the best of weren hunters found it difficult to smell through a breath mask, even one that enabled its wearer to pick up scents while protecting him from the thin, frigid air. If he tried turning his bare face toward such a wind on Arist, his nostrils would quickly freeze, and he would smell even less. The weren in the colder parts of Kurg often used masks made from the bladders of the trub fish, but nothing with such a weather resistant organ swam, walked, or flew on Arist. This miserable moon was far colder than even the harshest Kurg winter.

At least his electrically heated goggles allowed him to see the harsh, windswept terrain. The goggles were costly, but the weren of West Lodge had a geothermal electric plant to recharge their lanth cells. The price of charging them offworld or at one of the human settlements every half-season would have reduced the weren of Arist to their bare fur in a very few years.

Just above the crests of the Gumad Mountains, a tiny hint of blue sky squeezed above the horizon. Sullen gray clouds hung low overhead, heavy with imminent snow.

As if we needed anymore, Kuhudag grumbled to himself. In every direction there was nothing but an endless expanse of low rises and shallow ravines, a landscape scattered with cold and broken boulders and all of it blanketed with eons of snow and ice.

That, the warrior told himself, made little sense—not if he had truly heard something out there. If strangers were close enough to hear, they should have been close enough for Kuhudag to scent them—unless the same wind that forced him to wear the mask was also playing tricks with his hearing.

He crouched and studied the boulder field ahead. Perhaps his eyes would do what his ears and nose could not. When Kuhudag stood, stretching his full two and a half meters above the ground, he could see as far as a human standing on a boulder, but standing up in plain sight for any enemy to see would be inviting folly. Kuhudag had hunted too long on too many worlds to be so foolish.

Crouching to avoid becoming a conspicuous target, he could scarcely see anything at all. Remaining in such a position too long would freeze his limbs to the ground. Only his thermal suit and the fur of his torso lay between his vitals and the heat-eating surface of Arist.

At times like this, Kuhudag wished that he had never heard of this cursed place. Still, as the youngest of five brothers, he had not relished the idea of spending twenty years on Kurg fighting for family dominance. Just out of adolescence he had traveled north to the Orlamu settlements with great reluctance, then on to their university. The Orlamu worshiped the Divine Unconscious, or drivespace, as it was known to outsiders, but for him it was only a way of leaping from system to system and seeing a thousand times more than he could ever have seen on Kurg.

Even during his tenure under the relentless Orlamu teachers, the thought of becoming a priest had never appealed to him. As the years passed and he had earned a reputation as a scout, a guard, and even a mercenary on world after world, what little of the faith he'd learned had slipped away. Sixty years had passed since he had last set foot on Kurg, and he was finally beginning to miss it.

Though he had been on Arist for three years now, he was, in a sense, still a stranger there. Most of the weren on the frozen moon had come there to escape the servitude of VoidCorp. They were willing to endure the killing atmosphere to live as a free people. Though Kuhudag had never experienced the domination of anyone, he shared their love of freedom and was willing, if necessary, to fight for it.

Such a need, he knew, might well come again. Indeed, that moment might be upon them now. The weren of Arist had lost some of their hunting grounds to the human settlers in Red Ridge and the settlements farther north. And while the weren had received a good price for the land at the time, they desperately needed more land. Habitable land was scarce on Arist. Unless settlers wanted to live in domes, a luxury that none of the weren could afford, the only habitable regions of Arist were along the equator. Now the weren of West Lodge wanted to see how far south the outlaws, hermits, and other humans from Red Ridge had pushed into the weren hunting grounds. That was a task fit only for an experienced hunter and warrior, an apt description of Kuhudag himself.

Kuhudag pushed the musings of the past from his mind, fixing his attention on the task at hand. Most of the tall, massive rocks on the white landscape were covered with gray beards of ice. Nothing broke the boredom of the boulder field except howling swirls of snow. Kuhudag shaded his eyes with one gloved hand. Nothing and more nothing—an infinity of nothing!

Were the old shamans of Kurg right? he wondered. Did those who went into the "Great Sky" reach the end of being and fade in nothingness? Heresy among the Orlamu, but he had heard the tales whispered around more than one hearth fire in his youth.

Kuhudag shrugged and swept snow from his chest, irritated with the turn his thoughts had taken. If he had not swallowed the complex rites of the Orlamu, he could easily have forgotten the simple fears of his people. Still, crouched in the desolation of Arist, it was easy enough to turn the moans of the wind and the ghostly swirls of snow into monsters that haunted a weren child.

Kuhudag consoled himself with the fact that while he was having difficulty spotting any living thing on the frozen plain, any creature out there would have just as much difficulty seeing him. Under normal conditions, the thick fur that covered every centimeter of his body was a blend of white, black, and gray, but like all the weren, he could change that color to match his background. Now he was as white as the wasteland itself, and his white thermal hunting suit helped him become even more invisible in his environment.

While there was nothing in the barren landscape he could see, smell, or hear, Kuhudag had been a hunter too long not to trust his inner senses as well. He had stayed in one place long enough. It was time to get back to the ravine where he had begun. He had checked the western quadrant, now he would check the area to the east, and if there was nothing there, he would move into the most dangerous quadrant of all, the one that lay straight ahead. With a final check of the landscape, he gripped his weapon against his chest and raised up slowly, moving away from his hiding place. He loped as swiftly as he dared, taking great care to seemingly drift with the swirls of snow.

If any creature spotted him now, it would know something was there, but it could not be sure just what it might be. The thick, padded hunting suit masked his true form, hiding his great, muscular body, his deadly claws, and his fearsome face.

Even another being accustomed to the weren often found it hard to look eye to eye with such a creature. From the sloping, furry forehead, past the pointed ears to the small yellow eyes, most humans found a weren's face disconcerting at best. From there, though, its visage became a nightmare for beings from other worlds. The underslung jaw and upward-protruding tusks would instantly remind a human of mythic tales of the prehistoric tigers of ancient Earth. The demonic-appearing claws of the weren and their loping, animal-like gait would uncover primal dreams of a creature born of wolf and ape. There were surely more unusual-looking beings in the galaxy, but none, if any, could match the strength and appearance of a two hundred kilo weren on the prowl.

Yet those who knew the weren were aware that these folk possessed a complex, strictly structured society, and when they were not fighting an enemy or a member of the family, they were very tolerant of other species and were even capable of embracing new and interesting ideas.

Kuhudag slowed and then paused above the shallow ravine. He listened and sniffed the air. He could smell nothing that shouldn't be there. Holding his rifle above the sharp snow, he crawled on his belly the last few meters. He stopped then and gave a low, nearly subaural growl that only another weren could hear.

His call was answered, and Kuhudag crept over the ridge and slid down inside. The dark muzzle of Grutok's stubby rifle met him and held there, a centimeter from Kuhudag's eyes.

"Good. At least you are awake," Kuhudag muttered, sweeping the barrel aside. "You must have learned something, though I doubt it could be a great deal."

Young Grutok's face twisted into the weren equivalent of a smile, an expression that quickly vanished when he saw the chill in his elder's eyes.

"I have been most alert, Worthy," Grutok said with great respect. "It was you who taught me that a weren call might be imitated through a mechanical device."

"It might, though only a whelp like yourself would be taken in by such a foolish ruse. Have you anything to say to me, anything you might have seen or smelled prior to your winter's nap?"

"Nothing, Worthy. If any creature had approached my post, I would have killed it at once, sacrificing myself in order to warn you of its presence."

"Yes, fine," Kuhudag said. "The proper thing for you to do, of course, though it would be a prideful thing."

Kuhudag looked down to check his weapon, or more plainly, to hide his expression. Grutok was a whelp, and an annoying one at times, but he had to admit there was talent of a sort in the lad. Otherwise, Kuhudag would not have taken on the solemn task of attempting to teach the whelp the warrior trade. The fact that he was Medlyna's whelp and therefore had the blood for this kind of life only strengthened Kuhudag's resolve. There was no female he knew who could match Medlyna in a fair fight—and certainly no creature outside the weren species.

"I am going to check the western quadrant now," he told Grutok. "I expect it will get colder still. The weather always gets worse, no matter how bad it is at the time. Lesson One of the day: you will think you are freezing to death. This will be true, but you will not give in to the temptation to sleep or worse still, die. I will not tolerate either of these excuses. You understand this clearly?"

"Yes, Worthy. I will not dishonor you in any way."

"Lesson Two: a weren warrior does not *think* and certainly does not *speak* of the possibility of . . . the word that you said. Never let it come from your mouth again."

"No, Worthy." Grutok lowered his head. "I feel great shame within my being. I feel—"

"Stop it. Just don't do it again. Do you have enough food and extra ammunition?"

"Adequate food, Worthy, and four extra clips."

"Good. Eat sparingly, and do not shoot anything unless you have to. If you must shoot, shoot to kill. Ammunition is expensive."

He let his gaze sweep over the whelp for an instant and saw all he needed to see. Grutok was adequately dressed and properly equipped. He was also cold and doing all in his power not to show it. He knew he should tell the whelp that it was good to endure pain but stupid not to take measures to save your life. Dying was useless if you wasted it in a senseless gesture. Still, he decided to keep his silence. There had been enough lessons for the day. Grutok would likely get cold enough to learn to move his various parts without exposing himself to an enemy. If he did not, then he would likely die. That would be a waste, Kuhudag thought, because this one had a chance to become as good as his mother and his dead father. It would be a shame not to see that happen.

"I go now," Kuhudag said. "Should I not return, which is a most unlikely event, you will remain at your post until you are relieved or until you are set upon by an enemy force. If such a thing should occur, you will save one final breath to signal the others."

"Yes, Worthy," said Grutok, and he patted the stock of his rifle in a gesture of respect.

Kuhudag grabbed a frozen slab of meat, shoved it in his pocket, and slid back the way he had come.

* * * * *

The western quadrant looked remarkably like the area he had covered in the east. Kuhudag would have been greatly surprised if he had seen anything remotely different from ice-sheathed rocks and howling swirls of snow.

After half an hour of crawling to the new position on his belly, he reached the spot he was after. The rock was not the best cover on the white plain, but neither was it the worst. Seeking the safest place in which to wait was often a fatal mistake. The enemy watched for movement near good cover, as Kuhudag did himself.

As he had predicted to Grutok, the weather did seem to be getting worse, either that or he had been exposed to the terrible cold too long. If Kuhudag was freezing, the whelp, even in the protective hollow of the ravine, was likely worse. No time to think about that, he told himself. Let your mind wander to someone else, and the next thing you know you'll—

Kuhudag suddenly came fully alert. The instant the thought touched his mind, the wind brought him the smell of warm-blooded life, and in the same moment, the unmistakable sound of a boot heel scraping on rock. He crouched lower still as he searched the boulder field that covered the landscape upwind.

His own insulated boots kept the rocky ground of Arist from stealing all of his body heat, but they kept him from extending his toe-claws as well. Still, even on Arist, few weren traveled the wilderness without slits cut in the tips of their gloves to allow the use of their claws. He used them to grip the edge of the icy rock and ease his head the slightest centimeter into the open.

There was nothing he could see or smell. The sound of the boot—if that indeed had been what it was—did not come again. Only the wind, and the eternal field of snow—

Kuhudag ducked instinctively as an incandescent green laser beam slashed the air over his head. Steam and ragged chunks of rock erupted from the stone behind him.

Kuhudag was moving almost before the sound of the weapon fell away. He ran and rolled to the right and the rear, knowing that direction took him on to a slope leading down and out of his enemy's field of vision. Of course, it might take him directly into someone else's vision as well. A warrior learned very early that certainties were rare in battle. A warrior who didn't take this lesson to heart seldom lived to old age.

A fast, wild tumble took him down the slope past jutting boulders and into the ravine. An unprotected human would have broken bones in such a fall, but stout weren frames could take a lot more punishment. He landed intact, cushioned by snow an arm's length deep. Counting precious seconds, he leaped out of the drift to more solid ground.

At once, he began to circle forward and farther to the right, hoping to discover the enemy's flank. There was no visible sign of anyone, but during his tumble down the hill, weapon fire had broken out elsewhere. Most of it came from his right, but some came from straight ahead where the enemy had seen him sticking his head up from the rock. He was glad Grutok had not seen that. In his head, he mentally titled the incident as Lesson Three.

He knew where the others of his kind were waiting, to the left and to the rear of Grutok's position. Now every few meters he reported his progress and a warning to his comrades by using the low-pitched hunting calls. It would have been simpler to use one of the tiny human radios that could easily fit inside the ear, but such devices were not cheap. With proper equipment an enemy could locate the radio's user. To compensate, the weren of Arist had developed their own language of hunting calls that few humans understood. On the other hand, no human was going to hear his call against the cold wind shrieking through the rocks.

Even if Kuhudag did not truly believe in such things, he hurriedly vowed an offering to the High Hunter if no enemy heard him. Even when he had been halfway faithful to the Orlamu religion, he had tried to stay in touch with the older powers of his home world—just in case they were actually there.

As he called and crept forward, the fighting around him seemed to grow more intense. To his left he could hear the intermittent crack of weren rifles and the sizzle and hiss of human energy weapons. It sounded as if the humans might be running as low on energy as the weren were on cartridges. Both sides seemed to be playing a cautious game, staying under cover, remaining where they'd been when the shooting began.

Kuhudag unslung his own rifle and made sure nothing had frozen since he had unwrapped it from the fur sheathe, then he dropped a cold round into the breech. In blowing snow, he felt that his rifle might actually outrange some of the human energy rifles, and any advantage was worth pursuing in an environment that was certainly no comfort to either side.

He began stalking the enemy's flank and rear, moving swiftly and keeping low, trusting that the moan of the wind, the hiss of driven snow, and the firing to his left would cover the sound of a careful weren warrior.

Fwoomp!

Fwoomp!

The sound, distorted by distance and wind, gave Kuhudag a chill that did not come from the winds of Arist. The humans had used grenades! Whether they had used them to cover a retreat or to prepare the way for an attack did not matter greatly. The weren had no such weapons, no means of replying. Kuhudag's party did not carry even a charge of ordinary blasting powder for clearing rubble from ice caves.

A third grenade exploded in the distance as Kuhudag entered a boulder field where the rocks were nearly the size of small hills. The gaps between the boulders were enough to allow three weren to pass through abreast—or more than a few human soldiers.

Fearing the worst, Kuhudag increased his pace. The weren concept of battle honor required that one allow an enemy to retreat from a fight begun by bad luck, but the humans did not sound as if they were retreating. He knew what he must do: reach the enemy's rear so that they would have to look over their shoulders and fight in two directions at once.

Drawing in a breath of cold air from his breath mask, he charged through a gap between two boulders, then stopped cold in his tracks as four human soldiers burst through from the opposite side.

Kuhudag fired from the hip. War luck was with him. A human fell, clutching his leg and screaming curses in a tongue Kuhudag could not understand. The fall of one soldier unsettled the others. They hesitated, uncertain what to do next. Kuhudag had no such problem. He darted for the protection of a boulder before his enemies could sear its face with their lasers.

Swirling steam and bits of rock showered Kuhudag as he ran from cover again, making for the narrow gap to his right. He stopped, went to his knees, sighted, and fired again. He was careful not to hit the wounded human. That one was clearly past fighting today and might not survive the journey home through the frigid Arist night. Honor also forbade him from shooting the human kneeling by his wounded comrade.

Kuhudag was tempted to simply put the next bullet into the snow in an effort to remind the enemy that they were in the open, and he was not. Still, for his own sake and that of his comrades, he could not risk human determination outlasting his ammunition. There was only one reasonable choice. He squeezed the trigger and shot one of the two remaining humans mercifully in the head. The heavy bullet shattered the target, sending a fine red mist spraying across the snow. Kuhudag nodded in tribute to his foe. It was an honorable end for any opponent, one he would gladly accept himself. He left others alive to tell of his victory and laud his honor as well.

Kuhudag had also been taught never to fire twice from the same place against an armed opponent. Remembering this lesson, he ran quickly to his right, swerved to his left, and rolled behind the protection of a sharp-edged rock that was half buried in the frozen ground.

He doubted the surviving humans would care to follow. They would tend to their dead and wounded and retreat from the field—either that or stay under cover and use their radios to call for help. This meant that Kuhudag could not simply nap behind his small rock. He would have to retreat himself, at least back to Grutok's position, and let his comrades know there might be a sizeable force of humans on the plains. This fact, he decided, they might already know themselves.

He crouched and listened, hearing nothing but the crackle of distant fire. Keeping low, he sprinted back the way he'd come, watching the boulders to the left and to the right.

The grenade came from behind, soared past his shoulders into the snow a few meters in front of him, and exploded in a burst of orange fire. Kuhudag had the smallest part of a second to see the dazzling burst before his eyes, to feel the terrible heat burn through his protective suit and reach his fur and skin. In the instant he had left, he thought that this, surely, would have been the basis for a good Lesson Four for Grutok, and he was sorry this was something he would never get the chance to teach the young whelp.

Chapter Three

September 21, 2501

Damion Witzko stood on a rocky ridge that led to the highlands of Rimfire Island, watching as the last shuttle dropped off the remainder of his platoon. With a nearly silent whisper, the shuttle lifted off and turned into the wind.

The island of Diandes was only eighty kilometers west of Rimfire, but the topography of the two were as different as night and day. The hills of Diandes sloped up gently from sandy beaches, scarcely high enough to be called hills at all. Rimfire was a ragged intrusion thrust up from the sea. Pinnacles of stone rose to dizzying heights above a lush, tropical forest, a steamy, nearly impenetrable tangle of brush, creepers, and thick-boled trees. The few patches of bare ground on the island were riddled with angles and fissures that were treacherous to walk upon when they were dry, and deadly when they were soaked after a tropical rain.

It was nowhere anyone would ever want to be, Witzko thought to himself, in other words, a small, isolated hell, a near perfect site for training Concord Marines.

Witzko was proud of his platoon—doubly proud as he watched them move into position for the first tactical maneuver, crossing D2 Ravine. They had moaned, groaned, and likely cursed their first lieutenant when they learned that their "off" day was cancelled and they'd be going to Rimfire for a fun afternoon. Still, when they jumped off the shuttles in full combat gear, they were one hundred percent marines.

Whatever the reason they were there, they would do as they were told and do it better than any other platoon in the Corps. There were forty-three NCOs and enlisted personnel down there, and only nineteen had been in Recon less than a year. It was a good group, but not yet as good as they could be. Overestimating your own abilities, Witzko knew, was the way to get people killed.

One thing they *weren't*—and Captain Savant's words still burned in Witzko's head—was a lazy, sloppy outfit. Witzko knew it, and Savant damn sure knew it, too.

"We've got most 'em over now, Lieutenant. That water's full of spider leeches, so no one's lagging behind."

Lance Corporal Julie Travino pulled off her helmet and gave Witzko a weary grin. She was a tall, lanky trooper, a redhead in her mid-twenties, slim for a native of Austrin-Ontis, whose people leaned to the stocky side. The standard carbon fiber battledress seemed to hang on her in scarecrow fashion, but Witzko knew she had earned her rank.

"Tell Sergeant Kran I want First Squad through that tangle in record time," Witzko said. "Standard entry isn't going to cut it today. If I know Bad-Guy Company, they'll pull something extra out of the hat."

"Sir!" Travino showed Witzko an offhand salute, then turned and ran back down the ridge.

She hadn't said a word, but Damion knew his people

and was well aware that word of his trouble with Captain Savant had quickly made its way around the platoon. They knew why they were out there on this miserable exercise, and they knew who had sent them there. Irina Lavon wouldn't have told them, Witzko knew that, but this was a Concord Marine platoon, and you didn't have to be a mindwalker to get the inside dope three minutes after it happened.

How much they knew about the trouble between their lieutenant and their company commander Damion couldn't guess. More than likely they knew too much. There were not too many old timers in the platoon; soldiering wasn't a trade that encouraged a long lifetime. Still there were a few, and Damion didn't have to guess twice who'd been responsible for spreading the latest trash around. Master Sergeant Jacques Belier was so old and overweight he looked more like a combat tent than a marine. The only reason he was still around was the fact that he'd followed Captain Savant's postings for most of that officer's career. As far as Witzko was concerned, the two were well suited to one another.

Belier loathed Damion Witzko simply because his captain did, and if Belier despised Witzko for that reason, he had reasons of his own to have it in for Master Sergeant Irina Lavon. Belier was the only other master sergeant around, and he knew that in spite of anything Captain Savant could do, he would never—in this lifetime or the next—take Irina Lavon's place. Even if she were killed in action—probably a recurring fantasy of Belier's—Colonel Seymoyr would never allow Savant to put a relic like Jacques Belier in her place. He couldn't take her job, but he could do all he could to make her life extremely difficult.

Witzko was well aware of the reasons Savant didn't like him. In the first place, he didn't like anyone except Belier. More than that, however, was the fact that Savant had come up through the ranks and Witzko hadn't.

Damion Witzko, Concord Military Academy Class of 2496, had flowed into his rank with little effort. He was good, and he was sure he would have made it on his own without his ancestry. His grandfather was Jonathan Kramer Witzko (General, Concord Marines, Retired), his father was Maxwell Harding Witzko (Major General, Concord Marines, Retired), and his aunt was the famous Francine Marie Witzko (Colonel, Concord Marines, KIA). Added to that was a string of uniformed ancestors and relatives leading back through the years until the records ran out.

That kind of background, Damion knew all too well, could be an asset or a hindrance. Right now, he fervently wished he had a name no one could possibly recall. Somewhere above him, in a shuttle hovering over the exercise, Captain Woodlaw Savant was watching, hoping that Lieutenant Damion Witzko would make some incredible, unforgivable error and screw up this exercise in every possible way.

Without activating his tactical display, Witzko saw that his platoon had already achieved a major advantage over "enemy" forces. The first elements of the platoon were crossing the ravine in record time, slogging across the narrow river and starting up the sides of the steep ravine. On the other side of the ravine past the big stand of trees lay the platoon's initial target: a simulated ultra low frequency comm grid. In a non-simulated situation, such an installation would be crewed by people who could make sensors out of trip wires and old socks in their spare time. Witzko hoped his crew assigned to Opposing Force remembered that. If a Recon Platoon had one particular axiom burned into their heads, it was "What can be seen can be hit—and what can be hit can be killed."

Witzko turned his display on passive and ran down the steep path from his post above the action. Platoon Sergeant Jobal Kran saw him coming, turned, and walked toward him through the grass.

"No problems so far," Kran said, "but I got your message from Travino. I'm thinking you're right. Those bozos are sending out peculiar comms, trying to make me think one thing and doing the other. They've got something up their sweaty sleeves."

Witzko nodded. He knew Jobal Kran had mentioned his message only out of courtesy for his lieutenant. No one needed to tell Jobal Kran what was coming down. He would have sniffed it out the minute he dropped off the shuttle. If there was combat marine equal to Irina Lavon in the platoon, it had to be Kran. Tall, with craggy features and dark skin, he was clearly of Solar African ancestry. His stony face made him look a bit older than he was, but no one who'd worked out against him would doubt his condition. A devout Orlamu, a fitness fanatic, a mountaineer, and a ten year Recon Marine, Kran was what you'd ask for in a platoon sergeant if StarMech could build one for you.

"You have any idea what they'll try?" Witzko asked.

"No, sir. Might be they don't either. We've got random numbers built into our plot; they've got the same. They'll most likely tune us on *react-2*, set up one counter, make it look good, and then go for something else."

Witzko frowned, looking at the camouflaged troopers taking up positions in the brush. "This time, I've got an idea it's going to be something we *haven't* seen before. Keep your eyes open, Sergeant Kran, and send out extra outrunners. Double up on the RPVs overhead."

"Sir!" Kran said.

"Let's do it," Witzko said.

To the west, the ravine's floor was too steep, too wet, and too overgrown to be passable. Farther east it was in plain sight of any Opposing Force outposts watching for a crossing there. Straight ahead, Witzko and Kran agreed, was the widest possible front at the closest place to the enemy. Maybe it wasn't perfect, but under the circumstances, it was the "least worst" of the options open to the platoon.

Witzko hand-signaled to his flankers. One was providing backup comms, the other security, and both knew to stay far enough from Witzko and Kran to avoid giving hostile observers the chance for valuable targets. On the modern electronic battlefield, any team with less than five-meter intervals might as well be bright red holo readings labeled "Command Group."

Witzko stayed low and crawled backward ten meters. From that position he could move quickly to either side to avoid incoming fire or join whatever section of the platoon might suddenly need help from himself or Kran.

Peering out through the roots of a yellowknife tree, he saw the platoon was doing exactly what they were supposed to do. Each squad had divided into teams with one team advancing down the slope and the other observing, ready to provide covering fire.

Witzko considered recon by fire, plastering the far side of the ravine with a long barrage of heavy fire, but thought better of it. Shooting to see who shot back was noisy and not all that effective with individual weapons in heavily overgrown terrain. A heavy weapons barrage would make an impression on the enemy. A Recon Platoon on deep penetration generally carried a couple of heavy sluggers but didn't have the firepower to maintain effective action for long.

Still, there was a way to feel the Bad Guys out, one that wouldn't pose a threat as chancy as starting a firefight. Considering that the good Captain Savant was running this show, Witzko's idea might rattle him some, throw him off guard.

Witzko signaled a marine who was crouched down to his right. The trooper crawled over at once, cradling his weapon in the crook of his arms.

"Grecko," Witzko said, pleased he'd remembered the new replacement's name, "get up to Sergeant Kran, tell him I want Second Squad to make a thrust forty meters east, no farther. Forty meters, hold there thirty seconds, then back the hell off quick."

"Yes, sir. Second Squad, forty east. Thirty seconds, get the hell back."

"You've got it. Get over there double time."

Private Grecko gave Witzko a puzzled look, then obviously decided that was a bad idea. Lieutenants could do anything they wanted, no matter how dumb, impractical, or totally unnecessary it might be. Keeping his mouth shut, Grecko belly-crawled through the thicket and disappeared.

Witzko waited. Drawing fire was a risky business even in simulation, but a forty meter jump was likely safe enough—especially if the squad got out of there fast. Their presence would register on the enemy sensors, and with any luck, the Opposers would open up before they learned the motion was a feint. If the marines didn't fall back in time . . .

Witzko waited, counting the seconds in his head. Stones rattled and vines crackled as the advancing squad made their way up the hill. With such a small group moving as a body, only the heaviest airburst weapon would get them if they were spotted. The scattered piles of boulders along the way wouldn't hurt either, unless, Witzko reminded himself, they were booby-trapped or concealed sensor arrays. This operation had been set up too quickly, he felt, to organize something like that. Unless . . .

Witzko felt the hairs crawl up the back of his neck . . . unless Captain Savant had had this "punishment exercise" in the works for some time. If he had, he'd have a lot of fun tricks waiting for Witzko's platoon.

Witzko broke electronic silence with a quick coded signal. The signal told the comm marine with Second Squad to utilize his electronic countermeasure gear to locate any concealed sensors. It was a risk. Even the weak signal of the gear might register somewhere, but it was a risk he had to take.

A quick reply came back from Lance Corporal Planke. *All clear, no problem.* Witzko signaled "Roger," and breathed a sigh of relief.

The major elements of the platoon were across the ravine and the river, and Second Squad was nearly in position. Witzko watched hand signals wag back and forth. Advance teams picked the spots where they'd go to ground, and the "tail-end Charlies" and sniper teams moved up and took position. Last of all, was the so-called "heavy weapons" squad, which wasn't heavy enough to cause any Opposers much pain.

Still, it was that squad that would guard the floor of the ravine as long as possible. The floor itself was navigable for ground vehicles, especially hovercraft. OpForce's optional equipment included three of those craft, if Savant chose to use them. If there was ever a day to watch out for "optionals," this was surely it.

Witzko sensed it before he heard it. One of the other troopers shouted it first: "Incoming! Incoming!"

The shells screamed overhead, then exploded in an orderly line of harmless, but impressive yellow plumes to the right of the second squad. The squad had waited out its thirty seconds and was on its way back down. Witzko let out another breath, relieved he'd guessed right. The shells were ten meters off, but the snoopers in the shells would remedy that with the next volley—which arrived four seconds later, right on the spot.

The rest of the platoon responded at once, running up the ravine in the opposite direction of the volley, taking quick advantage of Witzko's feint. The teams scrambled quickly up the steep wall, Platoon Sergeant Kran encouraging them with the ancient signal for "double time," a big fist moving rapidly up and down.

"Leeman! Hardy!" Witzko shouted at the team on his right, signaling them to follow him toward the heavy weapons team. He didn't want to get too cozy with such a prime target, but he needed to be close enough.

Kran left the ravine and raced toward him. He suddenly paused, looked up, and then leaped in a hole beside his lieutenant as an armored hovercraft stormed into the ravine, raising a cloud of dust. A stubby-nosed particle cannon in the craft's bow turret swept across the field, sniffing out targets. A portal in the craft snapped open, and a squad of multilegged shapes swarmed to the ground.

"Man, I hate that," Kran muttered, twisting his mouth out of shape. Witzko had to agree. Even though he knew the twisted, alien shapes were holograms that were someone's idea of the infamous "klicks," the effect was real enough.

Both Kran and Witzko shouted a warning. No one could hear, and no one needed to. The platoon had gone to ground at once, laying down a defensive volley as the klicks dispersed and the turret weapon opened fire.

The sound of heavy weapons and unceasing rifle fire was a deafening roar. Witzko saw Kran shouting, but nothing reached his ears. From the alien hovercraft, non-lethal lasers stitched the floor of the ravine. The marines fought back with a withering fire, but Witzko knew it wasn't enough, not against the wicked blue beam that sizzled everything in its path. Too late, the platoon's heavy weapons team tried to move out of the cannon's path. Their weapons flared with a disabling hit. Before the gunners could escape, one of them took a "lethal," and the sensor on his helmet blinked a bright red.

"*Damn*!" Kran cursed, pounding one fist in the other. "I told those clowns to hold the *low* ground. It doesn't take a two dollar sensor to spot somebody perching up there like a bird on a limb. Morrek and Ogata have to answer to me!"

"They did," Witzko said, pulling his helmet down low.

"What's that, Lieutenant?"

"They did keep to low ground, Sarge. Look." Witzko tapped his hand display. A green line pulsed bright, nearly running off the grid. "That OpForce simulation was overpowered, about ten points above regs. They couldn't miss with a shot like that."

Platoon Sergeant Kran stared, then suddenly understood. "Are we talking cheating here, Lieutenant? You telling me that?"

Another volley of shells whined overhead. This time three marines took simulated kills. Kran stood, shouted at Lance Corporal Travino, then ducked down again as Travino led her squad out of the kill zone into a stand of trees. The enemy volley ended as quickly as it had begun. The hovercraft backed off and disappeared through the dust of the ravine, leaving half a dozen simulated klicks behind. Marines came out of the holes, stunned for an instant before the NCOs shouted them back in order again.

"That's what I'd call it," Witzko answered Kran's question. "The power blips are all over the place—ten, up to fifteen over the max. This platoon's going to have a mess hall full of simulated KIA marines tonight, Sergeant Kran."

"You going to do something about that, Lieutenant?"

"Yeah, I am, Platoon Sergeant."

Kran removed his helmet and wiped a layer of dust from his face. "You'll need backup on that mission, sir. I'm with you. I hereby witness unauthorized power blips, sir."

Witzko thought about Captain Savant's actions and knew at once that he would never try such a blatant trick unless he had some way to cover what he'd done. Colonel Seymoyr would demand ironclad proof. Lieutenants did not make such formal accusations against captains without proof. Witzko's word, even with Kran's confirmation, wouldn't quite cut it. He'd have to have a lot more than that.

"Thank you, Sergeant," he said, "I greatly appreciate that."

Yet he knew that might be all the satisfaction either he or Sergeant Kran would ever get.

* * * * *

As Witzko stepped out of the shallow hole, two marines ran out of the dust where the hovercraft had disappeared. Kran raced to meet them, talked to them a moment, then turned back to Witzko.

"Something happened," he said, grinning from ear to ear. "That buggy full of uglies stalled out back there. It's still operating, but it's not going anywhere."

Witzko felt a sudden elation. "What I'm thinking—"

"I'm thinking that too, sir. That overpower trick backfired on 'em. All that juice they used glitched up the works, and OpForce can't get them back."

"Well, that *is* a damned shame, Sergeant," Witzko said with mock sympathy. "Let's go give them a hand."

Kran ran off, signaling the squads to him. Witzko checked his weapon, glanced at the display screen again, and followed.

It didn't take long—three minutes flat—to work out the maneuver for "Operation Sack," as Witzko dubbed it at once. First and Second Squad split and moved out through the trees. When the squads reached the hovercraft, Second Squad loosed a ragged volley, then backed out fast. The stubby turret whined around and sprayed the woods, setting simulated fires. "Klicks" poured out of their portal again and fired at the vanished marines.

The cannon fire was somewhat erratic, Witzko noted, and the "klicks" moved in a jerky, twitchy kind of walk.

The simulation was still intact, but it wasn't working right. The craft and its alien troopers were low on juice, and OpForce didn't know how to get them out.

As the cannon and the "klicks" concentrated on marines that weren't there, two troopers from First Squad suddenly appeared above a stand of rocks, each with a satchel charge in hand. At the same time, both the First and Second Squad riflemen opened up with a withering fire. The troopers acted quickly, tossing the satchels down the turret and leaping away.

The charges exploded with a muffled *whooook!* Even a simulated charge had a tremendous force of its own, and two of the lethal packs had done their job. When the smoke cleared away, the hovercraft had come to a halt. The turret was blackened, and every "klick" in sight was officially dead. "Disabled" lights blinked frantically everywhere.

Witzko didn't waste time on a victory party. The Ultra Low Frequency installation was still their target, and Witzko was certain Captain Savant and his OpForce wouldn't make the same mistakes twice. Even if they didn't cheat on power flow again, the stalled hovercraft had given them extra time to get ready for an attack. It didn't seem quite fair to Damion Witzko that Savant's cheap deception had bought the OpForces extra time—but war, even simulated war, wasn't supposed to be fair.

"All right, get going," Kran shouted. "I want First Squad up front, Second on the flank, I want—"

Kran was interrupted by a loud squeal from Witzko's radio. Witzko nearly jumped out of his skin.

"*PRIORITY URGENT—PRIORITY URGENT*!"

"Werewolf Five-Anna," Witzko answered. "I read you clear."

"This mission is canceled, Lieutenant," a mocking voice said over the comm. "You and your platoon will report to shuttle points at once. You are on Boarding Alert as of 2130 hours. You will not debrief. I repeat, you will not debrief. You will shower, change into combat ready uniforms, and report to Embark Niner on the double. Out."

The marines moaned as one. "All right, that's enough," Kran shouted. "As you were!"

"We're already in combat-ready uniforms," someone said.

"Yeah, but you haven't showered," came the answer. "I'm real sure of that."

"Pipe down," Kran yelled, turning on his crew, "Back to the shuttle point. You got your orders, marines!"

"He didn't say a thing about eating," someone said, and Kran didn't bother to call him down.

Witzko was glad the platoon was too angry to notice him. If they had, he was sure they would have seen the bright red anger in his face, the cords rigid in his neck. Even transmitted over a combat radio, the voice was unmistakably Captain Savant's. For Damion Witzko, the message was loud and clear: you win this round, Lieutenant, but this fight's just getting started.

* * * * *

Witzko scrambled down the slope. The platoon was double-timing back through the ravine, Platoon Sergeant Kran urging them on, biting at their heels like a dog after a herd of reluctant sheep. A member of the heavy weapons crew was tending a "dead" weapons marine against a tree. Witzko recognized her as one of the satchel throwers, Private Stosser, who'd recently transferred in from the Combat Engineers.

"Good piece of work," Witzko said. "You dropped that egg very nicely, Private."

Stosser shook her head. "I didn't check my footing before I threw, sir. I should've been—*ow*!"

"Relax," said her teammate as he began to strip away the CM guards around Stosser's lower leg. "You're not going to get a big medal out of this."

"I don't want a medal," Stosser said. "I want to get up and get out of here." She remembered Witzko's presence then, looked startled and added, "Thanks for stopping, sir."

"I don't think it's any problem," said her teammate. "I'd guess a sprain—mild fracture, maybe."

"It better not be a fracture," said Stosser. "I don't need that!"

Witzko recognized the teammate as Private Phelan, who was crosstrained as a medic. Phelan stripped off Stosser's boot and pulled a first aid kit out of his field pack. He pulled on a medical gauntlet and ran his hand over Stosser's ankle. The scanner beeped and showed three purple lights.

"Freezo's okay for now," Phelan said, "but you get a lift to Urgent Care when we land. Don't enter any marathons until we get back, either."

Stosser sat up, suddenly forgetting her pain. "I can make the mission? It'll be okay?"

Private Phelan nodded at Witzko. "You'll make it, Stosser," Witzko said. "No one's going to leave you behind."

The two privates snapped off salutes. Witzko answered the gesture and followed the platoon down the ravine.

Chapter Four

September 21, 2501

Master Sergeant Irina Lavon set her fruit soda down with one hand and picked up her blinking comm with the other. Across the table, Sergeant Reeman rolled his eyes and made a pleading gesture, part of his daily, unending pursuit of Irina Lavon.

Lavon ignored him, stifled the impulse to laugh, and clicked the comm's audio.

"Lavon here."

"We got a new bunch just reporting in. You want to take them, Queenie, or shall I debrief them?"

Lavon bit her lips and counted to ten. Counting forever, she knew, wouldn't improve Jaques Belier's manners and would only be a waste of time. She vowed, however, to one day find a way of curing Belier's habit of using her hated nickname, preferably before the heat-death of the universe, but she wasn't betting on that.

"When is Recon coming back?" she asked. "Their little exercise still on schedule or not?"

Belier laughed—an all too familiar, high-pitched laugh designed to torment Irina Lavon. "You haven't heard, have you Sarge? Hey, I would've called, but I thought you already knew."

Irina gripped the comm. "Knew what? Spit it out, Belier."

"The exercise was *canceled*, Lavon. Your lieutenant goofed it, as usual."

"He what?"

"By the way, you better get packed. We've got Boarding Alert at 2130. Not a lot of time."

"You're nuts," Irina said. "We're leaving at 0630 in the morning, not tonight."

"You think so?"

"I don't think so, I know so. I've been running around all day getting the T.O. & E. straightened out, which, by the way, *you* got so fouled up I could hardly—"

At that instant, the Troop Alert bell began to howl in the hall. Irina looked up, then stared at Sergeant Reeman.

"Now hear this! Now hear this! Boarding Alert is now scheduled for 2130 hours this day. Repeat. Boarding Alert is 2130 hours. The following units will stand ready at once . . ."

Irina could hear Belier's unnerving cackle over the comm. She switched it off with a murderous glance at Reeman. "He *knew* it! He was right there at HQ, his finger on the button, ready to sound the alert as soon as *I* bit on his little joke. Damn him, I will murder that snivelling little bastard. I will chop him into little—"

"Forget it," Reeman said. "Besides, 'little' is not a description I would give Belier anyway. What's all that about Lieutenant Witzko? I don't see the lieutenant goofing up the exercise or anything else. There's got to be more to it than that."

"There is," Irina said darkly, "and if you don't know the answer to that one, you've been asleep about a year."

"Oh, right," Reeman said with sudden understanding.

"Yeah, 'right' indeed. Now get out here, friend. I've got more than I can handle *without* this charming news."

"Well, my luck." Reeman gave her his best kicked dog look. "I had major fantasies for tonight."

"You've always got major fantasies, Sergeant Reeman. Go have them with someone else. You and I have shared so many ditches and D-rations, anything stronger than a buddy hug would feel like incest with you."

"You don't know what you're missing," Reeman sighed. "That extra stripe doesn't make you immune to my charms."

"No." Irina grinned. "It makes me real careful, though."

She blew him a sisterly kiss and scurried for the door, pausing at the mirror on the way out to make certain her uniform was within reason and regulation for greeting newcomers.

On her way across the mall she thought about Witzko and knew that there was little question who was behind whatever had happened on Rimfire Island. Belier, Captain Savant's pet sergeant, must have known all about it, too. He was too ready and too eager to contribute *his* part to the whole mess.

Great. Just what we need, Irina thought, a little more hassle besides getting the platoon ready for a combat mission. A small war was bad enough without dissension in the ranks. Master Sergeant Irina Lavon had been around the Concord Marines a long time and knew what could happen when everyone wasn't working together to keep each other alive.

She offered a silent prayer, hoping there weren't too

many newlies. She wished that she'd insisted that Belier take them himself, but she hated to see newcomers get their first impression of the Concord Marines from Belier. They might, she thought, simply desert on the spot.

Long legs and the sound wind that comes from a ten kilometer run before breakfast brought her to Battalion HQ in ample time. Luckily there were only three newlies—two humans and a t'sa. She glanced at the t'sa's identipad first, giving him the once-over from the corner of her eye. The ID confirmed that the t'sa was indeed a *him*. Gre-Ikwilisan Thumn was male, and if he belonged to the Thumn clan he had more family background than even Lieutenant Witzko did. The question in Irina's mind was, so what is he doing here with the Concord Marines as a civilian technical adviser?

Whatever he'd been doing, he'd done it rather well, Irina thought. His personnel file contained a list of commendations, awards, bonuses, and general praise of his talents. Talent, of course, didn't show on the surface, and to Irina's eye he looked much like the average t'sa—a bipedal reptilian about a meter and a half tall, covered with orange-brown scales. The usual flexible plates and spikes of bone jutted from his head and back. He wore a sleeveless coverall that halfway met Concord Marine regs, and he carried a backpack and a bulging shoulder bag.

"Welcome, to the 26th," Lavon said. "I'm Master Sergeant Lavon."

"I rejoice in being among your most honorable company," the t'sa said in surprisingly good Standard.

"Well, we're glad to have you," Lavon replied.

The two humans were a newly promoted sergeant named Ajayla Chen and a corporal called Hurik Lee who looked a good deal older than his rank suggested. Lavon brought up his file and decided that if Lee had left a trail, he'd covered it very thoroughly, either that or being a corporal gave him chances for deals and scrounging that he would lose at a higher rank. Lavon knew from experience that this was more than a possibility for a supply specialist.

Lee had the look about him, all right. His alert, bright eyes said he could hardly wait for a chance to start some new scam in the battalion.

"Whatever you do, Corporal Lee," she told him with a glance that said she was quite familiar with who and what he was, "remember that you do it for the benefit of the Third Battalion. I expect you to act with discretion and steal in moderation. If you don't—and I assure you I will *know* if you don't—I shall land on you with both boots. Those few who have survived my attention tell me it is a most unpleasant experience."

The color drained from Lee's face, and for a moment he looked as if he might pass out. Gathering himself together, he nodded politely at his new leader.

"Yes. Understood, Master Sergeant."

"Fine. I am so pleased to hear it."

"Now, Sergeant Chen." Irina read from the record. "This says you're a communications specialist, qualified to operate everything from a portable comm to a dreadnought's main rig. Very impressive."

Irina read on and raised a brow. "This part's *not* that impressive, Sergeant Chen. Apparently the reason you're only a new sergeant and not a warrant officer is that you are quite fond of, ah, company in bed and high stakes gambling, everything from cards to top-of-the-line virtual battles."

Irina studied her new sergeant with a dubious eye. "Looks to me like you don't have the character to rise from the ranks, but you're too good at your job to throw away. What do you suggest we do with you here?"

"I hope you don't think my past is any indication of my desire to do my duty, Master Sergeant," said Chen. "I have changed my ways and learned to control myself. I will do a good job for you here."

"You will? I'm so pleased to hear it, Sergeant. All you have to do is show me. Please note that this is a Concord Marine field battalion, not a circus on a tourist planet. As long as you remember the difference, we'll get along fine. Otherwise, my warning to Corporal Lee applies equally to you."

Chen lowered her eyes and tried to look contrite. She didn't succeed very well.

"Report to supply, all of you, and draw your gear. Don't waste any time. In case you didn't hear the alert just now, we are out of here at 2130 hours. That's today, not next week. Dismissed."

The two humans departed as quickly as they could. Before departing, the t'sa gave Irina a deep, ceremonial bow, a gesture normally reserved for the dominant clutch sibling of the clan.

Irina left, crossing the mall again. A heavy skyfreighter droned overhead, sending a tremor through the ground and shaking every window in the quad. It landed out of sight, but not too far to raise a cloud of sand. Irina Lavon sneezed. She thought about the newlies. Whatever their virtues or vices, their presence promised that any cruise with the three would be anything but dull.

Chapter Five

September 28, 2501

Kuhudag opened his eyes. His first impression was that the afterlife was no warmer than the one he'd left behind. His face hurt, and his chest felt as if he'd just been roasted. Worse still, he noted that Grutok had died too. How could this be, he wondered, when the whelp had not even been close when the human's grenade exploded? Undoubtedly it had been a very large grenade.

"Worthy, you must please speak to me. You cannot cease to live. I will be chastised severely if I report your demise!"

Kuhudag squinted. It was truly Grutok, looking much as he had when he was alive. This could only mean that he *was* alive, since the Old Ways taught that the weren were greatly transformed in the afterworld.

"What happened? I believe I had a severe accident."

"Yes, Worthy, you have indeed," Grutok said, covering Kuhudag's face against the biting wind. "It is most fortunate that I was able to drag you back to our position. At first, I thought you had passed on to a greater life, then you made a noise of sorts—"

Kuhudag forced himself to sit up, biting back the pain

so Grutok would not be humiliated at such a sight. "You dragged me back here? By yourself?"

"Of course, I take no credit for this act," Grutok said quickly. "I was helped by higher powers. I could not have managed such an effort myself."

"No, certainly not. Still, whatever part you *did* play is to be lightly praised."

"An honor I can scarcely accept, Worthy."

"Indeed."

Kuhudag pressed his face into the snow to cool his skin and fur, then raised his weapon and looked it over from end to end. Clearly while he had lost consciousness Grutok had cleaned it thoroughly. He was careful not to seem to notice. Saving an elder's life had given the whelp more than enough attention for one day.

Peering over the edge of the hollow, he looked out onto the wintry plain, trying to recall exactly where he had been when the explosion occurred. Grutok quickly confirmed that Kuhudag had not been out for long. Ten minutes at the most.

This told Kuhudag a great deal. The situation out there had surely changed, but apparently not so much that they were threatened with an immediate attack by the humans. He could still hear the chatter of human and weren weapons in the distance, but no more grenades. He sniffed the air and turned to Grutok.

"I intend to take a look. Again, if I do not return you know what to do."

"Yes, Worthy," Grutok said. Kuhudag could see the beginning of a protest in the whelp's features—that Kuhudag might not be in condition to go back into the field—but he did not dare voice such a thought. Kuhudag was thankful for that. The young one had been most helpful, and it would be a shame to discipline him now.

* * * * *

Another half hour of crawling among the ice-covered terrain taught him nothing new, except for the fact that he was certain the grenade had broken something vital and that he would never be warm again.

Checking his rifle once more, he began to withdraw to Grutok's position. He avoided retracing his path in case some crafty enemy had somehow managed to get behind him and was lying in ambush. Carefully scanning the terrain, Kuhudag headed back in the general direction of the hollow.

Again sending the low-pitched signal ahead, he waited for Grutok's reply. Grutok answered, and Kuhudag pulled himself over the edge of the shelter. At once Grutok handed him a hot, steaming tin of Killberry tea.

Kuhudag was astonished. He made no effort hide his surprise. "Ulaak's Eyes, lad, where did *this* come from?"

"My mother sent it with us," he answered. "It was for a most needful moment."

"Yes, well, this would certainly be the time she was speaking of, I imagine."

He gratefully brought the cup to his mouth and let the hot, spicy liquid flow down his throat. At once, the warmth spread through his body, miraculously warming parts he felt he would never feel again.

"I must remember to thank your mother," he said. "This was an act of unusual kindness."

"Yes, Worthy. She will be pleased at your approval."

That, Kuhudag thought, was truer than the whelp imagined. It was very unlikely that he understood this was another subtle gesture on Medlyna's part—another small, near ceremonial act—that told Kuhudag she might be willing to show more than a formal interest in Kuhudag's friendship, that she might very well care to take that friendship to a much higher level.

That idea, Kuhudag thought, had occurred to him as well, one that would not be all that unpleasant to think about on the way back to camp.

* * * * *

By the time Kuhudag and Grutok rejoined the hunting party, the clouds had blown away and from a darkening sky the blue glow of Platon washed across the snowfields. The rest of the party challenged them three times in the last four hundred paces of his approach, but no one showed any pleasure in their survival or expressed the slightest interest in Kuhudag's battle.

"All has not been well," Alaagh, the third best hunter, told him. "We have not had a fortunate day."

Kuhudag followed Alaagh's glance and saw the two cloak-wrapped bodies lying stiff on a patch of trampled snow with the first few stones for their cairn already piled beside them. He understood even more clearly when he heard the moans from inside the one tent the party had brought. Apparently the healers were doing what they could for four badly wounded warriors.

Kuhudag did not have the heart to ask how much harm the weren had done the humans. Even if it was more than the weren suffered, this was not a day for boasting. If the humans had inflicted more harm than they had sustained, it was a day to be remembered in silence until it could be honorably avenged.

* * * * *

Late in the day, after he'd had a chance to eat and warm himself, Kuhudag relieved a sentry who was nearly frozen on the outer edge of the camp. His vantage point lay behind a boulder that partly hid him from the plain but still gave him a good view across the flatter ground in three directions.

The silence grew heavy, and twilight drew near as he watched the frozen wilderness slowly fading from sight. The sun's muted light was now completely gone, and Platon hung behind a dim haze. The heavy clouds that had covered the sky earlier had drifted north and were likely covering those broken lands in a fresh blanket of snow.

As ever, he was careful not to watch any one spot too long, lest he see movement where there was none or enemies where there might be friends. Still nothing but twisting eddies of snow moved in all the barren wasteland before him.

The silence seemed to thicken as Platon sank beneath the horizon. Shortly before midnight even the wind died to a breeze, and the moans from the tent came only now and again.

It was Burwab who came to him in the darkness. Despite his strong gait, the weren chief's broad shoulders sagged, and it seemed as if his tusks had grown more yellow, his ruff thinner, since the morning. Kuhudag was not surprised. Burwab had served as Council Chief of West Lodge for seven years; Kuhudag knew more than most the toll that took. All things considered, he would rather have fought a duel once a week than wear the cloak of leadership.

"The others have told me what occurred," Burwab said. "As I could not be present when you returned, I would be grateful to hear your ventures myself."

There was a less than subtle plea in the leader's voice, a hope that Kuhudag might confirm that the weren had inflicted some hurt on the humans. Kuhudag understood, but he feared to be thought of as boastful if he went too quickly to that part of the tale.

Beginning at the beginning, he told his leader the complete story. He left out only that part concerning his refusal to fire on the retreating humans and their wounded comrade. His reasons were good and sufficient, but he doubted Burwab would see it that way. The chief had slightly different feelings about the path of honor, and Kuhudag respected those feelings.

"It is good, the work you have done today," Burwab said when Kuhudag was finished. "Did you recognize any of the humans?"

"No."

"Were any close enough that you would recognize them if you saw them again?"

"I had the best look at the wounded man's face, but I would not give the Iron Oath that I would recognize him again."

Burwab seemed disappointed, but Kuhudag could not be certain of that. The chief's breath mask and goggles hid his face except for his intent brown eyes.

"Will you be one of those who will march to avenge this day?" Burwab asked. "If you are among them, perhaps we can punish those truly guilty of weren blood and honorably leave those about whom there is doubt as to their own shame."

"None of those I faced—" Kuhudag began, then stopped. He realized Burwab did not care to hear that he could not assure him the opponents he had faced had shed weren blood.

"I cannot be certain, Burwab, who the particular humans were. I heard them speak to one another, but it was no speech I recognized. That tells me next to nothing, of course. The humans speak many tongues beside Standard."

"Yes, indeed," Burwab said, stomping his feet on the ground and wrapping his arms about his chest, "but the way they were dressed, perhaps, something in their manner . . ."

He knew what Burwab wanted. The leader readily assumed these humans were from Red Ridge or one of its outlying settlements. Kuhudag could not honestly give him that assurance, though this was what Burwab wished to hear.

"I will say this," Kuhudag went on, "though I have no way to prove my thoughts. I suspect the humans I faced might be new to the field, that we have not faced them before."

Burwab looked up quickly. "Oh? Why would you say this, Kuhudag? You have just told me that you did not recognize the humans, that you had no idea just who they might be. Now you tell me something else?"

Kuhudag didn't miss the irritation in Burwab's voice. This, as he had known before he spoke, was another thing the leader did not wish to hear.

"It is only a thought for the moment," he said, "but I am duty-bound to express my feelings on this. The humans I faced used laser weapons. We have seen this weapon before, as you well know, but it is not a common thing on Arist."

"Lasers tell you these humans are different, that they are not Red Ridgers trying to keep us away from yet more hunting grounds?"

Burwab's eyes narrowed behind his goggles, and he continued, "It is possible that the hermits and outlaws of the Ridge could obtain laser weapons from somewhere else. Everyone—including the weren—trade off-worlders for whatever goods or weapons they can get."

Kuhudag did not reply. Burwab spoke truly, but Kuhudag's instinct told him that the chief was wrong.

Staring out across the the dim snowfield, Burwab shook his head and said, "I appreciate your thoughts, but I can see no reason to think the humans you faced were any different from the rest."

"In my mind, the fighting skill they showed demands a great deal more training and discipline than I have seen from the Ridgers. I respectfully stand by what I have said, Burwab."

"I repeat that I appreciate your thoughts. I simply see no merit in them, Kuhudag. Is there any more you wish to tell me?"

"I think that is all," Kuhudag replied.

Burwab muttered something Kuhudag couldn't hear, then turned and stalked off through the snow.

Kuhudag stared after the leader, angry and startled by Burwab's words. The leader had come very close to an insult that could not be ignored short of a duel, and that was an unthinkable act—two leaders of West Lodge set against one another—especially at a time such as this, when the weren faced enemies of another species.

Kuhudag took deep breaths to bring his rage under control. Burwab was not thinking clearly. His mind, his judgment, had been clouded by the events of today and the days before that. Kuhudag was uncertain how to handle this new problem. Burwab was clearly wrong in his behavior, but there were others who would side with him if it came to a challenge of leadership. The chief had many supporters, weren who had voted against the selling of hunting rights to the humans. Such a decision, many would argue, had been a choice the weren should not have taken. With council elections only half a year away, this could well be a factor in keeping Burwab's followers in power.

"I don't want the damnable job," Kuhudag said aloud, "but I am not at all certain he should have it, either."

Still, Kuhudag knew that whatever happened, he would fight alongside his people, no matter who was leader. His honor, his reputation as a hunter, demanded it.

For the moment, he did not feel the cold, did not feel the cutting bite of icy flakes upon his skin. He was a weren, and he was a warrior. He threw back his head and lifted his face to the sky. From deep within him came a howl that drowned out even the moaning of the wind.

Chapter Six

October 09, 2501

Lieutenant Colonel Seymoyr had missed dinner, and *Stormbird's* captain Ela Myklebust was so eager to get past the business at hand that she forgot to order drinks, let alone snacks. A Star Force captain outranked a marine lieutenant colonel, and Seymoyr had suffered worse handicaps than an empty stomach.

"I still don't agree in principle," Seymoyr told the captain in his most respectful fashion. "I thought we were supposed to do all of our coat-trailing in the Hammer's Star system. Who exactly gains from a slow cruise around Bluefall for a couple of days to see who trails us?"

"You trust Admiral Skorbo, I hope?" Myklebust asked. The task force commander flew his flag in the squadron's other heavy ship, the Concord dreadnought *Revealer.*

"Completely, but trusting him doesn't make such a long cruise to starfall logical."

The captain looked down at her hands, but Seymoyr didn't miss the half smile "You wouldn't be disagreeing even in principle if you'd seen the messenger who brought the, ah, call it a *request,* to both me *and* Skorbo."

Seymoyr squinted at the ceiling. "Let me guess:

medium-sized woman, slim, red-haired, with enough cybernetic augmentations to get her shot as a cykotek on some planets?"

"She's wearing her hair black now, but otherwise that's the one." Myklebust looked if she'd bitten into something sour.

Seymoyr understood the look and knew the question of a slow cruise out of the system was no longer open to discussion. The "messenger" worked for both the Concord and the Hale Regency, the government of Bluefall. When she brought a request, it had the force of a direct order from both. Even a "request" from the Regency would have carried enough weight. Without its base on Bluefall, the Concord's operations would be crippled in the Verge.

"All right," Seymoyr said. "I hear and obey. Who do they expect to trail us? The Thuldans?"

The Empire was the most logical suspect. They were a major menace to the peace the Concord was trying to bring to the Verge, and they had actually tried to take Regency Island a few years before. True, they got their forces blown into hot gas for their trouble, but it took more than that to discourage a Thuldan.

"Probably," Myklebust said, "Skorbo and I did insist on one thing. We and *Revealer* cruise in supporting distance until we starfall. We won't try to tempt the Thuldans into attacking by pretending weakness. We save that for Hammer's Star."

"Suppose the Thuldans' trailer calls in heavy reinforcements once we're out where there's enough space to hide the bodies?"

"We'll get your marines out—if possible—onto something solid."

They shook hands on that. Seymoyr had not qualified for command after twenty years of staff duty only to get half his battalion wiped out by bad luck in a space battle.

The chime on the cabin door sounded. Two stewards entered, one with a loaded tray and plates, one with two pots. Behind them came one of *Stormbird*'s marine detachment, the captain's messenger.

The smell from the tray and pots was so enticing, Seymoyr had to force himself to listen. He was glad he did. Shuttle 198 was on the way up with Recon Platoon and most of HQ. That was the last of his marines.

"Captain," he said, pouring himself a hot cup of mythleaf tea, "would you care to honor my battle group by attending their welcome aboard?"

Myklebust nodded, then bowed as gracefully as she could with her mouth full. Seymoyr looked at the captain's plate and realized that he wasn't the only senior officer who had missed a few meals lately.

* * * * *

OCTOBER 11, 2501

Bluefall lay thirty hours astern. As the dull gray durasteel door of the lift slid open, Damion Witzko could see the image of the planet's dazzling oceans and deceptively white cloud formations on one of the bridge's holodisplays. *Stormbird*'s main navigation array was focused on *Revealer.* Even three hundred kilometers away, her massive bulk dominated the image. The big dreadnought looked like a metallic egg laid by an asteroid-sized reptilian, then hammered at randomly by meteorites. A Galactic War II veteran, some the ship's additions were repaired battle damage, but most were postwar refits. Eleven hundred meters long and three hundred meters wide across her docking collar amidships, she spouted pods and arrays for every weapon and sensor a marine lieutenant should be able to recognize, plus a few Witzko had never seen before.

Damion might well have followed his career aboard such a ship, but his Tactical Intuition scores for ground combat were so much higher than those for space combat that he'd not fought too hard against family pressure to join the marines rather than Star Force. Still, he'd devoured all sixteen files of *Galway's History of the Driveship* before he was fifteen. He loved fine ships and thought that the marines might give him the best of both possible worlds. He could fight on the ground but get a lot of free ship time on the way to the fighting.

He was so taken with the dreadnought that he realized a moment too late he'd been gaping at the display instead of standing at attention. His companion, Captain Kira McRae of 2nd Company, was looking stun charges at him. Colonel Seymoyr was too polite to glare. He simply cleared his throat twice.

"Permission to come on the bridge?" Seymoyr asked the ship's marine detachment.

The guard turned to Captain Myklebust and shouted, "Visitors requesting freedom of the bridge!" McRae and Witzko were only taking their turn at the standard courtesy visit expected from officers of embarked marines, but ship detachment marines announced everyone as if they might be a fleet commander.

"Good morning," Myklebust greeted the marines.

She looked as if she had slept soundly, which was more than Witzko could say of himself. After getting

Recon quartered, he had been so full of tension from Captain Savant's "training exercise" that he had exercised in the gym until he was tired enough to go to sleep.

"Good morning, Captain," Seymoyr said. "May I introduce Captain McRae of 2nd Company and Lieutenant Witzko, Recon Platoon leader?"

"I'm afraid there's nothing exciting going on," Myklebust said. "If there were, we'd have to chase you back to your quarters and lock down for Battle Stations."

"What about our trailer, ma'am?" Seymoyr asked. "We've, ah, heard we have some company."

Myklebust suppressed a smile. She knew there were few secrets aboard a ship that lasted overnight.

"Display Four, maximum magnification," she said.

A holodisplay flickered on, showing a metallic speck against the starscape. The view suddenly enlarged, and Witzko recognized a Thuldan light cruiser, Hero class, with some curious-looking sensor arrays sprouting in nonstandard places.

"Imperial Thuldan cruiser *Diomedes,*" Myklebust said. "She's been on our trail since two hours after we left Bluefall orbit, staying just outside legal distance where she can detect us changing a roll of toilet paper without going to active scanning."

"Why us?" McRae asked. "Or is it the whole squadron she's snooping?"

Witzko turned the question over in his mind. It would be just like Seymoyr to ask him to answer that, just to see if his juniors were on the alert.

"I've heard the Thuldans snoop-trail half the ships leaving Bluefall," he put in. "I suppose that's because a Thuldan warship much farther in toward the Stellar Ring here would stand out like a fly on the Emperor's scalp."

McRae actually cracked a smile at that.

Seymoyr nodded, adding, "The Thuldans can afford to lose ships and men, but they don't like to lose reputation. They lost a lot of that when they tried to take Regency Island and got blown out of the sky. Ever since, they've been trying to prove that neither the Concord nor Hale can tell them what to do around Bluefall."

"Yes," Myklebust said, showing a good many teeth with a grin that reminded Witzko of a hungry Moore's shark, "but neither we nor the Regency will let them play games with anything larger than a cutter in Bluefall orbit, so they have to play their tricks well out in the system. Can anyone guess why they're after *Stormbird?*"

McRae looked blank. Witzko didn't want to seem pushy, but both senior officers looked as if they'd value intelligence more than manners.

"*Stormbird*'s the first *Fortinbras* transport in the Verge," he said cautiously, "and they think she may be on a new kind of mission. Also, unless I miss my guess, the Thuldans aren't used to seeing StarMech designs bearing Concord colors."

Myklebust frowned. "I very much doubt that they are, and I'm just as glad they're surprised enough to be curious."

StarMech had licensed the design as part of their initial contribution to the Concord. They were perfect fast transports once they'd been stripped down to defensive armament.

"We can starfall with *Revealer,*" Myklebust concluded, "and there's a quick-change kit being designed that can turn the troop spaces into missile storage in ten days."

McRae shrugged. “Just as long as you let us ground-pounders debark before you load the missiles. I’ve never bunked with a plasma warhead before, and I’d just as soon not start now.”

After morning coffee, before they were scheduled to leave, Witzko asked a final question: “What happens if *Diomedes* tails us right out to starfall?”

“The Thuldans are tough and arrogant, but they’re not stupid,” Myklebust said. “They’ll probably stay at a safe distance. If they don’t, *Revealer* will take good care of us.”

Witzko wanted to ask how but couldn’t quite get up the nerve.

Myklebust guessed his question and smiled.

“We dump garbage.”

“Ma’am?”

“Isn’t that illegal?” put in McRae.”

“Exactly. It’s so illegal they’ll cruise up close to document it for their complaint. It’s not often that they have a chance to bring charges against the Concord. They’ll survive what happens after that, but they’ll be less than eager to spy on us again.”

Chapter Seven

October 12, 2501

West Lodge, the largest of the weren settlements on Arist, lay deep on the side of a valley beside a narrow, slow-moving glacier. The great river of grinding ice ran down from Mount Guthru, a huge pinnacle of snow-covered rock that overshadowed all the surrounding land. In seasons when the sun reached the bottom of the valley, a thin skin of flowing water sometimes covered the ice during daylight hours, but the inhabitants of West Lodge preferred to take their water from the wells bored slantwise into the rock. These kilometer-deep shafts reached the glacier far below its surface, where the ice was purer and the hot springs used to melt it were closer to the surface.

On Arist, daylight was absent a good part of the year, but the West Lodgers did not miss it as greatly. Shelter from the wind and the cold was of primary importance on such a frigid world, and for that both the weren and the human inhabitants depended on the great network of caverns that burrowed deep beneath the surface.

Early in its geologic history, volcanoes had restructured the planet, leaving a near endless maze of burrow-like tunnels in its wake, empty tubes where lava had flowed for millions of years. Life had just begun to start on the small moon when Arist settled into its final phase of planetary life as a frozen, windswept world with a thin, frigid atmosphere.

When sentient races arrived, they found only two reasons to venture out onto the inhospitable surface. One was to hunt the tough, fur-clad *damool*, the wily *trac*, and the dozen or so other species of animals and birds that had adapted to the harsh environment. During the so-called "summer" of Arist when the ice along the equator thinned somewhat, many of the weren took the chance at hacking through the ice to catch and eat an occasional *raasha*, a fine-tasting fish. Yet even this required a certain amount of determination. An average raasha was three meters long and covered in thick, armor-like scales. More than one intrepid fisherman seeking dinner had received more than he bargained for and ended up as dinner himself.

The only other reason to roam about the surface was to fight. Killing would surely be more comfortable in the warmth of the caverns, but neither the weren nor the humans of Red Ridge would ever consider such a terrible breach of manners. Whatever was built on the surface during combat—and whoever ventured there—was fair game, but the caverns were home. The caverns were where you lived. Both the weren and the humans knew the limits of their territory beneath the cold surface, and each respected the other. Any other behavior would bring chaos. Not even the best trailmaker of either race knew the extent of the caverns. A war down there might begin, but it would surely never end.

* * * * *

The temperature in the sheltered valley was bearable without several layers of clothing, if not exactly comfortable. Wearing boots and hood, but with his arms and legs clad only in their natural fur, Kuhudag walked out in the grayness of a cloudy dawn, sniffed the air, and crossed the narrow stretch of rock to the cavern entry just below.

Above, on the rim of the rocky valley, twists of low-hanging cloud crept across the leaden sky. The wind above the ridge was light today, but Kuhudag wore thick fur and leather head protectors to guard his ears against the wind. Many of the weren scouts claimed Kuhudag could hear two snowflakes kissing a hundred paces upwind. He had never been asked to prove this, but he knew that he had acute hearing even for a professional hunter. Everyone in West Lodge would eat better if he kept that hearing for many years to come. Game had always been scarce on Arist, and it was now scarcer still after the sale of the hunting grounds. The underground breeding pens produced only a fraction of the weren meat requirements; the rest had to come from the fishers and hunters.

The moment he ducked through the cavern entry, the temperature began to rise. By the time he passed the outskirts of the underground settlement, he was ready to shed his outer wear.

At the shooting range, he found himself alone except for the two guards who kept children and fools from wandering into deadly fire. They waved him to Post Two and raised the red flags.

"Clear to shieldward!" one shouted.

"Clear to maceward!" the other said.

Kuhudag took off his hood, adjusted his earmuffs,

and loaded the first round from his pouch into the breech of his rifle.

He fired five rounds, sitting, lying, and standing, all at five hundred paces, then he stepped forward to three hundred paces and repeated the sequence. The third round of the sequence misfired.

He opened the breech and found the cartridge bulging at one end and beginning to split at the sides. One faulty round out of more than twenty wasn't bad. Still, it could have blown out the breech and exploded in his face. It had happened to weren before.

"Careful, warrior," said a voice behind him. "Everyone knows how Toorhat One Tusk got his name."

Kuhudag turned to face Grutok's mother, Medlyna. She was a striking female, Kuhudag thought; it was always a surprise to see that she was almost as tall as he was. Wearing the high-peaked cap she favored, she overtopped him.

"I greet you, Honored Mother. May I inquire into your well-being?"

"You may," she answered, "and I thank you for your concern. I am glad to say that all is well with me, in body and in mind."

"I am pleased that this is so."

The formal ritual over, Kuhudag paused and decided to chance a more intimate greeting. Nodding slightly, he thrust out his low, underslung jaw and raised his tusks a bare inch or so.

Medlyna accepted the gesture; she had once before, which gave him the nerve to try it again. Kuhudag was both pleased and relieved; this time, her return bow was a trifle lower than when they'd met before, telling him plainly that she would be open to a still more intimate interchange upon their next meeting.

She was equipped much the same as he was. Fur cloak and hood, open now in the comfort of the cavern, heated mask and goggles on a clip at her waist, and pouches of ammo across her chest. In a leather sheath she carried a knife with a blade of human-forged steel and a handcrafted bone grip. Slung across her back was her favorite weapon, the eight gauge shotgun that would have enabled her to bring down whole flocks of birds on Kurg. The shotgun was an unusual weapon among the weren, especially among female warriors. No one, though, questioned Medlyna's ability to use it.

"Young Grutok," Kuhudag continued, "I have not seen him since our patrol together. He is faring well, I trust."

"He is faring *too* well, I believe," Medlyna said with a scolding voice that hid a weren smile. "He will speak of nothing but his war venture with the Worthy Kuhudag. You have touched him deeply. He feels a closeness to you."

Kuhudag felt his heart quicken and tried to hide his feelings as honor required. If the mother spoke of her child's feelings, she was expressing hers as well. That was the weren way.

"I am honored by those feelings," he said. "Please inform the lad that I would . . . return . . . that closeness, as well."

"He will be grateful," she said, bringing her claws together at a peak. "I think I can assure you of that."

After this exchange, Kuhudag felt any further attempt at hitting a target would be futile. For the moment he had lost all interest in marksmanship. He had certainly given serious thought to Medlyna in the past, but lately those thoughts had greatly intensified. Now, with Medlyna's obvious encouragement, he saw their friendship was entering an entirely different stage—one in which they would both have to consider the obligations and responsibilities of taking the relationship further.

* * * * *

Kuhudag, on his walk back from the range, suddenly stopped as he was struck with a new and staggering thought. By Great Hootak, it was quite possible they had, just moments before, *already* taken that new, somewhat unnerving step.

Since the battle in the north, Kuhudag had been relieved that the humans had stayed away from the werens' surface quarters and its outlying settlements. Whether Burwab agreed or not, Kuhudag still questioned whether or not the Red Ridgers had participated—or even condoned—in the battle that had taken both weren and human lives.

You could never truly trust a human, of course, and it was entirely possible the Ridgers knew about the laser-armed warriors to the north and were even pleased by their actions. Perhaps they even *gave* the others those weapons. How was one to know?

Drawing his cloak closer about him, he walked back into the outside world. The wind had grown stronger, and icy bullets stung his face and hands. He drew on his gloves and set his goggles firmly in place.

In the near distance, he saw four warriors slogging toward him, backs bent into the wind. In the lead was Burwab himself, followed by the warrior Magtan and Shubud, West Lodge's senior priest. Devout Orlamu were fewer on Arist than in most weren communities off Kurg. In West Lodge, however, Shubud was not only a permanent resident but a member of the elected council.

"We have decided upon the time and strength of our journey to the Red Ridge," Burwab said, wasting no time on formal rites. "I trust you will be with me in the lead, Kuhudag. You are too valuable a hunter and warrior to march anywhere else in the column. Besides, you know more human languages than the rest of us, a talent that may be most useful."

Kuhudag was in no way fooled by Burwab's flattery or the fact that the chief now totally ignored their quarrel—and Burwab's humiliating remarks that bordered on a Challenge. Leaders had a way of recalling and forgetting what seemed convenient at the time.

"It is the time," said Magtan the warrior, raising a closed fist. "Our Brothers and Sisters must be avenged."

"Even in blood?" Kuhudag replied. He looked at Burwab. "This, too, has been decided?"

"If need be, yes," Burwab said.

"So without further hesitation we will show the humans that we have handed their race a blood debt."

"Do you see that we can do any less?" Burwab's teeth clacked together with a sound that drowned out the wind. "You continue to bewilder me, Kuhudag. I see you, but I do not know what you are."

Kuhudag held himself back, controlling the anger within. Shubud stepped quickly forward. His muzzle was gray with age, and he was as tall as either Burwab or Kuhudag. Stepping between the two ended the threat of violence almost before it began.

"To march against the humans, to teach them that we

can defend our honor and avenge our dead, is the decision of the Council," Shubud said. "To join us or not is every warrior's choice. It is true, however, that anyone who can help make our march a victory but decides not join it could well be considered dishonorable to his Brothers. This is the way that *every* weren knows."

The warning was anything but subtle. Naming no names, Shubud had made it clear he would neither condone nor counsel against a warrior challenging Kuhudag. Kuhudag knew, even if he didn't go, there was a good chance no one—including Burwab—would rise to that occasion.

"That is certainly the weren way," Kuhudag said calmly. "As for myself, Shubud, I doubt that any right-thinking warrior would desert his Brothers in time of need, even if he did not entirely agree with all of those Brothers." He turned his dark eyes on Burwab. "I cannot imagine that any among us would take the accusation of cowardice lightly. Such a thing would call for a reckoning at once, would it not?"

Burwab met his gaze. "It would, Kuhudag. I cannot question that. Nor would I imagine it would be necessary for such a thing to occur among those loyal to the weren, no matter their feelings, one way or another."

"It is as I have said," Kuhudag answered, then pausing for an instant to let the moment pass, "How ready are we to take blood for blood?"

"As ready as we must be," Burwab said. "We must be prepared to do what we must in order to come back safely." His tone said he recognized an offer of compromise.

Perhaps, Kuhudag thought, this had always been his intent. Burwab had not been one to think with his talons for many years.

"It is my opinion that we should first warn them by destruction rather than death," Kuhudag said. "Let them know we have the power to take blood vengeance or hold it back. In this way, we preserve honor in refusing to shed innocent blood, yet we do not refuse to challenge the dishonor done to us. Perhaps the wise among the humans will counsel the fools to sit with us and talk. They may lack hair and size, but they are not without wits."

Shubud nodded in agreement. "We will slay no one without arms in hand. We will slay no elders, women, or children unless they show violence to us. Even then, we will act only to defend, not to kill. We will destroy nothing whose loss might mean death to a human through cold or hunger."

This last hardly needed saying. The priest was merely repeating a dictum common among all folk on Arist, weren and human alike. It had long been understood, by word and tradition, that leaving another shelterless in the winds demanded restitution. Doing such a thing by deliberate action carried a death sentence that had, at times, been carried out by parties drawn from both human and weren.

Whether all this talk had been Shubud's intention all along, or in the sly thoughts of Burwab, Kuhudag felt he might indeed have made himself heard fairly this day.

Chapter Eight

OCTOBER 13, 2501

Bluefall now lay sixty hours behind, starfall barely an hour ahead, and the game of baiting *Diomedes* was nearly done. Irina Lavon stalked down the passageway toward Recon Platoon's quarters hoping to catch Jobal Kran before he entered his meditations.

A devout Orlamu, Sergeant Kran shared his faith's belief that the true nature of the cosmos would be revealed in drivespace. However, he had also been popping in and out of drivespace as a merchant space hand Concord Marine for twenty-five years without having any revelations he would admit to. His meditations were more of a precaution to prepare his mind and body in case some secret did come to him during the next one hundred and twenty-one hours.

Lavon entered after a his terse—"Enter"—and found him not yet in the lotus position but stripped to his shorts. Lavon admired the muscles rippling beneath his dark skin. It was, she thought, ridiculous to pretend not to notice.

As a platoon sergeant, Kran had a small cabin to himself. His quarters consisted of little more than a bunk that folded into the wall, a small table with a computer console, and three or four drawers set into the wall beneath the bunk.

"Greetings and blessings, Irina," Kran said. "What brings you here?"

"I'm trying to finish my list of problem children before we starfall."

Kran did not need to ask why this pertained to him. She had held him through many starfall-induced nightmares, an experience profoundly disturbing to a devout Orlamu who believed that starfall was a benign, even blessed state. In turn, he had brought her herb tea and cleaned up the mess when starfalling turned her stomach inside out.

"My soul is overwhelmed by your concern," Kran said in the formal Orlamu manner, then quickly returning to his marine persona, "You start throwing up a whole year's rations, Master Sergeant, give me a buzz. I'll come pull you out of the sink and hold your hand a while."

Irina made a face. "You don't *have* to be so graphic, Kran. I do remember what it's like."

Kran looked in the general direction of the Orlamu afterworld. "This time, it will not be so bad. You will scarcely wish to die."

"What a relief. As ever, you've made my day, friend."

"It is my task on this plane of being to take care of you, Irina," he grinned, "a pleasure, not a burden."

"I'll hold you to that, Platoon Sergeant. Happy journey."

* * * * *

Maybe he will have a revelation this time, she thought, as she made her way through the narrow hallway, and maybe I'll be able to eat like a human being again. Hey, anything could happen.

Lavon was so totally absorbed in her thoughts that she nearly collided with Lieutenant Witzko who was headed the other way. She drew in a breath and flattened herself against the bulkhead. Witzko reached out to protect her from the collision, and for an instant he was grasping her shoulders, holding his master sergeant a great deal closer than regulations permitted.

"Sorry, Sergeant," he muttered and pulled away.

"Oh, my fault, sir. Wasn't looking where I was going."

She didn't miss the fact that backing away, he managed to look her up and down with polite appreciation. Irina found she was rather pleased, certainly not insulted at all. In fact—

She quickly tossed the thought aside. Now where did that come from?

"Sergeant, are you all right?"

Lavon suddenly realized she was not all right. Aside from surprising herself with embarrassing thoughts about Lieutenant Witzko, her stomach was beginning its regular revolt. The stardrive and mass reactors weren't yet in starfall mode, but her body was acting as if the decks were already vibrating with the shifting strains of the power. It was bad enough being sick for an hour or more after starfall. This was ridiculous. Being sick out of anticipation for the last hours *before* starfall was something else.

"I'm sensitive to starfall," she said, deciding honesty was the only way to go. "I spend the first couple of hours in drivespace with my head in the toilet. That's if I'm lucky. If not, I spend a day in the infirmary."

Witzko looked concerned. "Have you tried Skaminine 92? It seems to work pretty well."

"I've tried everything authorized for the problem and a few things that aren't. I get two results: none, or it makes things worse."

"Ow!" Witzko cringed. "I thought I had trouble. I nearly ended up in the CDC because of low zero-g adaptability scores. It turned out I needed minor ear surgery, so they chopped around and gave me three months to recover, then tested me again. Here I am, a genuine Concord Moron by the grace of MedCorps."

Irina laughed. "Thanks for the kind words, Lieutenant. I think I'm going to be all"—a sudden fit of trembling took her—"uhhh, be all right, soon as I can . . ."

"Uh-uh, I can see that." Witzko caught her as she started to slide gently down the wall. She folded into his arms, a lighter burden than he'd imagined. Though Irina Lavon was a very lean woman, he'd imagined the famed master sergeant's strength and agility must weigh something. Instead, he found himself carrying a very limp lady whose form was perfectly soft at the moment, not even close to combat ready.

"Sorry," Irina said. "Guess I—" Her eyes got wide as she realized where she was. "Oh, listen, Lieutenant, I'm fine, really. You don't have to do this."

"I don't think you're going to make it by yourself, Sergeant. It's no problem, really."

Irina let out a breath. "Uh, try me. Okay?"

Witzko let her down. She was shaky for a moment, then nodded to show him she was fine. One step down the hall, however, told him she was wrong.

"Come on," he said, "I'm not going to have my master sergeant passing out in the hall. It won't look good on my record. Where are your quarters? This is NCO country, but I don't—"

"That way." Irina pointed. She stopped protesting and let him guide her. Two conflicting thoughts ran through her head: His presence was nice. His arm holding her squarely upright felt fine. The other thought was: damn it all, I feel too bad to care.

* * * * *

From his cabin, Witzko watched the tiny holodisplay show him the fate of the Thuldan follower, *Diomedes.* The proximity flares *Revealer* dumped along with the ship's garbage temporarily blinded several hundred crewmen but did little more harm than that. However, the Thuldans would likely hesitate the next time they wanted to collect incriminating evidence from a Concord squadron's garbage.

The bulkhead vibrated slightly, and Witzko knew the cutter *Activity* must have docked with *Stormbird.* The cutter would be hitching a ride on the hull the rest of the way to the Hammer's Star system. The escorts accompanying *Revealer* had long since done the same.

Witzko lay on his bunk and pulled the strap down from the overhead. Even though he usually did well on starfalls, it was always wise to keep the strap hooked down. Solid sleep was the way to get through starfall—unless you were an Orlamu and cared to stay awake and watch the black infinity of drivespace, hoping you would see something else.

As Damion Witzko drifted into sleep, his last thoughts were of how he had last seen Irina Lavon, curled up peacefully in her bunk with a restful smile on her face, mumbling something that he couldn't quite make out.

Chapter Nine

October 24, 2501

By the time Kuhudag finished bundling up his tent, the brief sun of Arist was more than halfway below the horizon. Platon would ride high tonight, but its clammy blue light barely let a weren cast a shadow.

Kuhudag found a rock that thrust itself farther out of the snow than its mates. He sat down on the chilly stone and began lacing on his trail boots. The weather had been against the raiders, and they were only now within striking distance of Red Ridge. To Kuhudag's pleasure, the lack of any human contact along the way had begun to stir certain doubts among the Council. In truth, no human had attacked a weren anywhere since the battle in the mountains.

An armed weren outpost to the south had a human radio and reported some sky vehicles passing north from Red Ridge, but the craft were not close enough to identify.

It seemed likely to Kuhudag that Shubud, the other Council members, and perhaps even Burwab, knew that if they continued ahead, they did so with imperfect knowledge. Honor might demand retaliation, but it also called for an effort on the part of the weren to perfect their knowledge of the enemy as soon as possible.

Honor and truth were two sides of the same coin, and one could not exist without the other.

* * * * *

Darkness was upon the frozen land when the raiders sighted the outskirts of Red Ridge. The weren scattered outward across the snow in a broad, loose wedge they would hold unless the enemy sighted them there.

Kuhudag unslung his rifle and took his place in the vanguard of the wedge. Keeping low, he peered over an icy ledge and looked down upon the settlement. The humans, like the weren, kept their above-ground structures for the convenience of hunting, trading, and the loading and unloading of equipment. The structures also served as outposts during a conflict such as they were engaged in now. Most of the actual settlement lay underground. The low stone and steel buildings scattered haphazardly across the sheltered valley looked remarkably similar to those the weren had left behind.

Sometimes war began with a sudden barrage, a terrifying onslaught of sight and sound that shook the world and shattered the soul. This time it began with a single shot, a signal from Burwab that brought a volley of rifle fire down upon the human settlement. In an instant, the war cries of the weren warriors echoed across the frozen land.

The attack seemed to terrify the humans. Even those Ridgers who had encountered weren before had never seen them quite like this—great tusked creatures over two meters tall, running across the snow field, roaring out their anger and waving their weapons above their heads.

The humans turned and ran. The weren encouraged their retreat with scattered shots over their heads. The warriors stormed through the settlement, shattering windows, blasting chimneys into ceramic shards, turning comm towers and power lines into a sizzling array of sparks.

Running down a back alley with a few warriors behind him, Kuhudag found only one human actively resisting. The man got off a shot, then quickly turned and fled. The weren stitched the ground at his feet with a stream of bullets but otherwise let him flee unharmed.

Pausing before buildings that were obviously aboveground dwellings, Kuhudag reminded his companions that they were to take no life unless they themselves were threatened.

"Anyone who disregards this warning will answer to me," he said.

The young warriors had the glaze of weren battle lust in their eyes, but they nodded in assent. Kuhudag left them, following the sound of rifle fire to his right. The rattle of human weapons was growing now; the Red Ridgers had been caught by surprise, but they were rallying now to defend their settlement.

Kuhudag joined a band of warriors storming down a main street, kicking down fences and torching vehicles as they went. Kuhudag stopped as screams came from inside a human house. The house was afire—he could see yellow flames through the broken windows. Burning humans was not the reason he had come, even though others might tolerate such behavior. He would have fought three duels a day to avoid taking part in such slaughter.

He sprinted for the door and aimed his rifle at the lock. One shot blew the mechanism apart. The door flew open, and a human male stumbled out, nearly falling into Kuhudag's arms. Kuhudag held him up, dragging him safely away from the fire.

The man stared up at him, too terrified to speak. After a few moments the shock began to pass and he finally began muttering words Kuhudag couldn't hear above the roar of the leaping flames.

"It's all right," Kuhudag assured him, knowing the man likely didn't understand. "You're not hurt, just singed a little. I'll find you some—*huuuuuk*!"

Kuhudag staggered, felt the pain swallow him, drag him to the ground. He tried to look up, wanted to see who had killed him, but only collapsed facedown in the snow.

Chapter Ten

October 14, 2501

Lieutenant Witzko took a shortcut to the gym past the troop recreation lounge, spotted Sergeant Kran, and stopped. Kran, running a finger through his meticulously trimmed beard, nodded as Witzko came near.

Witzko stopped. "Something I can do for you, Top?"

"In a manner of speaking, yes, sir. I believe there is."

Witzko waited. Platoon Sergeant Kran moved like lightning in the field. Out of combat, he took on a nearly priestly attitude in keeping with his Orlamu faith.

"It's in there, sir." Kran said as he gestured into the recreation lounge.

"In there?"

Witzko looked past him through the open door of the recreation lounge. The game tables were full. Off-duty crewmen and marines were busy with a number of virtual challenges, including the new, advanced holographic version of "Battlecruiser."

Witzko thought he spotted the trouble at once. Two of the major players were Sergeant Chen from Headquarters and Corporal Barbara MacKenzie of Recon's Squad Two. Chen looked glum, which was so rare when she was playing games that Witzko had to look twice before he realized MacKenzie looked positively cheerful. That was even rarer for one of Chen's opponents.

"I"m not accusing the sergeant of cheating," Kran said, "but she's losing, now, and I don't like that. Chen doesn't lose, and MacKenzie can't afford to lose."

"Chen's drawing her in."

"I didn't say that, sir."

"No, of course you didn't. In fact, you quite emphatically did not say that. Are you going to explain, Sergeant, or do I have to guess?"

"Neither, Lieutenant. Follow me, please."

Witzko followed him to a small storeroom where the t'sa adviser Gre-Ikwilisan Thumn sat cross-legged on a packing crate.

"All right, let's hear it," Witzko said.

"Sergeant Chen wanted to play MacKenzie for money," replied Kran, "not much to start, but the pot's getting bigger."

"How big?"

"Over five hundred dollars. More than MacKenzie can afford, if she loses."

Witzko let out a breath. "She's not though, right? Chen's cheating, and MacKenzie's winning?"

The t'sa gave a meditative smile. "I have no evidence I would care to offer. Still, I feel justice might be served if I altered the game somewhat so that the energy shields of MacKenzie's ships remain strong."

Witzko stared. "You can do that? Yeah, of course you can. Was this your idea, or did the sergeant here put you up to it?"

"Ask no questions, sir, that I cannot truthfully answer," said the t'sa.

"Okay, so the hacker ought to get hacked. I can't

argue the justice in that." He glanced back into the room. "All right. I'm not here, I know nothing about this. Understood? Cut off the game when Chen loses a hundred dollars, not one dollar more. The fewer people who have any reason to be curious about this, the better. Now if you jokers will excuse me, I have a workout date in the gym."

* * * * *

Three marines were crossing the overhead bars and nets, and two Star Forcers were working out on the machines at the forward end of the gymnasium. The dojo end was empty except for Sergeant Lavon. Witzko watched her a moment, a longer moment than he'd intended, but the memory of holding her close, carrying her to her quarters—strictly in the line of duty, of course—was difficult to set aside. In her body-hugging workout gear, no one could say the sergeant was anything but . . . fit.

It was too late to pretend he wasn't watching; instead, he walked toward her as if that had been his intention all along.

"Morning, Lieutenant," Irina said, kicking one leg higher than her head. "You up for some combat flips today?"

"Possibly. If you'll give me a couple of handicap points. I know your record, Master Sergeant."

"Hah!" Irina showed him a saucy grin. "No offense, sir, but I know yours as well. The officer wouldn't be taking advantage of his NCO, would he?"

Witzko turned away with a phony sneeze, hiding the sudden rush of color he could feel on his face. Her grin and the way the words came out were likely unintended, but they had clearly struck home.

"Lieutenant, you all right?"

"Yeah, fine. Must be a little pollen in the air."

Irina raised a brow. "In a starship? I don't think so, sir."

"Dust, maybe. Lot of dust in the air."

"Yes, sir. I guess."

* * * * *

It took three freestyle passes for Witzko to be sure he had a hair's advantage in speed, but not enough to compensate for Lavon's edge in reach. She'd seen him work before, but apparently wasn't aware of his ability to move without warning, either forward to strike or backward to evade.

After twenty minutes they were tied with two downs each.

"Try for the odd one?" Lavon asked. She had the beginnings of a bruise on one cheek and seemed to favor her left leg.

"No thanks," Witzko said, "I've had enough." He knew he might take her, but he also knew his bad wrist was beginning to throb again. Whatever the doctors thought, he knew that the rock climbing accident had left the wrist just a little readier to quit than its mate.

"We could do a great exhibition bout for charity sometime," Irina said, touching her knees to get her breath. "Know any worthy causes?"

"Yeah, us."

Irina smiled and ran a towel over her face. "You're good. You never signal a move. I don't think I've seen it done any better."

"Thanks. I've had a lot of practice," Witzko said, "not all of it voluntary either. When your name is Witzko, a significant population in your middle school feels compelled to try and take you down. It helps you develop a thick skin and a poker face from the start."

"That explains a lot," she said. "Time for the massage table?"

Witzko sincerely regretted turning down this comradely offer. "Sorry. I'll have to shower and get down to Ordnance for final suit inspection, then you can try your hand on my muscles, if I'm not too dead to notice."

"Understood."

"Later then, Sarge."

Witzko wrapped his towel around his neck and left the gym, thinking about Sergeant Lavon and the promised massage, thinking, for a moment, somewhat further than that.

He paused, let out a breath, and wondered if he was possibly losing his mind, thinking what he was thinking about his master sergeant. He'd always thought her attractive. Who didn't? This was something else, this was—what? It was disaster, is what it was, a perfect way to destroy his career in the Concord Marines, and hers as well. He ground one fist in the other. If only she hadn't gotten that dizzy spell in the hall. If he'd . . . if he'd just let her fall on her face, everything would be all right.

Witzko shook his head. What was he thinking about? He wouldn't do that. He'd done what he had to do, what anyone would do under the same circumsta—

"Lieutenant Witzko?"

"Huh? What?"

Witzko turned to see Master Sergeant Jacques Belier facing him in the corridor. Belier looked a great deal like two marines struggling to get into one uniform. The man truly had no business in the Corps; he should be spending his pension somewhere, annoying civilians instead of Concord Marines.

"What is it, Belier?" Witzko said. "I'm in a hurry right now."

"Yes, sir, I see you are, Lieutenant, sir." Belier gave him a pumpkin grin that nearly closed his tiny eyes. "Thing is, sir, you're wanted in the colonel's Ready Room, sir. The old man wants to talk to you, sir." Belier paused, and the grin grew broader still. "Him and Captain Savant, *sir*."

Witzko felt his stomach take a flip. Seymoyr *and* Savant—not good at all.

"I'll be right there," he told the sergeant. "Soon as I change and get into some blues."

"Oh, I'd just go in my sweats if I was you," Belier told him. "I don't think the CO and the captain want to wait that long, sir."

Chapter Eleven

October 25, 2501

Kuhudag awoke. He decided he was getting used to the unconscious state. This time, he didn't feel dead. Everything hurt too much for that. He had no grievance against the humans. They might have used a more lethal weapon or chopped him into pieces.

Opening one eye, he saw that he was in a very small room. The walls and floor were cheap plastic sprayed over stone. The front wall was a lattice of heavy metal bars with no visible door. On the back wall was a water tap with a cup. Next to that was a flush toilet that looked rather small and flimsy for a weren.

The imprisonment, then, was within the bounds of law and honor. If they didn't torture him or kill him—and if he could conceal his knowledge of several human languages—he might learn much that his comrades would never hear. He would have to be careful, of course, pretend to understand a little. When they came to question him, he did not wish to be thought either brain-damaged or a fool.

He slept, then woke again when the healer came. He mumbled that he was thirsty, and the healer handed him the cup. She was a young woman with pale brown skin and shiny black hair. She apparently didn't fear him. She went to work at once on his head, trimming fur, sealing skin, and spraying medications. She stepped out, and the bars descended from the ceiling to the floor, sealing him in.

When he awoke again, the guards were gone. In their place stood two other men. One looked so much like the healer that Kuhudag wondered if they were kin. The other was taller and nearly as broad as a young weren. His beard was red and thick. Both men wore outdoor clothing with the hoods thrown back; both were openly armed.

Kuhudag listened, his eyes nearly closed. Apparently, they were sure he couldn't understand them since they were speaking Japanese, but it was in fact one of Kuhudag's favorite human languages, the first he had picked up after Galactic Standard.

Both men, it seemed, worked for the same corporation, one trying to establish itself on Arist. Kuhudag suspected that it was VoidCorp, the largest of the corporate stellar nations and the one that most often turned up in unlikely places. This news would be less than welcome among Kuhudag's people, since many of them were escaped VoidCorp Employees. The men also disagreed on how to handle the new situation on Arist, but Kuhudag was not sure why.

"We haven't done them near as much harm as they did to us," the bearded man said. "Treece is dead, and Hrenich is going to have to go back to Spes for transplants."

"Their bonuses will be paid."

"To the Pit with the dollars! We can't put up with this!"

"No, we cannot. On the other hand, we cannot act without caution until we know more."

"I know enough right now," the bearded man growled. "I don't see any sense in stalling around if they're going to pull stunts like this."

"The weren would be insulted to hear their raid called a 'stunt,' " the smaller man said. "I know them, and it is clear they feel there is a matter of honor here at stake, though I can't begin to guess what it might be. Speaking of honor, I want your word that your workers will not come close to this prisoner. I will not have him harmed."

"Huh! Oh, sure," said the man.

"Dimmock, remember that we have an agreement. If your people down their tools over this, they will be in breach of contract."

The bearded man shook his head and mumbled to himself. The other man smiled and gripped his companion's shoulder. "You are a stubborn man, Paul, but a good man, I think."

The two men left. Kuhudag still pretended sleep. After a while, he no longer needed to pretend.

* * * * *

When Kuhudag awoke, he was certain he had slept several hours because he was hungrier than ever. He had just finished washing when the guards stepped aside and the bars rose again. The healer woman appeared, pushing a small cart. It held a steaming jug, a large covered bowl, and a plate of trail biscuits.

"Greetings, worthy guest," the woman said in Standard. "Do you understand my speech?"

"Greetings and thanks, worthy host," Kuhudag said, deciding at once there was little profit in playing the fool. "Am I permitted to eat while we speak?"

"Most certainly."

"My thanks increase."

The food decreased even more rapidly, although Kuhudag had no utensils but a large spoon. The hot drink was strong tea; the covered bowls held a thick soup with chunks of real meat.

Kuhudag knew the woman might have reasons for her apparent friendliness, reasons that might go beyond her duties as a healer. If she was indeed the daughter of the more honorable of the VoidCorp officials, she might be obeying his orders.

Once he had soaked up the last drop of soup with the last piece of biscuit, the woman put on a diagnostic glove and ran it over his head and his body, then pushed the whole array back through the gap in the bars.

She then sat on the floor and assumed the cross-legged position the Orlamu teachers called "lotus." She smiled at Kuhudag, the smile designed to set him at ease. It worked rather well, Kuhudag decided.

"My name is Doctor Christine Ohito. You have met my father, Alexander Ohito. We have been given the right to ask why your folk attacked Red Ridge. One of our people was killed, another gravely hurt. What grievance did you have against us that you attacked us in such a fashion without giving us a chance to speak? We might have been able to save the lives that have been lost among us as well as any that have been lost among your people."

"I can give you ample reason," he told the woman. "Only days ago, I was present in the north when *we* were attacked with no warning at all. Several of my folk were killed, and I tell you I myself dispatched several of yours."

The healer frowned. "I cannot believe this is so."

"Believe it, woman," Kuhudag said evenly. "I was there." He touched his face and bared his chest. "I was burned by a grenade. There were also laser weapons used."

The woman closed her eyes a moment. "Where was this?"

Kuhudag gave as accurate a position for the battle as he could, then concluded with, "There are some among us who suspect the worst of humans after you gained hunting rights that once were ours. A fair price was paid, but some think hunting rights are a matter of honor, not to be bought or sold."

Doctor Ohito looked as if she knew perfectly well she was not being told the whole truth. Despite his desire for the hostilites to end peacefully, Kuhudag did not intend to shame Burwab, Shubud, or the Council in a way that would give any one of them the right to challenge him.

"I am greatly concerned," the healer said. "I must speak to others. I know of no such attacks."

"Well, they happened, whether you know of them or not."

She shook her head. "I have no reason to doubt you, but this does not mean the humans were from Red Ridge. The people of Red Ridge are not the only humans on Arist. The attackers could have been bandits, the unwanted, those who cannot live by the rules of our community."

Kuhudag felt his fur rise at that. "They could have been," he said darkly, "but I don't believe it for a minute. They were well-equipped, disciplined warriors. I have fought all my life, healer, and I think I know when I am facing outcasts and vagrants. These were trained fighters—men who were good enough to face *me*!"

Doctor Ohito drew in a breath at that. "I did not mean to offend."

"Surely you did not, but I know what I saw. We were attacked in force, and there have been several skirmishes before. I think, indeed, you should talk with these *others* you mention. Perhaps there are things you have not been told. It may be that females are not honored among humans as they are among the weren."

She colored at that, her eyes narrowing in anger.

Good, Kuhudag thought. Now we have both shown our tempers. Perhaps we can talk to one another now.

Before Dr. Ohito could reply, the ceiling shook with the rumble of heavy vehicles, moving fast along the surface roads above Kuhudag's cell. Above the roar, he could hear the whine of skycars as well.

"What am I supposed to make of that?" Kuhudag asked. "Another peaceful gesture by the innocent humans of Red Ridge?"

"I think it's best that I see," said Dr. Ohito.

Somewhat shaken, she rose quickly and shouted to the guards to let her out. The bars were raised, and she scooted under before they were scarcely off the ground.

The guards stared at each other, looked at the shaking ceiling, and turned their weapons on Kuhudag.

"Don't look at me," he said. "In case you didn't notice, I'm down here."

The guards didn't seem impressed. They continued to keep their prisoner covered in case he decided to tear down the bars.

Less than a minute later, Doctor Ohito burst into the room again, her brown-tinted skin almost gray now, covered with dust from above.

"Damn Paul Dimmock and his stone-brained friends!" she shouted, clenching her small fists. "I should have known he'd pull something like this!"

"Explain, please," Kuhudag said.

"Dimmock and my father work for VoidCorp. I know what that name means to you, and I'm sorry. My father is not responsible for . . . for slavery of workers, things that occurred in the past. Dimmock is here to plan possible projects in this region. He's a hothead and he doesn't understand what we have here. Now his people have taken most of their air and ground vehicles and are heading in . . . in the direction of weren territory. I'm sorry. I don't know what to say."

Kuhudag wasn't greatly surprised. "If this is so, I would say this Dimmock human has been in weren territory before. I expect I have already met these *workers* of his."

Doctor Ohito didn't answer.

"Do they have armed skycars?" Kuhudag asked. "I saw none during the fighting."

"No—I don't know. They could have weapons outside of town." She shook her head, then looked him squarely in the eye. "I don't know how much I can trust you. The things you've said about the attacks on your settlement. They happened, I'm sure, but how do I know there wasn't some reason for that? You're . . ."

She stopped and quickly turned away.

"We're weren," he finished, "not human, big, furry creatures with tusks, ugly as any *animal* in your eyes. Everyone knows that animals kill for fun, that they have no high moral standards—like humans. We are incapable of understanding your kindness, your great achievements—"

"Stop it, please!" Doctor Ohito stared at him in horror, then stood and fled across the room. Almost before she got there, the armed guards were raising the bars, pointing their weapons at Kuhudag.

"Hurry!" he called behind her. "You know that animals attack when they are cornered."

Doctor Ohito didn't answer. In a moment she was gone.

* * * * *

A young man came to change his dressings and replace the healing spray with a simple pad to protect the wound. He was clearly frightened of Kuhudag, and one guard came in the cell with him to point his weapon at the prisoner's head.

More food and fresh water arrived in time. Kuhudag was well rested but slept anyway. He woke some time later. Nothing had changed except that he now had new guards, so he slept again. By now he was almost certain there were drugs in his food and water. If there were, there was little he could do about it.

Waking again in what he felt was the middle of the night, he saw Dr. Ohito sitting in the lotus position, waiting for him, watching.

He sat up and stretched, then drank a cup of water.

"Back to the zoo again, is it? What do you expect to learn from my habits this time?"

"Don't, please." The healer closed her eyes, then opened them again. "I regret what I said, worthy guest. I apologize. I think we both spoke under . . . strained circumstances. I do not ask for an apology from you."

"No, but you have it. Honor calls for it, and for

restraint—especially under the *strained* circumstances you speak of."

The healer nodded, then looked down at her hands. A blue sheet of paper was crushed in her palm.

"I do not need to look at this," she said. "It says that Dimmock's workers have bombed a weren iron mine with skycars. One of the weren was killed, four more were trapped in the debris and are assumed dead. There was major damage to the mine. Your people are sending out messages for help. The force you came with is on its way back."

Kuhudag waited. He was beginning to be able to read her feelings, the language of her body. "There is more, is there not?"

"Yes. There is more." This time she looked right at Kuhudag. "Casualties would have been higher at your mine, but the weren in that settlement were a good ten kilometers away at the time. They were fighting off a raid by another party of humans. Casualties were heavy among the weren."

Kuhudag sat up straight. He could feel the rage coursing through his veins. The healer drew in a breath.

"You see?" Kuhudag roared. "These are the outcasts you spoke of. The heavily armed vagrants tossed out of Red Ridge. Ask this Dimmock of yours who these warriors are. *He* knows!"

"I have not asked Dimmock," she said, looking away from the weren's wrath, "but I have spoken by radio to one I trust. Our raiders were as surprised by the presence of these other forces as you are."

"So they say," Kuhudag snorted. "Woman, what would you *expect* them to say? Now, tell me truthfully, if you will. Did Dimmock's forces try to find and drive off these *strangers*? Did they cheer at the news?"

The healer looked up. "Some protested. Some cheered, as you say. You asked me for the truth."

"Thank you. Though you are my enemy, you do me honor."

"I do not wish to be your enemy," she said, and Kuhudag was startled to see there were tears in her eyes.

"Well then," he said, "the answer is easy, is it not? Go and tell the others of your kind that the loathsome weren are your friends."

Again, the healer left. This time, though, Kuhudag did not sleep. He wondered if Doctor Ohito was telling the truth. He decided that it mattered little if she was. Her father was the senior VoidCorp human on Red Ridge, but the man Paul Dimmock was clearly the power here. Power, as any warrior knew, could easily overcome reason. It had always been so.

Chapter Twelve

TRANSCRIPT OF HEARING:
Log of the Commanding Officer, Lieutenant Colonel Wilm Seymoyr,
Third Battalion, 26th Regiment, Concord Marines
October 14, 2501
EXCERPT: ENCODED, EYES ONLY

PRESENT: LT. COL. W. SEYMOYR
CAPT. W. SAVANT
MSGT J. BELIER
IST LT D. WITZKO

SEYMOYR: Understand at the outset, Lieutenant, this is an informal hearing, an inquiry. You are not under trial oath, but you are, as ever, under oath as an officer of the Concord Marines. You are duty bound to answer those questions put to you by those present. If, at any time, for any reason whatsoever, you feel you cannot or should not answer these questions without legal representation, you may request such representation to be present. Do you understand these procedures, Lieutenant?

WITZKO: Yes, sir, I do. What I don't understand, sir, is why I'm here. To my knowledge, I have not committed any—

SEYMOYR: No one says you have committed any offense, sir. I would ask you to hold your, ah, protests until the facts are presented.

WITZKO: Yes, sir.

SEYMOYR: Master Sergeant Belier, would you please describe what, if any, unusual activities you observed in or around the Non-Commissioned Officers' quarters yesterday, October 13?

BELIER: Yes, sir. I did see an unusual activity, sir. I was returning to my quarters at 1700 hours when I saw Lieutenant Witzko here enter Master Sergeant Lavon's quarters, sir.

WITZKO: Just a minute, Sergeant—!

SAVANT: At ease, Lieutenant. You'll get your chance to speak.

SEYMOYR: Continue please, Sergeant Belier. And no more outbursts from you, Lieutenant.

BELIER: When I saw Lieutenant Witzko enter Sergeant Lavon's quarters I was, uh, shocked, sir, to say the least. It's against regs for an officer to enter any NCO's quarters unless that officer is on official business.

SEYMOYR: Why didn't you think this might be official business on Lieutenant Witzko's part?

BELIER: Sir, it didn't seem like official business to me, sir. Lieutenant Witzko was carrying the sergeant—in his arms, sir.

SEYMOYR: Did the lieutenant then enter the sergeant's quarters, Sergeant Belier?

BELIER: Yes, sir. He did. He went in and laid her on her bunk, sir. And then—

SEYMOYR: Go on, Sergeant.

BELIER: Do I have to, sir?

SAVANT: Do your duty, Master Sergeant. Just tell the colonel what you saw.

BELIER: Yes, sir. I saw Lieutenant Witzko and Master Sergeant Lavon in—in an intimate situation, sir.

WITZKO: That's a lie! That's a damned lie, Sergeant, and you know it!

SEYMOYR: Sit down, Lieutenant, or I will have you removed. You can then listen to the rest of this testimony on a speaker in the other room.

WITZKO: Yes, sir, but I want it read into the record, sir, that this man is lying. He is giving totally false testimony to this court.

SEYMOYR: Noted, Lieutenant, and it's an inquiry, not a court. Continue, please, Sergeant.

BELIER: Uh, that's about it, sir. That's all I saw. I don't have to . . . go into details, do I sir?

SEYMOYR: Not at this point, Sergeant, no.

SAVANT: May I ask the sergeant a question, Colonel?

SEYMOYR: If it's pertinent, go ahead, Captain.

SAVANT: Sergeant, you've testified that you witnessed these . . . intimate relations between Lieutenant Witzko and Sergeant Lavon. I ask you, Sergeant, you didn't . . . stand there and, uh, watch these relations, did you?

BELIER: Oh, no, sir. I did not. I left as soon as I saw what was going on in there, sir.

SAVANT: So you wouldn't have any idea how long the lieutenant was in the sergeant's quarters?

BELIER: Yes, sir. I would.

SAVANT: How's that, Sergeant?

BELIER: Sir, I knew I had witnessed a violation. I figured it was my duty to report it, as much I regretted doing so, sir. I waited down the hall a ways until the lieutenant emerged, sir. I waited a good hour. I never did see him come out, sir.

SEYMOYR: Is that all, Sergeant?

BELIER: Yes, sir, except that I reported this incident at once to Captain Savant, sir.

SAVANT: As you know, colonel, this incident took place right before starfall. There was no time to take any action on this until that was over.

SEYMOYR: I understand, Captain. Lieutenant, you've heard Sergeant Belier. What, if anything, do you have to say in answer to these rather serious accusations?

WITZKO: Sir, at this time I respectfully state that I don't wish to answer any more questions without legal representation, sir.

SEYMOYR: Under the circumstances, I think that's a sound idea on your part, Lieutenant.

Chapter Thirteen

October 28, 2501

It was seven hours since the mission had truly begun with the squadron's starrise into the Hammer's Star system. *Revealer* had undocked her escort of a cruiser, two frigates, and four heavy cutters, while *Stormbird* undocked her modest escort of two light cutters. Thirty seconds after achieving formation, the dreadnought and her companions went to full power, now visible to everyone in the system who wasn't biologically or electronically senseless.

Starrise was always a hassle to everyone aboard. Damion Witzko was no exception, and he had little time to think about Sergeant Belier or Captain Savant and how he could possibly defend himself against their charges. He saw Irina Lavon in the distance during a drill, but he was under strict orders not to speak to her until she gave testimony. When their eyes met, she merely shook her head in wonder, letting him know that she had been informed of the charges and was just as angry about it as he was.

He knew that she would tell the truth, as he had, that nothing improper had happened between them, that he had left her cabin at once. The only trouble was, of course, she had likely gone directly to sleep after that.

Worse still, when he had returned to his cabin to change from his sweat gear, there was a note blinking on his display telling him the ordance session he was to attend had been called off. Witzko was relieved and went right to bed himself, which meant that he, too, had no alibi. He had obviously been set up but had no proof. It was his word and Lavon's against Belier's.

Colonel Seymoyr had told him to go about his duties and to speak to no one except his legal counsel. At the moment, Witzko had no time to worry about that. Savant, he was sure, was having a laugh with Belier somewhere, considering Witzko's punishment when he was convicted. Belier would undoubtedly vote for dismissal from the corps. Savant would vote for something more unusual—like holding your breath outside the ship without a suit.

Witzko watched, along with nearly everyone aboard, as *Revealer* presented a spectacular weapons test, a deliberate effort to distract watching eyes in the system while the squadron slipped away into the fringes of the Revik belt. Plasma and particle guns, plus long-range lasers tossed out enough energy to power a small planet for a week. Colors flashed through the spectrum: red, green, violet and blue, silver and gold. At last someone fired off a high-intensity flare, the kind that would light up a hundred square kilometers in ground combat, and the show was over. By that time the squadron was well into the asteroid belt and doing their best to remain hidden.

Witzko met with Kran to finalize the platoon's boarding party plans and to go over the T.O. & E. one final time. There was plenty to think about—assault craft readiness, e-suits, weapons control, and a thousand other details. If *Stormbird* had to launch her marines, they would either go in their own suits or in assault landers. The last would be a tight fit if everybody was in full armor. However, the landers had enough firepower to make up for their lack of amenities, and if a combat assault ran beyond the limits of assault craft support, the marines were usually dead from other unnatural causes.

Witzko and every Concord Marine aboard knew things could get messy out there. Every settler anywhere close to the area of space where the Silver Bell colony had disappeared was understandably nervous. Now, with the answer to that massacre partially answered, Concord could put a name to the killers responsible. There were insectlike externals loose in the Hammer's Star system. Survivors had named them "klicks" from the sounds they made, but little more was known about them. They were intelligent, combative, and neither surrendered nor took prisoners. They had sophisticated weapons, some superior to anything the marines had seen. To any thinking being, it seemed likely that the klicks had not simply suddenly appeared in the Hammer's Star system. The swift, well-organized attack on Silver Bell suggested that a large base existed somewhere near the system. A few small outposts had been annihilated by Concord forces, but no sizeable base had yet been found.

Bone tired, Witzko left Kran, returned to his cabin and eased himself into his bunk. He slept and dreamed Savant and Belier had turned into klicks and were eating him piece by piece. They shrieked and laughed as they devoured him, tearing him into bits, tossing legs and arms about.

Witzko sat up in his bunk, sweat pouring down his chest. The shrieks were coming from the speaker overhead, blaring out a message to every corner of the ship.

"*Attention all hands! Attention all hands! Unidentified ship sighted, range 71,000 kilometers, emission profile external—not actively scanning at present. Readiness Condition Three. Repeat, RedCon Three.*"

Witzko came to his feet, slipped into combat gear, and headed down the corridor with a horde of other marines. Two minutes later, RedCon Three went to RedCon One—All Hands to Battle Stations. Witzko could feel the tension spreading throughout crowded hall. No one needed to tell a Concord Marine about RedCon One. RedCon One began with glory and ended with medals and body bags.

* * * * *

Sergeant Lavon's battle station was aboard one of the landers in command of the all-marine boarding party. In the pressurized steel cave that was Lander Bay Green, she spent the first ten minutes of RedCon One pulling on her soft e-suit, checking the readouts and her weapons load, then making sure that the other eleven boarders had done the same.

The mystery ship had scanned *Stormbird,* refused to offer ID—to no one's surprise—and finally accelerated away from the Concord cruiser. *Stormbird* and her escort cutters accelerated from .2 AU per hour to something closer to 3.0 AU. The fleeing vessel stayed well ahead and clear of her pursuers, well beyond range of the *Stormbird's* weaponry. Meanwhile, one of *Revealer*'s cutters had circled around and was headed on an intercept course for the mysterious ship. *Stormbird* threw every sensor beam available at the craft in an attempt to distract it from the cutter's approach.

In the fourth hour of the standoff, Lavon had a vaguely traitorous thought that this coat-trailing mission through the Hammer's Star system could have used fewer marines and more ship weaponry. At the beginning of the fifth hour, the chase suddenly ended. The ship seemed to be powering up for starfall when *Revealer*'s cutter dove in with weapons blazing. The magnified display of the other ship blazed with white light, nearly blinding the watchers on *Stormbird* before the filters came up. When the the filters dimmed, the ship was several million scintillating fragments of debris.

The display showed that some sizeable "pieces of something" were drifting near the ship's last position. Lavon had been around long enough to know what that meant. *Stormbird* would send out snoopers to see what the stranger had left behind. It was standard procedure with any debris found in space—and with possible externals involved, there could be no doubt about taking a look.

Irina Lavon sighed, squirmed into a new, even more uncomfortable position aboard the lander, and settled down to wait. There was nothing out there to fight now, but command would likely keep the marines on alert until someone took a look at the other ship's debris.

Extra time to sit and think wasn't exactly what Irina needed at the time. She wished she could talk to Lieutenant Witzko, but that was impossible until after her own inquiry. Surely, she thought, they wouldn't push this ridiculous charge, not with her record, and Witzko's as well.

Right, and Captain Savant and Master Sergeant Belier are just having a little fun. Any minute now they'll tell the colonel it was all a big joke. Sure, Lavon, and you'll make major general by Tuesday afternoon. . . .

* * * * *

Captain Myklebust frowned at the message and dropped it on her desk. "I'm not absolutely opposed to heading for Arist," she said, "but this message doesn't tell me enough to justify forgetting the asteroids. Spes may have more data on this, and they certainly have more ships."

"They may not have any ships closer than we are, however," Seymoyr said. "We have to consider that."

It was not much of a try, but it was the best he could do. Myklebust hadn't exactly ignored the plea for help from the weren settlement on Arist, but she was determined to deal with the "space trash" left by the possibly external ship. First the debris, then the asteroids, and Arist last—if, indeed, as she continually pointed out, Arist really needed help in the first place.

Maybe, he thought, he'd feel the same way if he was responsible for a major Star Force ship and her marines. Still, Star Force had a habit of giving priority to problems in space, and Myklebust was Star Force all the way.

"The message was fairly clear, Captain," Seymoyr tried again. "Something's wrong down there. There's no doubt the signal came from a weren-operated station. Their equipment's not the best, and the signal was weaker than it ought to be at this distance."

"In other words, on the lower limit for receiving, and garbled as well. There's another reason, Colonel, for not assuming we have enough data to justify abandoning our mission in favor of Arist."

"The garbling might have been jamming."

"By whom?"

"Whoever is fighting with the weren. I don't say we're getting the whole truth or the real case for either side, but I doubt they're making up the fight out of pure vacuum."

"You seem to think the weren all respect the majesty of the Concord," Myklebust said with a wry smile.

"The ones who don't respect the Orlamu Theocracy," Seymoyr replied. "The Theocracy tends to be on our side. Weren sending a false distress signal would find themselves with few friends at home or abroad."

Myklebust sighed and sipped her hot tea. "I don't want to neglect a civil disorder call, but I have to retrieve that material floating around out there. If it wasn't possibly external, I'd consider another course of action. It's what we call the 'big picture,' Colonel. I don't need to remind you of that. They may have had an in-system destination and only gone into starfall when they realized that they couldn't outrun us."

She hesitated and looked at Colonel Seymoyr. "Off the record, Wilm, I don't have a lot of choice. You know how the brass back home feels about Silver Bell, your people and mine."

"I didn't say you were wrong," Seymoyr said. "I just said I didn't like it."

* * * * *

Witzko and the other four members of his recon team floated in the black abyss between the stars. This far out in the system, even Hammer's Star was nothing more than the brightest light in an infinite sea of jewelled suns. Two other parties of marines and two cutters were searching the rest of the debris field left behind by the mystery ship. Witzko saw occasional flashes of weapons fire as *Vigor,* the farthermost of the cutters, sniffed out the larger floaters. Forty kilometers away, *Stormbird* hung against the starscape, keeping watch over all her children.

Witzko and his team had gathered around the most precious find so far: a two-meter-long cylindrical container made of some metallic alloy that didn't show up on the meters at all. Gre-Ikwilisan Thumn, floating nearby in an e-suit modified to fit a t'sa, had cheerily pointed out that planting bombs among debris was fairly common among many known races and was very likely practiced by externals as well.

Scanning showed this particular container held something with considerable mass and high density, hard rock or even a heavy ceramic or metal. No one wanted to torch the thing to see what was inside.

After consultation with *Stormbird,* it was decided to bring the thing back and carry it in a shuttle in *Stormbird's* wake until someone who did that sort of thing decided to open it up.

"That's the way I like to collect souvenirs," Platoon Sergeant Kran put in, "from *way* off somewhere."

"It's probably loaded with precious gems," said Witzko. "Flip that thing open, and we'll all be rich as star kings."

"Rank has its privilege," Kran suggested politely. "You go first, sir."

"Okay," Witzko said, "you talked me out of it. Next time, though—"

A voice burst into the circuit, seemingly loud enough to fracture eardrums half a light year away.

"Revealer *to boarding parties. Get back to* Stormbird, *now! Use your suit jets and get out of there. Go, go, go!*"

"Uh-oh," Witzko said. "I'm guessing someone's coming over to play."

Kran didn't answer. In a moment, a flash of encoded comm unscrambled itself, confirming Witzko's guess. *Stormbird* had an unidentified contact, two or more ships with external signatures closing on *Stormbird's* position on roughly the same course as the unidentified ship they'd pursued.

Witzko looked at Kran. Kran didn't have his comm on, but Witzko could read his words through the faceplate. "Great. *Now* what?"

Chapter Fourteen

October 26, 2501

Doctor Ohito arrived with Kuhudag's morning meal. At least, Kuhudag assumed it was morning. It was easy to lose track of time underground. A hunter sharpened his senses through a lifetime of living under the sun and the stars. He had never been comfortable indoors on any world, and he particularly disliked the deep caverns of Arist. There was too much rock, too much solid matter between him and the open world above. Many who had to live in the caverns became accustomed to it. As far as Kuhudag was concerned, a true weren could strangle in such a place, gasping for fresh air.

He didn't recognize the instrument on Doctor Ohito's belt until she pressed the top and twisted at the same time—much like opening a bottle. The moment she began speaking aloud in Common Weren, he understood.

"This device should scramble any audio surveillance within a five meter radius," she said. "We can speak plainly now."

"Hey," one of the guards called, "speak Standard!"

Ohito froze the man with a glance. "He cannot speak enough Standard to be clear about his symptoms. Do you wish me to report that you insisted I deny this detainee adequate medical care?"

The guard shrugged. He didn't want trouble. All he wanted to do was go off duty and sleep.

"I fear there is more bad news than good," Doctor Ohito said. "The trapped weren miners have been rescued, but two are seriously hurt. I mean no offense in this, but it may be their wounds are beyond the resources of your people. My father thought it would be a gesture toward peace if I flew to the mine and offered my skills."

Kuhudag shook his head. "My thanks, but I urge you not to go. Neither law nor honor demands this when you are not the only healer on Arist. I know my people, and they would not likely show you the usual courtesies at this time."

"I know, but why should I send another into danger I will not face?"

"Because another might not *be* in such danger. You are your father's daughter. Your death would weaken him twice over, and such a tragedy would not serve to bring your people and mine any closer."

Kuhudag paused. "I think there is more you have to say. Things you have saved until the last because you do not wish to say them."

The healer looked down at her hands then faced him again.

"The other humans, the ones you faced in the north. They have overrun a weren outpost. Several of your people—I cannot say how many—have apparently been killed. The others have retreated to the caverns. Some of the humans followed them there to . . . to pursue your wounded."

Kuhudag stood, spread his great claws, opened his mouth, and roared a weren challenge that shook the cavern. He tore at his chest, shook his tusks and slung spittle across the cell.

At once the guards brought their weapons to bear.

"No, *don't*!" Ohito shouted. "No! Hold your fire!" She quickly sprang in front of Kuhudag, as if her small form could shield him. The guards hesitated, backed away behind the bars, fingers still on the triggers of their weapons.

Kuhudag took a deep breath, moved away from the human, and stood against a far wall.

"You are brave and foolish as well," he told her. "You tell me to my face of an unspeakably dishonorable act. Neither weren nor human has ever broken the law of sanctuary. Neither your people nor mine have fought within the caverns. I must know—this Dimmock person who also attacks my people, was he involved in this massacre? Did he, too, break the law that has never been broken?"

Kuhudag watched her closely. He knew she feared him and did not blame her for that. There were few beings of any race who had seen a weren warrior in battle-rage and lived to describe it to others.

"I will not lie," she told him. "I would feel safer with you if I did, perhaps. I don't know. I have tried to find out if Paul Dimmock is working with these outcasts, but I do not know. That is the truth, Kuhudag."

"Yes," he said, "I see you and know that it is."

Chapter Fifteen

October 28, 2501

Witzko and his crew were scarcely aboard before the ship's alarm began to shrill again.

"*Readiness One! Red One! All hands to Battle Stations! Repeat, all hands to Battle Stations! Rig for engagement!*"

Witzko quickly led his Recon Marines to Damage Control Gamma, the closest troop spaces to Port Entry-D. DCG was a steel cubicle ten meters long with racked e-suits on the wall and crowded with emergency equipment. Without asking questions, the marines stripped out of their space gear and began helping Star Force hands with the damage control gear. There was every sort of device imaginable in the Gamma. Most important for the moment were the robots. Some were hull-repair units half the size of a shuttle, while others were small capsules of nanomachines that would put delicate electronics back together. A ship might survive without drive power or weapons, but when the electronics went, they took life support with them, and a ship without life support was a carrier of dead bodies which simply hadn't found a place to lie down.

They were nearly done with the robots when *Stormbird* took her first hit. From the lightness of the tremor, it was clear the hit was fairly far from Gamma. Witzko noticed that everyone who hadn't been sweating before was sweating now.

"Take it easy," he said calmly. "We're okay. They've got to shoot better than that."

A few marines laughed. Not too funny, Witzko thought, but what else is there to do?

"They likely know *I'm* here," said a voice from the back. "I owe folks money everywhere."

Laughter again—cut short this time by the second hit. This one shook marines like marbles in a box. Witzko found himself off his feet, pawing the air for something solid, but finding nothing but other marines flying about the room. He hit then, slamming into the floor. He lay there for several moments waiting for the ringing in his ears to subside.

A private helped Witzko to his feet. He staggered and shook his head.

"Everyone all right? Everyone okay?" He could hear his own voice in his head but little else.

He saw a private looking past him, and Kran was staring at the far wall, fists clenched at his side, anger in his dark eyes. Two marines were bending over another. The fallen marine was lying with his head at a strange, impossible angle, and Witzko knew there was no one alive who could bend his head like that.

* * * * *

The first hit was also a long way from Irina Lavon, whose boarding-party-turned-damage-controllers had assembled in Lander Bay Green minutes after Battle Stations sounded. Lander Bay Green now held four troop landers. Each was shaped like a fat, thirty-meter-long winged dart and was designed to let marines ride down to the dirt in relative comfort. They hung in pairs from two sets of rails that ran parallel down the entire length of the bay. Electromagnetic catapults could fling the craft down the rails and out of *Stormbird* at any altitude above two hundred meters.

Lavon had no idea what the hit had done. She cocked her head to one side, listening for tell tale sounds aboard the ship. It was hard to tell where the damage had occurred or what it actually was. A Star Force crewman might have told her, but there were no—

The second hit rocked *Stormbird.* Irina didn't have to ask where *that* one hit. With a deafening implosion, a section of the bay door sagged and gaped open. Atmosphere screamed out into space. The shock wave slammed marines roughly to the deck. Irina gasped as molten droplets from the bay door ripped through a trooper beside her.

Irina shouted out orders that nobody heard. Two of the multi-ton landers snapped their rail locks and flew across the room.

"Get down, move it!" Irina yelled, warning the marines as the big lander slid across the deck straight at them.

Three of the troopers scattered. Corporal Lucennes stared at her, too stunned to move. Irina knew she'd never reach him in time. Lucennes screamed as a hot chunk of plating took off his left arm.

Lavon finally got to him. "Take it easy," she said, "I've got you; I'll take you out of this."

The color had drained from Lucennes's face. He looked at Irina once, a frightened, frantic gaze, then closed his eyes.

Someone sealed the bay, and the last of the air pressure shrieked out into the void. Lucennes's suit displays said he was all right except for the arm. Lavon yanked a trauma pack off her belt, slapped primary treatment over the stump, sprayed a skinfilm over the melted end of the suit, then hit the emergency repressurization console.

A blinker on her own suit turned red. Not all the fumes from the hot metal had vented into space; some were trapped inside her suit. She turned the air scrubber to full. The light slowly flickered to green just as the third hit rocked *Stormbird.*

The white-hot light was intense. Marines were suddenly blinded in a thick veil of smoke. Even with the shock of the hit, they knew where to go. Everyone who could move ran from the port wall of Lander Green Four as metal turned liquid and spewed snaky columns of plasma about the deck.

Irina grabbed Lucennes with her right hand, the nearest other living being with her left, and sprinted for the nearest crew alcove. She pushed her two companions in just before the hot deck quivered as the bulky lander slammed into one bulkhead and then the next. Sparks and debris rained through the bay.

Irina waited. There was nothing more to do, no place to go. If the monster hit them, they'd end up as smears on the deck. If it didn't, they could still make pay call and pick up any mail, and if, Irina reminded herself, those particular sections of the ship were still there.

* * * * *

Colonel Seymoyr reached the Marine Tactical Command Center seconds before Battle Stations lockdown left him marooned in some sealed corridor. He was deep inside the ship, a long way from any hull breaches but cut off from the ship's internal 'net. Five hundred marines could talk to him, but he couldn't talk back.

As the tremors from the second hit subsided, he found he could raise a status report on his computer console. Their pursuers' drives had energy signatures of unknown origin and were out-maneuvering *Stormbird* on all points. Myklebust seemed to be using every trick in the book to put distance between her ship and the external craft, but so far they had matched her move for move and were still gaining.

The ships were large and so strange in appearance they almost appeared organic. The bigger of the two ships had more apparatuses and external bulges than any space vessel he'd ever seen. Their colors made them difficult to see with normal visual readings. They were either black or dull green, but they reflected no light.

Seymoyr watched hopefully as Myklebust launched four missiles. The enemy didn't blink. In answer they struck back with a blacklaser beam that took out the Concord cutter *Vigor.* Seymoyr clenched his fists but didn't look away. All those crewmen, gone in an instant, snuffed out just like that.

Another volley of missiles forced the enemy craft to high-speed evasive action that put some distance between them. *Stormbird* held on. Just then, *Revealer* and her consorts answered *Concord's* distress call, and the klick ships scattered when Concord reinforcements arrived. One klick vessel turned into a ball of white-hot gas as *Revealer* unloaded several turrets and weapon bays into it. Apparently seeing that it was drastically outnumbered, the remaining external vessel streaked away. *Revealer* shot after it but had only begun to close the distance when the other craft disappeared in a scintillating starfall of black and green.

* * * * *

It was a good hour and a half before Captain Myklebust asked Colonel Seymoyr to meet her. Seymoyr was expecting the summons, but he was pleased to have the chance to personally check out his marines. There were casualties—there always were—but less than he'd expected after the blows they'd taken from the klicks.

Myklebust was too calm, too controlled when Seymoyr found her in her ready room off the Bridge. It was a familiar guise for a commander; he was certain he showed the signs too.

"I've seen the reports," Myklebust told him. "You took some losses. I'm sorry. Star Force took some too. All in all, we got off pretty light. That's done. What concerns me is that we got off *too* light. I'd like to know why. Before *Revealer* got here, those clowns could've ground us to pieces. They didn't."

Seymoyr frowned. "You have any idea why?"

"I don't even know if I'm right. It's just the way I feel, Colonel. I've had the battle sequence run through all the probables. Those ships didn't behave like they should. Maybe that's the answer, of course. They're not *our* ships and they don't think like us. We don't have enough combat experience with externals to know what to expect."

"Seems to me if they wanted to get us good they would have sucked in *Revealer* and her cutters as well, taking us all out at once."

"Maybe they intended to." Myklebust gave him a weary smile. "Captains of vessels have made mistakes before."

"I've heard that," Seymoyr said. He paused, took a sip of tea. "Not to change the subject, but I will if you don't mind. I've got the reports on that debris we picked up from the other klick ship. Analysis says it wasn't something the klicks jettisoned, like garbage, before they went into starrise. There was a small, subsidiary ship in its wake. That's where our, ah, mysterious tube came from. Apparently, they were carrying it—and whatever else blew up out there—in a small cutter in the ship's gravity field."

"I thought you'd smell out that one. I'm curious about it, too. I don't like surprises, Colonel." She slammed her cup on the table. "That's what you get when you start out from scratch, dealing with something out there that doesn't like you but damned sure doesn't want to sit down and talk."

Colonel Seymoyr decided to go ahead and say what was on his mind. "I'll toss another wild guess in the hat. You don't think this aggressive behavior of the klicks has anything to do with that little package of theirs we picked up? As in, 'we want it back, and we'll kill to get it.' "

"You're right," she nodded, "it is a wild guess. However, it occurred to some of our people who are running all this mess through the computers. We've got the 'artifact' or whatever it is towed behind *us*, as you know—same as the previous owners did. We've been a little busy to mess with it. Still . . ." The captain leaned back in her chair. "From everything my high-priced snoopers tell me about the thing, there is no *way* they can open it up to find out what's inside."

* * * * *

When Lieutenant Witzko reached Lander Bay Green, two of the damaged landers had been bolted to the hull while the launch racks were repaired and the area repressurized. They were still taking bodies out when he arrived. The bodies were covered, and he couldn't tell who had been lost.

Looking past the grim sight, he spotted Irina Lavon. She was giving orders to Lee, Chen, and the t'sa—who somehow, Witzko noted, managed to stick together no matter what sort of chaos was going on around them.

Witzko let out a breath, relieved to find her still alive. There was no guilt attached to the feeling. He mourned when any marine was killed and rejoiced for those who made it out. That's what you had to do, and the Corps was like any other organization—you were bound to be closer to some members than others.

So how close am I to Master Sergeant Irina Lavon? he asked himself, but he didn't wait for the answer. He joined Lavon just as Chen, Lee, and Thumn rushed away.

"Those three formed their own platoon or what?" Witzko asked. "I never see one without the other."

"If things ever calm down, I'm putting a stop to that," Lavon said. She tossed an errant strand of yellow hair across her head. "You okay, Lieutenant? How'd it go at your end? We lost five, nine wounded, one amputation. Damn lucky it wasn't all of us."

"I lost one, three criticals." Witzko shook his head. "We've got some baddies out there, and they seem to know a hell of a lot more about us than we know about them."

"Yes, they do."

Witzko looked at her. She was holding up, but the strain was showing. He hadn't seen her since the inquiry, and he could see she didn't intend to bring it up.

"This is not the right time to say this," he said, "and if they see us talking together they'll toss in a couple of extra charges, but right now I don't give a damn. I'm sorry this happened. I promise you they won't get away with it. The colonel's new to the outfit, but he's no dummy. He's got my records and yours to lay down against Savant and Belier. Both of them have picked up a lot dirt since they've been in the service, and it's going to show. Anyway, I doubt they'll get around to us until this show's over. You won't have to worry about your end of the inquiry till then."

There was a look in Irina's eyes, an expression he'd never seen there before. Before he could identify what it might be, it came and was gone.

"I'll be fine," she said. "No problem, Lieutenant, okay? I've got to run. Got stuff to do."

"Right, Sergeant."

She was gone, then, leaving him standing there. Damion Witzko wasn't sure exactly what had happened, but he was certain he didn't like it, whatever it was.

* * * * *

Belier was waiting for her, standing silently in the hall outside her room. Irina stopped, close enough to smell his bad breath and count the broken veins in his nose.

"Sergeant, if you're still blocking my way three seconds from now, I'll jerk your spine out and beat you to death with it. One. Two . . ."

At that moment, Belier was sure she meant exactly what she said. He backed off, shaken, covering his fear with a laugh.

"No offense, Queenie. Just having a little fun."

"Call me that again, and I'll kill you, *then* pull you apart." Irina faced him, hands clenched at her sides. "Why did you do it, Belier? That was a cheap trick even for you."

"I call 'em the way I see them, Sarge. I mean, you and the lieutenant—"

"Were doing exactly nothing at all, and you know it. Did Savant put you up to it, or did you come up with it yourself and take the idea to him?"

Belier's chubby features widened into a smile. "You and me don't have to fight, Irina. We can work things out on this."

"Oh, we can, can we? Tell me how we can do that?"

Belier paused, then looked right at her with rheumy eyes. "You're going to be sergeant major of the Concord Marines one day. I know I haven't got a chance at that, but I figure I could screw it for you. I don't want to exactly, but I will."

"Uh-huh. I'll bet there's something I could do to stop that, isn't there?"

Belier almost blushed. "Yeah, coupla things, but I'll stick to the one I want the most. You'll laugh at me, but I don't care if you do." Belier hesitated, glanced over his shoulder. "I want the Big V. I want to retire, get the hell out of this mess, and take that sucker with me."

Irina was too disgusted to laugh. She felt as if something small and scaly had hopped from Belier and was slithering down her back.

"I can't believe it, you miserable old bastard. You

must be out of your mind. Do you actually think—"

"I don't think anything," he said, anger darkening his, face, "not a thing except I can ruin you, Lavon. You and that pet lieutenant of yours too. Neither of you will be marines when I get through talking, getting into the raw *details* of what I saw in there. You'll—"

Irina stuck the flat of her palm in his chest and sent him reeling. Belier yelled, tried to catch himself, and sprawled on the deck. Irina walked over him, opened the door to her cabin, and slammed it shut.

She stood there, shaking, holding back the anger that had come too close to the surface this time, the rage that she reserved for combat when everything let go and she became something more than the person, the woman, she knew herself to be.

Is it the other way around? she wondered. Is that other one, the killer, the real Irina?

Belier meant it, and she knew it. As outrageous as it seemed, that was the deal he was offering to get her off the hook. When they got in the field on Arist, she would recommend him for the Concord Marine's highest award, the Star of Valor. She would lie, write up the lie, and hand it in to the colonel.

If that was so, if that was what Belier wanted, Captain Savant wasn't in this at all. He hated Lieutenant Witzko, though, and knew the captain would buy the story at once.

A medal, the Star of Valor, for that demented, mean-spirited old man? They could ruin her reputation and toss her out before she'd desecrate the Corps with an act like that.

Right, she thought, and can you let them take Witzko down too? Can you handle that, Master Sergeant Lavon?

She didn't have an answer, and she didn't want to look for one right now.

* * * * *

Witzko had escaped the battle with little more than a new collection of bruises, slightly shaken nerves, and a strained muscle or two. Orders were that Recon Marines were to continue working with Star Force on clean-up operations until *Stormbird* was "in all respects ready to execute her mission."

When Witzko's platoon was finally relieved, he walked through the damaged corridors back to the ready room. Jobal Kran was there, looking even more solemn than usual. Witzko recognized the list in his platoon sergeant's hand, knew what sort of news he was going to hear.

"Final casualty list, sir. Corporal MacKenzie died of wounds received in the first hit. Sergeant Treko bought it. Russel, Deihudt, Sternwitz, Karlo, Biggert, Olafson, Morton, Reekmon, and Triman dead. Grusin's missing. Seven are wounded but likely to make it. Shall I pick an honor guard to bring MacKenzie back?"

Witzko didn't even try to pretend his eyes were dry.

He nodded and said, "Spread the word about passing the helmet for the dead's survivors. Standard Death Benefits never cut it. A little extra helps."

Kran didn't answer. He saluted as Witzko turned away.

Witzko wondered why it always happened. Right after members of your team bought it, it was hard to remember what they'd looked like. They all came back later, but at the time the faces in his mind were blank.

Moments later, new orders came through. Recon Platoon was to join the hull gang and the heavy robots for external hull policing and repair. After thorough suit checks, the platoon filed out into the passageway toward the airlock. They were only a few hatches away from the nearest exit bay when Sergeant Chen, Corporal Lee, and Gre-Ikwilisan Thumn hurried past in the opposite direction. Sergeant Lavon was on their heels, looking like a harried teacher taking three perverse students on an outing.

Kran stared after them. "Great. I wonder what the Unholy Three are up to now."

Witzko frowned. "The Unholy what?"

"The Unholy Three," Kran said. "Chen, Lee, and Gre-Ikwilisan. I think it was Lavon's idea. It certainly seems to fit."

Witzko shook his head. For the moment, his thoughts were on MacKenzie, dead out there in the void, waiting for an Honor Guard to bring her in, and Grusin, out there with her, or maybe turned to plasma somewhere. Sometimes the stars were friendly, but today they seemed malevolent, cold, uncaring eyes in the endless dark.

* * * * *

"I've set course for Arist," Captain Myklebust said. "We'll keep a good watch on our tail, of course. Any time you can't see your enemy, that's the time to look the hardest."

She took another forkful of salad and chewed with elaborate care. "We've had updates on Arist since we talked," she said, pausing to look across the table at Colonel Seymoyr. "We've been trying to get acknowledgements through, but either Platon is radiating, their satellites are down, or somebody is jamming."

Seymoyr didn't like the last idea and said so.

Myklebust nodded. "That's why I'd rather head straight for Spes. I'll send Arist an acknowledgement but nothing else. Somebody could match course with us and dump a load of frozen chewing gum in our path that would probably take us out. I hope old Adrianus allows *Revealer* to continue with us as escort to Spes, but I haven't received confirmation on that."

Seymoyr frowned. "We don't know that Spes has fire-power to spare, and we don't know if anybody else is in position to help Arist. We certainly don't know how much shooting's going on there."

"A light cruiser or a frigate would be better for scouting and low-altitude work," Myklebust said. "*Stormbird's* lost most of her ground-support capabilities to battle damage."

"We still have *Activity*," Seymoyr pointed out, "and we do have marines, which a lighter ship wouldn't. Besides, if we at least scout Arist and protect civilian lives and property, *Revealer* and her friends can go straight on to Spes. That should make Admiral Raastad kiss our feet."

Myklebust nodded slowly. "You've got a point . . . assuming the klicks don't come back and chop us off at the ankles. Let's check the landers' status board before we make any final decisions. I don't know if we can hope for a surprise landing, but I'd like to plan on that basis. The more landers, the more marines we can put on the ground."

Seymoyr couldn't resist a small jab. "Of course, the more marines, the less need for surprise."

Myklebust didn't smile. "A little more tea, Colonel? I believe yours is getting cold."

Chapter Sixteen

October 28, 2501

Kuhudag came up out of sleep at once, sat up, and blinked. A deep series of tremors shook the ceiling and the walls. He knew at once that it was the sound of battle raging somewhere above. He quickly used Orlamu deep breathing to bring his senses fully alert.

Through the din of charge rifles, explosions, and an occasional laser weapon, he could hear the crack and boom of more outdated projectile weapons. They were weren, his own people then. Who else could it be?

Once more he was glad that he had persuaded Doctor Ohito not to try for West Lodge, even on a mission of mercy. If the weren were angry enough to attack Red Ridge so soon, then they were probably desperate enough to take hostages.

After a few minutes, the battle seemed to get even closer to the prison. Now he could hear the unmistakable flat crack of weren hunting rifles. One of them fired so rapidly the weapon obviously had a magazine. Above the sound of the guns, he heard the sizzle and hiss of human energy weapons. All of it joined in with shouts, curses, and war cries in human and weren tongues to form a horrendous cacophony that shook the walls of the building. The whine and rumble of moving vehicles shook the earth. Obviously the battle was close enough now to be inside the confines of Red Ridge but still not close to the cavern where he was imprisoned in his cell.

Even if the weren didn't take Red Ridge itself, they might reach the prison and give him a chance to escape. He hoped Doctor Ohito and her father were not engaged in the fighting. They had treated him with honor, and he did not wish them harm. Maybe, if he were rescued, he could be of some aid them.

Air still flowed through a vent overhead, but now he smelled smoke along with the air. He wondered if it came from the above-ground settlement or somewhere in the cavern itself. Without one of the Ohitos present, he wasn't sure the guards would bother to save him from a fire.

The smoke was growing thicker now, strong enough to make him cough. The guards pretended not to notice, and Kuhudag was damned if he was going to show he cared.

A moment later he noticed that the sounds of firing and vehicles faded, then died away altogether. The air in the cell began to clear. One lone skycar continued to drone in endless circles overhead, but otherwise the night was silent.

Kuhudag stood straight as the doors of his cell slid began to slide up. The thick metal clanged against the ceiling, and the guards backed up, aiming their weapons at his chest. Two humans in drab uniforms marched into the room with weapons ready. A weren hunched along before them, turning now and then to snap his tusks in anger at his guards.

Kuhudag stared. By the great Opaaz! It was Grutok, Medlyna's whelp! His heart beat against his chest. The lad was obviously wounded; his right arm was soaked with blood, and much of the fur along the arm had been seared.

Kuhudag backed up as the humans pushed Grutok into the cell. Kuhudag caught him at once and laid him on the floor. He was hurt, but the wounds were not mortal, not if Kuhudag could get him help.

He rose and spoke to the guards. "In honor, you will give healing aid? You will receive my respect in return."

The humans seemed startled, then turned to each other. Kuhudag was old fashioned enough to believe it rude to watch enemies when they were debating a matter of honor, so he turned his attention back to the whelp.

Grutok wore only the remnants of thermal underwear and boot linings. There were minor fragment wounds along his body and bruises along his skull. Kuhudag guessed he'd taken several hits from a stutter rifle. His breathing was slow but steady, and it seemed unlikely he would die of any visible wounds. Still, invisible wounds often killed more brutally than those one could see.

Kuhudag turned to see a guard pushing a slim, plastic-wrapped parcel through the bars. Kuhudag nodded his thanks. Inside the parcel was a small metal tube he recognized as a miniature diagnostic scanner. There was also a clean shirt for bandages, a blunt-nosed pair of scissors, and a can of antiseptic pain-killing spray.

Grutok was awake enough to wince as Kuhudag started to trimming away the singed fur.

"Be still," Kuhudag growled in Weren. "Would you have the humans see you express discomfort in their presence? How could I face your mother after that?"

"I cannot face *you*, Worthy," Grutok replied. "As you can see, I allowed myself to be captured by smooth-faced dwarves. I did not even kill one before I was taken."

"You may not have noticed," Kuhudag told him, "but I, too, have been captured. We have not gone far enough in your warrior schooling to touch upon the subject of captivity. I will say only this much now. The manner in which a warrior is taken, and his behavior after that, determines honor lost or gained. Tell me what is happening above ground and who is there. I take it that our forces have been repulsed, unless, of course, your presence here is some clever ruse to help me escape."

"I'm afraid that is not so, Worthy. Yes, our forces decided to gracefully reposition themselves at a point farther back from the settlement, at least for the time being. I am sure this is a wise tactical move."

"No doubt," Kuhudag said. "Now if you would tell me in a somewhat more comprehensible manner how we happened to *reposition* ourselves, I would be most grateful."

Grutok explained how the weren forces had advanced upon the settlement, nearly taking them by surprise in a particularly blinding snowstorm, but the human sensors had found them out. From that point, Grutok said, there was fierce fighting in the streets with many victories going to the weren, until the humans brought their ground and air machines into play.

"It was most difficult to face them after that, Worthy. Though we disabled many of their devices, we were targets in the open. I must tell you that some of our people have left abruptly for the afterworld."

One of the guards outside the bars laughed at one of his companion's joke. Grutok didn't hear the joke, only the laugh. In his present condition, that was enough to snap his reason. With a roar that started deep within his chest, he came up off the floor and threw himself at the bars.

"Hairless weakling!" he roared in Standard. "White-face! I have not killed your kind yet, but I vow to you I will!" Grutok stretched his long, clawed arms through the bars and slashed at his captors. The guards shrank back, eyes wide with fear.

"Stop him!" yelled the first guard. "Get those bars closed, now!"

The bars were still a half meter from the floor. The guards had left the bars open in anticipation of the imminent arrival of the prison's cleaning detail that would be bringing around brooms and mops for the daily cleaning detail.

The second guard rushed to carry out his orders, and, his mind clouded by fear, made a big mistake. He threw the lever up instead of down, and the bars whined up to the ceiling.

"No, you idiot!" The first guard stared, then backed away, raising his weapon and bringing the barrel to bear upon Grutok's head.

Kuhudag moved in a blur. The instant he saw the guard's mistake, he knew what had to happen next. Sweeping Grutok aside, he rushed from the cell, grabbed the first guard's weapon, jerked it from his grip, and tossed it across the room. The second guard was slow. Grutok took him, lifted him off his feet, and held him high to toss him against the bars.

"Don't harm him!" Kuhudag called out in Standard. "Set him down, lad. Easy now."

Kuhudag spoke firmly but gently. He knew Grutok was in the warrior's state of battle-rage. He also knew he was still too young to control this fierce emotion.

Kuhudag grabbed Grutok's hostage and held both guards straight out in his claws.

"Now, what shall we do?" he asked the two. "If we fight, I feel our encounter is over at this moment. If we do not, we can search for a peaceful solution. I apologize for the young one's lack of honor. He is not experienced in the warrior ways. He has just witnessed the death of his people at the hands of *your* people. To a young, untested weren, this is a blood-call. As an adult, I require a greater push, but, I must remind you, not *much*."

"It was a-a mistake, I'm certain," the first guard said.

"It was certainly that," said the second.

"Good. I am sure we can—"

"Let them go! Now! Let them go or you're dead, weren!"

Kuhudag turned. The female human was standing in the door, a charge pistol aimed at Kuhudag's head. Kuhudag felt she was quite serious. Grutok didn't move.

"There is no need," Kuhudag said. "We have come to an understanding."

"Do it, now! I'm warning you!"

A new face appeared behind the woman.

"What's going on here? What are you doing?" demanded Dr. Ohito, her face pale with rage and fear.

"I'm going to shoot this weren if he doesn't do what I say."

"No," Ohito said, fighting to remain calm, "no, you are *not*. Put the weapon down, Deirta. There is no need."

"Don't bother me, Ohito. Get out of here."

"All right," Ohito said. "Have it your way."

She moved with a speed Kuhudag did not expect in so small a human. She chopped the edge of one hand across the woman's wrist and drove the fingers of her other hand into Deirta's stomach. The woman doubled up, gasped, and dropped her weapon

Ohito dove and came up holding the pistol by the muzzle.

"Witness!" she said. "I threaten no one with this weapon that has put law and honor in danger to no purpose."

Kuhudag let his hostages go. Dr. Ohito dropped the pistol's clip out of the weapon into her hand and snapped the bullet from the chamber to clatter onto the floor. She then handed it butt first to the guard whom Kuhudag had held.

"Please keep this safe for your comrade until she, ah, knows and understands her art."

The female guard used an eloquent obscenity. One of the men laid a restraining hand on her shoulder. She shook it off furiously, glared at Ohito, and stumbled out of the room.

"Now, is all in order here?" Ohito asked. She looked from the guards to Kuhudag and back. The guards mumbled and turned away.

"I think we have concluded our encounter," Kuhudag said. "Before you entered, I apologized for the young one's . . . *enthusiasm*."

"Fine," Ohito said. "Now, both of you back into your cell, and let's take a look at this *enthusiastic* young one."

The two weren and the doctor entered the cell, and the bars whined and clanged shut an instant later.

She unslung her medkit and kneeled beside Grutok. Grutok looked up at Kuhudag. Kuhudag nodded, and Grutok lay still, studying the human with interest.

Doctor Ohito ran a small, humming instrument over his wounds. Grutok winced—not from the pain, but from the fact that the human left large, hairless patches on his head and chest where she cleaned and dressed his wounds.

After she had finished with Grutok, Ohito came to Kuhudag and inspected his nearly healed scalp.

"Paul Dimmock's armed workmen are claiming several dead weren in the night's battle," she said softly. "They have also gained new friends among the folk of Red Ridge, now that the weren seem to be open enemies. However, my father and those who follow him believe we will have help from offworld soon. We have communicated with Spes. They will not say much, but my father thinks that is an indication some sort of force is in the area. We have also monitored a weren broadcast from West Lodge. Your people have sent a signal asking for help. One way or the other, we may be able to end this terrible mistake that has come to plague us."

Kuhudag looked at her. "Mistake? Is that what this is? Whose mistake is it?"

Doctor Ohito read the anger in his eyes. "I don't know, Worthy. I don't think you do, either. Someone started this, your people or mine. I don't think blame matters at this point. We have to stop the fighting somehow, before we destroy each other. The diplomats can assign blame later."

"No," Kuhudag replied. "It matters greatly. I cannot simply dismiss all this as a *mistake*."

Kuhudag shook off her words. He respected Doctor Ohito, but he no longer had the patience to listen. Grutok's wounds and his news of weren casualties had nearly swept reason aside.

"What of the other humans?" Kuhudag asked. "The ones in the north? Those who have now broken all laws and pursued my people into the caverns? No one seems greatly interested in these warriors, but I can tell you they exist. Grutok here can witness to their presence. He was there with me."

"Please, Kuhudag. I don't doubt they exist. I simply cannot discover who they are. Paul Dimmock thinks—"

"Huh! I give no credence to what this Dimmock human thinks. He does not show great concern for honor, much less the weren whom he pursues! *Darut-eg iermarkhta?*"

"I don't blame you for your feelings," she said, "but let me tell you what I think. The human raiders in the north have not attacked your people for days now. It may be that our first guess was correct. These people are probably outcasts and malcontents from Red Ridge or other communities. Now that Paul Dimmock has organized resistance against your people, these outcasts are laying low."

Doctor Ohito paused. "There is good reason for that, if this is so. Many of them are likely men and women who have committed some crime or have run out on their contracts with VoidCorp."

The mention of VoidCorp brought a rush of blood to Kuhudag's head. "Yes, I can imagine a VoidCorp Employee might become *disaffected* in some manner. My own people didn't have the choice of running away from these slavers."

"I know," she said gently. "I am sorry I brought up the subject. I am sorry in many ways, Kuhudag, for all that has occurred, but not all within VoidCorp are the demons you believe them to be. My father and I are both VoidCorp Employees. We are medical people, and we do not make policy. I'm sure you know that, though you may not accept it."

"You do me honor by your help and understanding," Kuhudag said. "I cannot deny this. I am grateful, as is Grutok here."

"Yes, Worthy," Grutok put in.

Doctor Ohito rose. "I'll be back when I can, and I will bring what news there is. Please get along with the guards." She turned to the two men. "I'm sure there will be no more trouble here."

The guards raised the bars for Ohito. At the door, she turned.

"You understand that if the Concord does indeed take a part in this conflict, they cannot allow your folk further revenge any more than they can mine."

"In return," Kuhudag replied, "I expect them to help us find those humans who lurk in the north and who may yet do further harm to all of us. I do not make this a formal offer. I only let you know what the weren may ask."

The doctor nodded. "You could hardly ask for less."

"Good," Kuhudag said. "Now I may offer you a little help. If Red Ridge is dividing into factions, is the woman guard, the one you called Deirta, is she one of Dimmock's folk?"

"I don't know. If she has violated her oath, she cannot stay on as a prison guard."

"She might be dangerous to you as well, Doctor, if she is running with Dimmock's band."

"I will most certainly consider your advice," she said.

Doctor Ohito left, leaving Kuhudag alone with dour, but reasonably calm guards and a drowsy Grutok.

He wished that he could be far away from dishonor and treachery. That, he knew, would take him a long way from Arist and his duties there.

He thought again about Ohito's words. There was little use in pressing the matter with her, but he did not believe the story she wanted him to believe—very possibly wanted to believe herself—that the well-trained, disciplined warriors he had faced in the north were merely vagabonds and miscreants from the human settlements. Kuhudag had seen such ragged, hollow-eyed humans before. Most were addicts, criminals, or both—and none of them were practiced in military tactics. They might have lice, fleas, and dull blades about their persons. Certainly they would have cheap narcotics and a bottle of spirits, but they definitely would not carry sophisticated laser weapons and grenades.

There was not a vagrant on any planet anywhere that could send a weren warrior diving for cover. Perhaps, Kuhudag thought, the woman simply could not see the truth in this.

Chapter Seventeen

October 28, 2501

It was a venerable custom among Recon Marines that operations up to company level were discussed in open, communal meetings. The thirty-five fatigue-clad men and women in Mess Compartment D listened to Sergeant Kran with acute attention. Each of them understood that this conference could mean life or death for them in the days to come. For this, Damion Witzko was grateful.

Jobal Kran ran the general situation and most probable Recon mission past his people with the help of a holodisplay that began with the whole globe of Arist, then focused on the area between the weren settlement at West Lodge and the mining community of Red Ridge.

"Since most of the fighting seems to involve patrols and raids back and forth across this area," Kran said, "the first peacekeeping job is to hold it against both sides, stop the raids, confiscate any weapons caches, and warn both sides against anything you can't stop. That's a job best done with a force landing from orbit with tactical surprise and a high-powered portable sensor net. Guess who's at the head of the line with those capabilities?"

"Recon all the way!" the platoon shouted in unison, Witzko along with the rest. It was a ritual that might seem silly to outsiders. Certainly no one claimed it was original, but it did the same for Recon Marines that it must have done for whatever long-forgotten elite unit had invented it. It made them walk a little taller and look out more carefully for one another. It made each of them feel more secure when the flares went up and the shooting war started.

Kran turned the meeting over to Witzko, again according to custom. Witzko laid out a rough plan for a Combat Assault from orbit.

"Collecting enemy supplies in the area is secondary to the first two jobs," he added. "Supplies are no good to an enemy who can't get to them. Don't forget this is a peacekeeping mission. We're here to stop a war, not start it."

"What if they shoot first?" somebody asked, another ritual question.

"We shoot back," the others answered in chorus.

"The maps, sir. They indicate a lot of caverns on Arist. I understand both the weren and the human populations live underground because of the weather."

Witzko spotted PFC Atanza in the rear of the room. "That's true, but we don't know if the caverns play any part in this conflict or not. The very brief info we've got reflects a number of raids on the surface."

Nadya Atanza was old for a private who'd only been in Recon for a year, but her file showed she'd taken a drop from sergeant in the Concord Defense Corps to join the marines two years before. She was qualified in sniping, demolitions, vehicle operations, was working on a medic rating, and generally came across as quiet but valuable.

"All right, Atanza," Witzko said, "you've got something on your mind. Tell us what you think."

"Well," Atanza said, "if we *do* have to work in caves of any sort, sir—I mean, if that were to be the case, we've got everything we'll need except caving gear."

That remark brought a few blank looks. Witzko glanced at Kran.

"Climbing gear covers most of caving, and that's built into the armor," Kran said.

"I don't want to start up the old quarrel between you climbers and those of us who are afraid of heights," Atanza said, "but you're almost right, Sergeant Kran. Full armor can be way too bulky for getting through tight passages. We'll need heated, light CM gear so people who have to change out of armor to go underground won't go hypothermic. We also need to be sure we have the ability to trace cave formations and find supply dumps underground—"

"There we may have to rely on ship capabilities," Kran interrupted.

"I've heard *Stormbird* can't operate at low altitude until she's seen a repair dock," Atanza said.

"She still has some capabilities," Witzko put in, "but you're right. We shouldn't count on her for heavy support. Star Force may surprise us, but we ought to be ready for a worst-case scenario. 'Hope for the best, but plan for the worst.' That's pretty standard operations for the Concord Marines."

A mutter of agreement followed Witzko's remarks. He turned the meeting over to Kran again to discuss supply inventory and systems checks on the overland suits.

Witzko had to admit to himself that Atanza had a point. Whether the caverns would come into play or not, they were there. It was something he couldn't ignore. In the marines, the one item you left behind was usually the one you needed the most.

* * * * *

Irina Lavon paused to look at the Third Battalion Wall of Honor. The wall was made of jet black durasteel so polished she could see herself in its reflection. Etched into steel was the list of Third Battalion's combat dead since its inception in 2487. There were forty-eight names in all—not a big total, considering—but enough, if you happened to remember some of the faces behind those names.

Four of the names were new, the etching still sharp and crisp: MacKenzie, Grusin, and the others who had died the day before. Their ashes lay in urns in a niche below their names. Lavon had served with battalions where the Wall of Honor was so large it had to have a separate section for the niches; she had seen those niches filled with urns of ashes from a single battle. She herself had earned her wound stripes from one of those battles, as well as her Rescue Commendation and Close-Combat Badge.

Is that what it's all about, she wondered, wound stripes, promotions, and then your name in cold steel on the wall? No, it was more than that, a lot more than that.

"Many old comrades are up there, Master Sergeant, more names than I like to remember."

Irina turned and came to attention at once. "Yes, sir. That's very true, sir."

"At ease, Sergeant." Captain Savant showed her his permanent scar of a smile, put his hands behind his back, and rested on his heels.

"I was hoping I'd run into you, Lavon. I thought we might talk."

"Sir?" Irina felt the color rise to her face. "About what, sir?"

"Perhaps I shouldn't discuss this with you before you appear at your inquiry, but since we're going into combat soon. . . ." Savant cleared his throat. "I'll simply say that I was most disappointed to learn you were involved in this *sordid* incident with Lieutenant Witzko, Sergeant, most disappointed. You have an outstanding service record and an enviable combat record as well. For your sake, as well as the unit's, I wish this thing had never happened."

"Sir, you'll be pleased to hear then that it never *did* happen," Irina said, eyes straight ahead.

Captain Savant mumbled something to himself. "Master Sergeant Belier tells an entirely different story, Sergeant."

"Yes, sir."

"You've spoken to Lieutenant Witzko, then?" Savant's easy tone disappeared. Now he was closer, in Irina's face. "Is that true?"

"I don't believe I'm supposed to, Captain, until my own inquiry."

"No, you're not. I'm asking you if you have spoken to him."

"Begging your pardon, sir, should your questions to me, out here in the hall and *not* under official sanction, be part of my testimony? Sir?"

From the corner of her eyes, she could see the captain's dishwater eyes close to tiny slits. "Are you being impertinent, Sergeant? Is that what you're doing?"

"Sir. No, sir. I am asking a question of my company

commander, sir. I am asking your advice on a very important matter, sir. I would appreciate your counsel."

Savant let out a breath and stepped back. "What I would like to think, Sergeant, is that you have better sense than to push me too far. I would also like to think—for your sake—that you perhaps did not willingly take part in the encounter with Lieutenant Witzko, that yours was not a voluntary action. That would make a great deal of difference in how this matter is dealt with, Sergeant."

Irina Lavon faced him, then, breathing hard to maintain her control. "I promise you, Captain Savant, that what you have said here *will* be repeated when I stand before you and the colonel, every word of it, *sir*!"

In the overly bright light of the corridor, Savant looked like a hideous clown. His face was white with strain, and his smile curved nearly up his cheeks.

"I, Sergeant, will swear that our conversation never happened, never. I don't think the colonel will be overly impressed that you are a moral offender *and* a liar! Think about it, Master Sergeant."

"Well, then," Irina whispered harshly, "since this conversation isn't really happening, you can take your advice and shove it right up—"

"Careful, Sergeant," Savant interrupted her. "Just because I'm not really here doesn't mean that I'm not your commanding officer. Your life can be made even more unpleasant. Remember that."

After he was gone, Irina stood in the corridor for a long time. She wanted to go and find Lieutenant Witzko at once. Maybe if they talked about this terrible thing they could do something, find some way to stop Savant and Belier before she and Witzko were both so smeared they would never survive in the Corps.

No, I can't, she told herself, not now. Maybe after this mission is over, if both of our names don't end up on the wall.

Irina walked back to her quarters. She wondered, not for the first time, how deeply Captain Savant was involved in this dangerous charade. Were they in it together, or had Belier brought him the story, knowing full well that Savant's dislike of Lieutenant Witzko would bring him into the conspiracy at once?

How could the man have such hatred? she wondered. She was well aware that Savant resented Witzko because he, Savant, had come up the hard way, and Witzko had a military family behind him.

No, it wasn't that, not entirely. There was a hatred, a bitterness that came from within, from the man himself. Savant couldn't live with what he was and had devoted himself to making everyone else miserable as well.

* * * * *

The command group briefing was a good deal smaller than Recon Platoon's. The six of them scarcely filled the Tactical Command Center. Myklebust, her executive officer, an officer from *Stormbird* Operations, and Lieutenant Commander Hammel represented Star Force. Attending from Battle Group Seymoyr was Major Pelletin, who was now acting as both executive officer and permanent Ops officer.

"The way it stands now," Captain Myklebust concluded, "Spes will be on standby if we need them. We'll evaluate the drop first, see what we've got down there. Frankly, I'm more concerned about klicks showing up again than I am this pocket war we've got going down there."

"If we did have klick trouble, could Spes get here in time?" Seymoyr asked.

"No," Myklebust frowned, "not if I waited until I *saw* any klicks, but I wouldn't, Colonel, would I? I would try to anticipate from the Far-Out drones and from our patrols and sensors if there seemed to be a need for our people from Spes. I cannot simply ask for an *armada* to stand by and hold my hand in case the baddies might decide to appear. Combat is a calculated risk. I imagine you know that from your experience."

Uh-oh, I punched the wrong button that time. Seymoyr felt his ears redden. Everyone else at the table pretended they were somewhere else. He was certain whatever was going on had to do with a hundred other worries on the captain's mind, but *he'd* been sitting there when the missiles started to fly.

"Uh, well, yes," said Ikido, Myklebust's exec, "since we have already encountered the klicks, you can be sure, Colonel, that experience is built into Battle Control. We'll have plenty of time to act, if we need to."

"I'm sure the colonel understands," Myklebust said, with a killing look at her exec. "Thank you, Ikido."

"Certainly," Ikido said, wondering if he could fit under the table.

"I take it then that you've received word that *Revealer* won't be joining the party?" Pelletin asked, trying to take some of the heat off of Seymoyr.

"*Revealer* will be departing to complete her mission immediately," said Myklebust. "I'll be surprised if she's still out there when we leave this room."

"As far as the initial drop is concerned," Seymoyr went on quickly, "we can drop Recon Platoon and some add-ons down first with a lander in reserve for the second wave of supplies. That leaves the other three free to return to orbit and reload. With *Activity* and three landers we can bring down a whole company on Red Ridge."

"Why Red Ridge?" Hammel asked. He looked like a cadaverous Buddha and was under treatment for nervous stomach. The fight with the klicks, plus working for Myklebust, had not improved his health.

"Because we have to be evenhanded," Seymoyr said. "Recon's going down in what we believe is weren territory. We can't be absolutely sure without breaking silence, so an educated guess is the best we can do."

"What about putting Recon down in neutral territory, then moving them across country into weren territory?" Hammel asked. "That would help keep us looking impartial."

"Negative on that," Seymoyr said. "That means two lifts. One company en masse will impress a lot more hothead humans *and* weren than a dribble of squads and platoons."

"Are you sure we can do it all in one lift anyway?" Myklebust asked. Whatever had gotten on her nerves seemed to be forgotten now. "*Activity* might be handy if you need air fire. She can operate low and slow. *Stormbird* can't."

Seymoyr raised a brow. "Just how slow is *Stormbird* now?"

"Fast enough to fight but too slow to win the races this year."

Seymoyr sighed. "I'll get some of my people together with Hammel. We'll work something out."

"Don't we always?" Myklebust said, and her weary smile was real this time.

Chapter Eighteen

October 30, 2501

The prison did not have a proper exercise yard since it was not intended for the long-term confinement of dangerous prisoners. Kuhudag would have preferred either no exercise at all or a larger yard. Both he and Grutok were within pistol range of a dozen Red Ridge humans, and a good many of those humans carried rifles as well. To the average human, the two weren probably looked exactly like the raiders who had recently attacked the settlement. Given the resentment against the weren that seemed so prevalent in Red Ridge, Kuhudag was not inclined to put too much trust in human honor. "Accidents" could happen out here.

Grutok's arm was still dressed in a thick cast, but he was determined to uphold weren honor. Kuhudag didn't have the heart to stop him and didn't try. A whelp had to learn the hard way. If he made it to full warrior status, then the chances a mentor took along the way were worthwhile. If he didn't—

BOOOOOOOM! BOOOOOM!

The sky seemed to split as a sonic boom struck Red Ridge, the sound rolling off one hill and then the other.

Rows of icicles crashed from the prison walls and shattered on the frozen ground.

The humans were all looking up, pointing their weapons at the sky. Kuhudag followed their gaze and saw a silvery shape flash by overhead.

"Did you see the markings on that ship?" one guard called to the another.

"Cursed right!" another shouted. "That's Concord!"

The first man muttered an obscenity.

"Perhaps we shall see some changes soon, Worthy," Grutok said. "I would like to meet a marine. They are said to be good fighters."

Most of them are humans, Kuhudag thought. If there were weren among the ranks of the Concord Marines, Kuhudag had certainly never heard of any.

"I suppose we shall see," he said aloud.

* * * * *

Witzko had turned off his comm and punched in the external audio pickups of his suit. He could hear the whine of the wind coupled with the metallic sounds of a lander stressed by high-speed, low-altitude operations.

The four landers skimmed over ridges and threaded frozen valleys to stay below sensor horizons; sometimes, Witzko thought, the craft flew low enough to pick up rocks. So far the crew had seen nothing at all. It was a blazing bright day with no clouds and little wind—only the frozen, never-ending surface below. All things considered, Witzko thought, his people would drop under conditions as ideal as marines could reasonably expect. Now all he had to do was set everyone down in perfect order, just like in the manual.

The Harkamp Overland Mark IV suits were good. Still Witzko felt the designers had gotten carried away with the dream of giving every single marine the capabilities of a sensor-surveillance post, heavy weapons team, demolitions squad, and armed skybike. A Harkamp soldier could drop in from high altitude, fly over any terrain, and survive two-thirds of any weapon made. Of course, that assumed that everything worked properly, and every marine knew that everything hardly ever did.

In addition to the killer weapons built into the suit, Witzko's platoon carried a double load of supplies. Every marine—even the medics—carried a charge pistol. Most of the ranks also bore the standard issue IF-3 11 mm charge rifle. The Encounter Squad carried stutter rifles in hopes of taking out targets without killing them. A precious few soldiers carried a 25 mm sabot cannon in case the platoon needed to blast anything into several hundred pieces. Every marine also carried an array of grenades, both of the nonlethal and deadly variety.

"Ready alert!" the co-pilot's voice squawked in Witzko's ear. "Thirty seconds."

"Station One," Witzko answered.

"Station Two," said Sergeant Kran.

The co-pilot was jumpmaster. Witzko didn't know him and prayed the man had done this before.

The lander's nose tilted abruptly, and the craft climbed to a thousand meters in a few seconds.

"All stand! Visual check on your jump buddy."

"Visual check, aye," replied Witzko. His buddy was Private Atanza. It took him longer than usual to check her; extra demo gear hung on her suit like bulbs on a waterfruit tree. Atanza checked him in turn, and they nodded okays through their plates.

The lander's drop hatch slid open with a hum that Witzko felt more than he heard. The wind shrieked like an enraged demon, and Witzko flipped his audio to low.

"Recon Five-Anna," he said, "initiating drop."

"Confirmed, Recon Five-Anna. Drop is a go."

"Red Light. Red Light. Countdown."

". . . seven, six, five . . ."

". . . four, three, two . . ."

"GO-GO-GO-GO!"

Witzko threw himself into the frigid wind, tumbling twice as he barreled through the lander's slipstream. He flipped on his suit's induction power and slowed to a tactical rate.

From above, Arist was a swirl of rock, snow, and ice. Witzko could well understand why the inhabitants of this tortured landscape lived in an underground maze. He also noticed there were enough hiding places on the surface to hide a dozen small armies. Good news or bad, depended on your point of view.

Witzko landed gently three meters from Private Atanza. What had appeared to be snow covering the ground was actually thick, hardened ice. As Witzko crunched his way over the arctic plain, he was grateful for once to have the thick armor that prevented him from feeling the ground beneath his feet. Despite his suit's state-of-the-art environment control, just *looking* at the frozen world around him made him feel cold. He shivered and increased his suit's internal temperature.

The platoon was on the high rim of a jagged canyon that stretched east and west—two kilometers wide and two hundred meters deep. The troops were in good order, spread no more than forty meters wide.

Witzko was about to hail Kran when a signal on the civilian distress frequency crackled in his ears.

". . . crashed north of . . . canyon . . . look for a black stripe on the . . . wall. Anybody . . . there?"

The message repeated several times. Witzko closed with Atanza and hailed Kran.

"I smell something," Kran said bluntly.

"Yeah, maybe," Witzko replied.

"It might be an old distress beacon," Atanza said, "still coming on after the—after the survivors stopped surviving."

"Huh-unh. This started right after we dropped," Kran said. "I don't like it, Lieutenant."

Witzko didn't either, but he also knew that he couldn't simply walk off and drop it.

"Home in on them. I want a squad with me on the north side, and I want one medic. Everyone else, follow the south rim. Keep tactical formation and tight surveillance. If so much as a snowflake moves out here, I want to know about it before it hits the ground."

Stealth was better on the ground, but that would take an hour. Witzko got his people in the air, holding three meters off the ground, just enough to keep off most of the rocks. In three minutes, his point man reported the sighting, and Witzko told *Stormbird* he had visual contact on a possible crash site.

A few moments later Witzko himself was over the site. Past volcanic activity had shattered a bit of the canyon wall, leaving a slightly inclining slope that was little more than a hundred meters deep. One small skycar lay half buried in a pile of broken ice and snow fifty meters below the marines. Two humans in cold-weather gear stood near the vehicle. At least one of them carried a large rifle. The skycar's engine was still giving off heat on the sensors, so they hadn't been here long. Witzko started down, using his suit's induction engine to hover less than a meter above the ice.

"Hold it, sir," said Atanza. "I've got some more heat coming in from the south."

Witzko checked his own sensor. Judging from the size of the blips, this new party consisted of five weren. They were now less than half a kilometer from the skycar and approaching fast. The humans had not yet seen the danger. All of them were armed.

"All right," he said, "let's do it. Track 'em, but don't engage unless they start shooting. Let's not start any wars just yet. Go to nonlethals."

He nodded to Nadya Atanza. Atanza sent a signal rocket arcing over the canyon. No one could miss it, but some of the people down there didn't seem to care.

Witzko swallowed a curse as the weren began to open fire on the humans by the skycar. The humans dived for cover. In a moment, they were returning fire themselves, blazing away with charge rifles while the weren fired everywhere at once.

"All right," Witzko said wearily, "prepare nonlethals, but wait for my signal."

He set his external speaker to maximum volume and shouted, "Throw down your weapons! I repeat: throw down your weapons! This is a Concord Marine peace-keeping force. Further resistance is illegal and will be met with extreme force!"

Again no one cared to listen. Witzko gave the order, and the marines opened up. It didn't take long. One concussion grenade went off among the weren, knocking them to the ground and burying them in a thin blanket of frost. The crash party vanished in a cloud of knock-out gas as a salvo of smokers landed in the snow around them.

Witzko landed a few meters from the skycar just as the squad rearguard caught up with the him. Two men coughed and struggled to their feet. Four marines surrounded them. Atanza disarmed the two humans while the other marines stood guard.

"Well, that's just fine," the man complained. "I've been rescued by the damned marines. I should've kept my mouth shut."

"You're not hurt, sir," Witzko said. "I regret that we had to use force, but we don't want any casualties here. We've treated the other party the same."

The man scowled and wiped his hands on his shirt. He looked to be in his fifties, a gnome of a man wrapped in thick winter wear and his beard frozen to his face.

"Weren filth," he muttered. "Should've wiped 'em out when you had the chance and saved us the trouble. Not worth a damn, living or dead!"

"Give us those weapons back, and we'll handle it from here," said the second man, who looked like a twin of the first. "Take care of those stinking, fur-covered devils quick!"

"Gentlemen, that's about enough," said Atanza.

She guided the pair to the side of the canyon wall, well out of Witzko's way. Witzko could hear them grumbling as he walked toward the four weren who were coming in under guard.

"All right," he told them in Standard, "you have surrendered to a superior force. Your persons, property, and honor are safe from the Concord as long as you give no further offense. We won't let you kill us, one another, the two humans, or yourselves. We *may* release you if you offer no more hostility. Allow us to search your persons and gear in an honorable fashion, accept our custody, and answer our questions. We demand no more of you now."

The weren looked at him then conferred with one another long enough to assert that they didn't *have* to do what they were told.

"We agree," the leader said finally. "There is clearly honor here. We mean no harm to you or your comrades. These humans have made us their enemy through their actions. However, we promise not to kill them while they are under oath to you. We do not bind ourselves beyond that."

"Thank you," Witzko said. "I ask for no more."

Chapter Nineteen

October 30, 2501

Since the cutter's sonic boom passed over Red Ridge, Kuhudag had heard or seen nothing of any Concord activity. It was frustrating to simply sit in captivity with no idea at all of the newcomers' intentions. What did they know about the problems on Arist? If someone in Red Ridge—like Paul Dimmock, for instance—had gotten to them and convinced them the "hairy devils" were running wild, then Kuhudag's people would be no better off than they were before, worse probably.

He had learned next to nothing from the Red Ridge humans. Perhaps he could glean something from the reactions he'd seen among the guards and prison workers. Some were loudly unhappy the Concord might stop them from settling their score with the weren. Many seemed relieved they didn't have to think about it anymore. Every sentient species had its share of those, Kuhudag thought—beings that welcomed turning over responsibility to someone else. Even the weren had an ample share, though he hated to admit it.

The prison guards were plainly split. Whatever their opinions, he was sure they would not defend their prisoners if Dimmock's people decided to go on a rampage.

If that happened, he and Grutok didn't stand a chance.

Kuhudag let out a growl of frustration. He remembered a teacher of history who said revolutions come not when hope is gone but when it has risen and then fallen again. Making another endless round of his cell, he decided that he was likely in that very situation right now, and he reasoned, if the Concord forces weren't coming close to Red Ridge anymore, it was likely the fighting was taking place somewhere else, maybe to the north, he thought hopefully. Maybe the Concord believed there were other human warriors up there. Maybe Ohito had managed to contact the marines and tell them how these "outcasts" had stormed the weren in their caves.

The very thought still made his blood run cold. If only there was some way to *be* there, to take some action himself—

"Worthy," Grutok said in Weren, guessing his elder's thoughts, "do not condemn me for expressing myself, but I must tell you I think we should consider attempting to escape from this place or die with honor trying. Either would be better than this."

Kuhudag bent low and whispered to the lad. "I am no more willing to die a helpless target than you. If you see a way out of here that has not occurred to me, please enlighten me."

Grutok bowed his head. "I cannot, Worthy, but I would be honored to give my life trying."

"Foolishness is not the path to honor. I have apparently not driven this lesson home to you. We will discuss it further when there is time."

"I must tell you, Worthy. My claws are itching. I feel a great rage in my heart."

"So do I," Kuhudag told him. "Retract the claws for now, but hold onto the rage. Rage is better kindled over a *slow* fire."

Though Kuhudag felt it was his beneath his dignity to address himself to the guards, he told himself it was a necessary thing to do in light of the situation. The guards, though, were more than a little reluctant to speak to him. Each time he approached the bars, the pair moved back a meter or so, pretending that they had intended to do so anyway.

"If I may intrude upon your arduous duties," Kuhudag said at last, "I would ask if there is news from above. I do not expect you to reveal that which you cannot, of course."

The guards exchanged a shrug. Neither moved closer to the bars.

"I don't think there's much I *can't* tell you," the first one said. "I just don't know a whole lot. The Concord has dropped marines in your territory. There's at least one Star Force cruiser in orbit, maybe more. Nothing's happened here since your people attacked, but we've heard there's action at other places."

"Where, do you know?"

The guard spread his hands. "Hey, who's going to tell me?"

"Have you heard of any action to the north?"

The guard looked at his companion. The companion shook his head.

"We haven't heard anything like that." He frowned at the weren. "If we get into a major war here, and I'm not saying that's what everybody wants, you understand—if we did, though, what'd your people do?"

"Fight back. What do you think?"

"I mean, I don't know much about the weren, and I don't have anything against them, you understand. How do your people feel about us?"

Kuhudag thought it was a foolish question but one that called for a reasonable answer.

"Much the same as you do," he said. "The weren would be pleased to cease hostilities—with honor, of course—if your people would allow it."

"Yeah, but you attacked *us*," put in the second guard. "What do you expect us to do? Lie down and roll over?"

"I do not wish to dispute you," Kuhudag said, "but I must tell you it is the other way around. It was you who began this fight. I cannot believe you are not aware of this."

"I think it's you that's got it wrong," said Number One. "I've got a friend who knows a—"

"*Attention! Attention! Concord Marines on a peace-keeping mission will be landing at Red Ridge in thirty minutes, that is three-zero minutes. I repeat, this is* a peacekeeping *mission. However, be warned that armed resistance will not be tolerated. Concord Marines on a peacekeeping mission in twenty-nine minutes. . . .*"

The loudspeaker faded, and Guard Number One turned to Kuhudag.

"I guess they'll answer questions now. Otto, you run up and see what's happening, all right?"

The other guard nodded and left.

"I assume your people will not resist," Kuhudag said.

The guard grinned. "Are you kidding? Against Concord Marines? Only if they shoot first. We're not going to start anything with them. If your folk have as much sense—"

Kuhudag held up a formidable claw. "I cannot let our

previous conversation go. It was not the weren who started this fight. It was the humans, not us. We do not move in an aggressive manner unless we are challenged."

"That's not what I hear, tooth-head."

"What?" Grutok broke in angrily. "What was that?"

"I said—"

"Do not say it again," Kuhudag said as he laid a restraining hand on the whelp's shoulder. With a possible resolution only a half-hour away, he didn't want anyone's temper flaring this late in the game.

Chapter Twenty

OCTOBER 30, 2501

Two minutes after Witzko's call, Colonel Seymoyr was ready to strip off his uniform and put on his full field gear, helmet and all.

Down there's where I ought to be, he told himself, down there with my marines, not up here watching on a damned holodisplay.

Moments after that he received further word from Lieutenant Witzko. The crash site was secured with both weren and humans contained. No casualties.

Seymoyr breathed a sigh of relief. Lieutenant Witzko was a good officer. He didn't need a field officer to help him blow his nose.

Seymoyr shook his head. A shame, too, such a capable officer getting himself into some kind of mess with his own master sergeant. To top it off, she was first class too, an experienced combat NCO with a splendid record. It couldn't come at worse time, either—for the lieutenant, the sergeant, and the outfit as well. Things like that happened, Seymoyr knew.

They don't happen in my command, and if they do, the marines involved will damned sure wish they'd behaved themselves when I get through—

"Colonel," a voice came over his comm, "Myklebust here. You available a minute?"

"Certainly, Captain. Right here."

Now why did she ask? he wondered. What if I'd said "no?"

"I'm putting *Activity* on low altitude patrol for a while. I knew you'd want to know."

"Good idea," Seymoyr said. "Anything special going on down there?"

Myklebust paused for a moment. "Nothing I can put my finger on. Not yet, anyway. Sensors are plotting some movement in an area where no fighting's going on. Maybe nothing, but I don't care for people moving around if I don't know who they are."

"I'll second that."

"Thought you might. Colonel, I'd like to see your company down in Red Ridge as soon as possible. We've got some pressing questions, and there's nothing like a couple of hundred marines knocking on your door to shake loose some answers."

"It won't be a couple of hundred," Seymoyr said, "not yet anyway, not with just three landers. Team Recon needs those supplies right now. We had an incident, a skycar crash. It should be on your console now."

"It is," the captain said."

"Good. Is the resupply lander ready to go?"

"It will be in a few minutes."

Seymoyr wondered if he should try to pack a few more marines in with the supplies and make the fourth lander part of the force going to Red Ridge. That would mean a longer flight at low altitude after unloading, however, and he decided to stick with three.

"Thanks for letting me know about *Activity.* If they see anything—"

"If they do, you'll be the first to know."

"Good, I'll be sending down the landing force in three minutes."

"I'll watch them from here."

"Ah, Captain, I don't think you gave me the grid on those blips."

"I don't guess I did. Seven-Seven-Niner. Like I say, that's an area where we're not supposed to have any activity. North . . ."

* * * * *

In the half-hour after the incident at the crash site, Witzko's Team Recon detected and intercepted five more small parties within twenty kilometers of the first skirmish. Two parties of humans surrendered upon being challenged. Two more groups gave up after marines laid down bursts of nonlethals. The last party, a squad of seven weren, ignored the nonlethals, but they laid down their arms after one of the marines opened up with a warning barrage with his sabot cannon. Weren were fierce and courageous but not stupid.

A fifth party simply seemed to vanish into the landscape. An intensive scan detected a cave mouth near where they'd disappeared and several other possible caves within a five-kilometer radius.

In Commmand Center aboard ship, the marines had studied maps of the surface of Arist. The world was honeycombed with caverns, and no one had ever even attempted to learn where they all were. In the first place, only the weren and the humans on Arist had any idea of the complexity of the caverns, and they weren't even telling each other what they knew, much less the marines.

Caverns were the havens of Arist's settlers. Many even had geothermal heat; others had been improved over the years. It was clear to Concord command that the uncounted kilometers of caverns were a blessing to the inhabitants of Arist but an enormous handicap to the marines.

That was pretty much the size of it, Witzko decided. In a short-term endurance contest, the marines had the advantage. In the long-term, the locals of both species would win; they could go to ground, evade and resupply, then return to fight whenever the notion struck them. Eventually the Concord would get tired of the game and go away, leaving Arist at peace until the weren and the humans decided to go at it again.

A deafening roar in Witzko's audio brought him out of his reverie. Turning quickly, he punched the safety off his rifle and sent out an alert to his platoon.

"Cancel, back to Oner," Witzko said wearily, as he beheld the action below.

One of the captive humans had apparently mouthed off to a weren. The weren, already uptight, was ready to defend his honor at the slightest excuse. With a savage war cry, the weren leaped at the human. Luckily, his legs were short in proportion to his torso, and the human missed being disemboweled by at least twenty centimeters. Before either of the combatants could react, two marines swept by Witzko from above, the stutter guns on full automatic. The stutter gun's bursts slammed into the brawlers, bringing them to their knees.

"War is hell, Lieutenant." Witzko saw a bulky armored figure waddling toward him. "I read that somewhere."

Witzko recognized Lance Corporal Julie Travino

behind the frosty faceplate.

"So I understand," Witzko said. "Peace is pretty exciting too, if you can get through the first day."

Laughter rang through his audio, and Witzko realized he'd left his comm on open channel. "Okay, back to it, marines. Watch yourselves out there. We don't send any medals home if a civilian shoots you in the head. It's too embarrassing for the family."

Witzko switched off, leaving the channel open to Travino.

"Keep an eye on this bunch, Corporal. Some of our people haven't done this before. I'd like 'em to leave Arist in one piece. Keep our two brawlers down there separated on opposite sides of the party with warnings that I'll bind and gag the both of them if they try anything like that again."

"Aye, sir, will do, sir." Travino saluted, turned and followed the group across the rock-strewn plain. Witzko had seen Julie Travino in the gym. There she was a slim, well-formed young woman. Now she looked like everyone else, an iron-clad gorilla.

Maybe, he thought, that was a good idea. A combat marine didn't need to know who was guarding his back—male, female, or someone he couldn't stand at all.

"Witzko," a voice broke into his private comm, "Seymoyr here. Priority, Lieutenant."

"Sir, on line, sir."

"Good. This is a Scramble-D, Witzko. No one else is on the channel. For the moment, that's how I want it."

"Yes, sir."

"*Stormbird* CO is sending *Activity* on a low-down, taking a look at a sector up north that's showing blips where nothing's supposed to be going on. That's fine with me, but I want *infantry* confirmation, Witzko, if there's anything there. Real footsloggers on the ground, you got me? I don't want a damned sensor showin' me a bunch of crawly dots. We got *dots* up here. I want to know their names, DNA, and what they had for lunch. You read me, Lieutenant?"

"Loud and clear, sir. I'm on it right now."

"Get on it *yesterday*, Lieutenant. Out."

Witzko didn't take the time to wonder what lit a rocket under Colonel Wilm Seymoyr. Seymoyr had transferred the rocket to *him*, and that's all Witzko needed to know.

"Atanza, Travino—to me, double-time."

Both of the marines responded at once. He could see their faces through their frosty faceplates, ready and eager as hounds on the leash.

"This is for you two only. Restrict your channels. There may be something going on in the north. *Activity*'s taking a look, but the old man wants ground sniffers on this. Take two weapon specs, any one you want. Take a look up there at seven-seven-niner. Go in low, go in max, but watch yourselves damned close. Keep on my channel at all times. Don't ask me what you're supposed to see. That's why you're going. Nobody's got any idea. Any questions?"

"No, sir," the marines said at once.

"Go then, and watch it out there."

In a moment, Damion Witzko was standing alone by a giant, ice-shattered stone. Atanza, Travino, and two weapons techs were now no more than snowy contrails just above the wind-blown plain. Witzko shot a clear "confirm action" beam up to Seymoyr in *Stormbird.*

Now that he had a moment, he wondered what it was all about. It was very possibly nothing. Nerves were strung tight on every combat mission, and eventually someone saw spooks on a holo or a sensor or hiding behind a bush. Sometimes you knew you'd found something when the people you sent simply didn't come back, then you sent *more* people, a hell of a lot more, knowing your unseen enemy knew you were coming now.

A few minutes later Atanza's voice came over their private channel.

"Recon Five, this is Recon Eye. We've got something here, Lieutenant. Are you reading me?"

"I'm here, Atanza," he said calmly, reading the tension, the strain in the soldier's voice. "What have you got? Let's hear it."

"It's . . . nothing's here, sir. No one, nothing. But they've *been* here. There's tracks, boot tracks everywhere. Hundreds of 'em, sir, churning up the snow right down to the ice layer."

Witzko could hear Atanza's breath blowing hard against her filters. "You can't, ah, estimate how many are in this force? Any idea besides *hundreds*? That doesn't give me much of a guess."

"Sir, may I break in, sir?" another came in through the comm. "This is Travino. I can't give you a number either, but the tracks are solid here, and the path is about forty, fifty meters wide. It goes back at least a kilometer or two, then disappears under new snow."

"That's back," Witzko said. "Where does it go forward?"

"It doesn't, sir," said Atanza again. "All the tracks lead into a narrow-mouthed cave. They go underground, sir."

Chapter Twenty-One

October 30, 2501

Irina Lavon felt like the proverbial sardine. She'd never actually seen one of the creatures, whatever it might be, but she was certain this was exactly how it ought to feel—poked, crunched, occasionally grabbed—though that last one was hard to prove.

The eighty marines of Recon Platoon led by Witzko had ridden down to Arist in full armor with room to stretch their legs among pallets of supplies. The two hundred who followed in three landers wore cerametal battledress, weapons, and packs, but were still wedged in too tight to move.

Slicing down through the equatorial atmosphere of the frozen moon, the temperature was only slightly unbearable. The landers dropped below Mach Two, plunging into high cloud. At 10,000 meters, they fell into the storm, and the world around them turned black. Wind shrieked, and blue tongues of lightning forked across the sky.

"Red Ridge four minutes, three-two seconds," Second Company's Top called out. "Heads up! Heads up!"

The last blur of clouds disappeared, and the landers

swept low over the ice-covered ridge of ruddy stone that gave the settlement its name.

Lavon knew the lander crews would have fingers close to weapon and decoy buttons now. *Activity* wasn't far away; she would scorch the sky to get there if the ground suddenly sprouted active weapons.

The landers went straight in without a hitch. Ramps and hatches flew open, letting in a blast of frigid air and the welcome glow of pale sunshine.

Goodson twirled his hand in a circle, the signal for "Form up! Keep it moving, people."

Double-time and spread out was safer, Irina knew, but that sort of entry panicked the locals, who were likely nervous enough watching armed marines land in their laps. Coming in easy was a chance, but marines took that kind of chance all the time.

As Irina's boots hit the snow, she unslung her charge rifle and stepped out onto Arist. To her left a lander was unloading fifty marines, forming them up in a useful, but non-aggressive square. Pointers were already walking toward the gathering civilians, looking as friendly as an armed marine could.

The lander took off again, slowly, without closing hatches. It slid at low altitude toward the uninhabited ridge to drop off two observer squads with mobile heavy sensors and an array of heavy weapons. An anti-sniper team stood ready to skybike into action at an instant's notice.

Getting her people in order, she walked toward the settlement itself. It wasn't much to see, a haphazard sprawl of stone and scrap metal shacks. Looks were deceiving, though, for every structure was built to hold in the warmth. Deeply slanted snow roofs kept the buildings sound. From every roof sprouted an array of chimneys, solar collectors, ventilators, and heat recyclers—much of this equipment third and fourth hand, and nearly all of it homemade to some degree.

"Company coming," announced Private Rewall.

Irina had already spotted the approaching figures, and she gave a subtle signal to tell the others—in case they hadn't noticed—that this bunch was armed. The marines remained friendly but were ready for trouble if it happened along.

"Afternoon," said the group's leader. "Nice day for this time of year."

"Yes," Irina said, "it certainly is."

It wasn't, but she was sure that was not what the person wanted to hear. The apparent leader was a short, squarely built woman with graying hair that curled out from under her heavy hood in peppery wisps. Irina also noted that the woman carried a holstered charge pistol, a Galactic War 2 model, but lethal all the same. The woman grinned and pointed to a small blue badge on her thick blue jacket.

"I'm Handerlast. Director of the Red Ridge Port Authority. Matter of fact, I *am* the Red Ridge Port Authority. I must inform you that your vehicles have landed in an unauthorized area. Would you care to move them to a marked port pad or pay the fine?"

"Neither," said Captain McRae, stepping up beside Irina. "I ask, with all proper courtesy intended, that you kindly step aside and let us pass."

"As you said it so well yourself, Captain. Neither."

Handerlast was still smiling, but her eyes now held a definite hard glaze. She stood her ground, crossing her arms across her breasts. Irina noticed that the second citizen, a middle-aged man with mud-colored eyes, kept his left hand hidden between the folds of his cloak. It was scarcely a subtle move. Irina could see the bulge of a hand weapon there. The third civilian was a girl no older than fourteen. A quick glance at the captain told Irina that McRae got the idea as well: the Red Ridgers were making a point, not provoking a confrontation.

"We have a legal obligation to bring our peacekeeping force down in a simultaneous landing," McRae said. "We also have an obligation not to disrupt Red Ridge life more than necessary. Bringing the landers down here lets us do both. I think you can agree there is *not* room on your regular pad for all of our equipment."

"Well, it's not too large, that's true," Handerlast replied. "However, the contract workers have promised us an extension for heavier traffic. It's not done yet."

"Yes, ma'am," McRae said patiently, "and your point?"

The woman granted McRae a toothy grin. "It's contracted for. It just isn't finished yet." She nudged a wooden stake with her foot. "They've got the plots up. We're callin' that the 'first phase.' "

"First phase?" McRae's expression didn't change.

"Uh-uh. That means the Red Ridge Port Authority extension is *legally* underway—"

"Right, I know what it means," McRae said. "You waive the movement order, and we'll pay the landing fee and the fines. Is that all right with you?"

"Why, that'd be quite satisfactory," the woman said.

"How much?"

"Fifty dollar fee and a hundred dollar fine—"

"All right."

"That's for each lander, of course."

McRae looked off into space for a moment. "Fine," she said calmly, "that's fine. I'll have Master Sergeant Lavon here get that to you as soon as possible."

"Good. Welcome to Red Ridge." The woman grinned, motioned to her cohorts and walked back down the street.

"Well, that's a new one," Captain McRae said. "Landing fees and fines for the Concord Marines."

"Yes, ma'am."

McRae turned on Lavon. "Sergeant, if you even think about laughing—"

"No, ma'am. Never occurred to me, ma'am."

"Good. Make sure it doesn't."

McRae turned and walked back to the lander. Irina did the best she could, biting her lip, choking, making strange sounds. In a moment, the urge died away. She knew, though, she'd have to watch herself. The next time she saw Captain McRae—

Something caught Irina's eye. She looked past the lander, past the retreating figure of Captain McRae. Her breath caught in her throat, as if a great hand had closed about her neck. Captain Savant and Sergeant Belier! What were they doing here? Neither was scheduled to come with the landers. Belier was strictly HQ, and Savant, the Company Commander, would never set up Ops this close to a settlement.

Irina Lavon turned quickly away, before one of them looked her way. A cold thought touched the edge of her mind, and she quickly brushed it away.

Stop it, Irina, that is absolutely crazy, strictly paranoid. They are not down here for you. This brush fire was not designed to screw up your life. Okay, that's what it's doing, but nobody planned it that way, not even

Belier. Though if anyone could—

She tossed out *that* thought as well. She had entirely too much to do to go nuts. Maybe later, when she had a little time.

Chapter Twenty-Two

October 30, 2501

At Witzko's instructions, Recon Eye left one marine and a sensor array two kilometers out from the underground entry, then gathered up a crew to join the others. On the way out, flying low and max, Witzko got Seymoyr on the scramble channel and quickly filled him in.

Seymoyr didn't stop and ask questions. He put Witzko on hold, talked for ten seconds to the *Stormbird's* captain, then shouted in Witzko's ear.

"I want sniffers in low, and I want pics of those boot prints. I'll run 'em through up here, tell you how many and what they weigh. We'll get a chem on the kind of weapons they're using. If they're fresh, the UV will tell us where they've been and track them back through the snow. Incidently, the captain's calling off *Activity* for now. They did their job. All they can do now is spook whatever's there. Okay, what else you got for me, Lieutenant?"

"One thing we don't need sniffers for, Colonel. The boot prints are clearly human. Not marine boots, but it looks like surplus combat footgear—most of it used, as near as I can tell. Stuff from GW2, common war gear you might see anywhere."

"Nothing else? No weapons, no trash?"

"No, sir. Just the prints. We've got a band of snow coming in on us now, if you want to get those sniffers in, sir."

"On the way. Lieutenant, I don't know what we've got here. If you have as many prints as I'm looking at now on the screen, you've got entirely too damned many people we don't know about wandering around down there. I'm getting Intel at Red Ridge to back some of those clowns against the wall. If those troops you're trailing belong to Ridgers, then somebody's lying to us, and somebody's looking for more than a tangle with the weren. We're talking a possible attempt at racial genocide here!"

Colonel Seymoyr cut the link. Witzko suspected that he had plenty more to say, but most of it Witzko knew how to do, and you don't tell your CO that. When he got off the comm, he got Kran, Atanza, Corporal Travino, and the best Point Squad he could find, including Stosser and Phelan, and guided them to the relatively wind free side of the skycar. He told him what he needed to tell them from his talk with the colonel, then told them what he wanted himself.

"I'll answer what you're getting ready to ask. No, we're not probing the cavern right now, not yet. We need more data, and the CO's taking care of that. What we're going to do is sit tight. We'll set down the resupply lander about ten kilometers out. We'll take what they've got and send them back for more—both live and hardware. A lot of that hardware will be ammo and sensor gear."

He turned to Kran. "Call in Rizzo, Kasuga, and the rest of Eye Three. Set up a surveillance perimeter no closer than three kays out. Whatever's in there likely knows we're out here, but I'm not handing 'em any marines on a platter. We go in there, we go in ready and hot. I don't think we can count on friendlies. Somebody's army is down there, and I'm certain it isn't ours."

"If serious hostiles show up," Kran added to the team, "follow the lieutenant's orders. Evade, watch, report. If you can, do it without being detected."

"Nobody's going to leave you hanging," Witzko finished. "We'll be here. You see anything more than a snowflake and you report in immediately."

The members of the squad all nodded. They knew their officers and non-coms. They knew if any rocks were flying, they wouldn't have to eat them by themselves.

"What do you think?" Witzko asked Kran, when the others had walked away. "What the hell went down that hole, Sarge?"

Kran sniffed the air. "I don't have to wait for the CO's sniffer report," he said, "I can tell you right now those clowns were walking heavy, carrying gear, lots of weapons, whatever. I wouldn't want to run in and check 'em out just yet."

"Someone's going to have to," Witzko told him.

"Hey, I *know* that, Lieutenant." Kran looked up at him and grinned. "I know what 'recon' means, too, and who's in it. I'm just not in any big hurry to carry out my sworn duty right now. What about you?"

"I've been thinking about leave," Witzko said. "I don't think that's the right marine attitude, Sergeant, so try not to spread it around."

"No, sir," Kran said. "They'll never find out from me."

* * * * *

Witzko broke off a conversation with Kran as a silver glint in the sky heralded the approach of the resupply lander. The pilot came in slow, easy and silent, as Witzko had instructed him to do, landing a good three kilometers from the no-approach zone around the entry to the cave. Marines ran to help unload. Witzko watched them a moment, then followed them as they approached, wondering who they'd sent down to support his team. He looked away, then turned back again as something caught his eye.

No, that couldn't be, he told himself. There is absolutely no way they'd send those goofs down here. They wouldn't do that to me.

They had, though. There was no mistaking the names "Chen" and "Lee" stenciled on the overland suits. And even if Witzko had been wrong about that, he certainly couldn't miss the peculiar hop-and-lope gait of the t'sa, Gre-Ikwilisan Thumn. The t'sa wore a soft e-suit, a cerametal vest, and a modified helmet that made him look like a character out of a bad cartoon.

"Sergeant Kran," Witzko said, "I hope I don't see what I think I see. If I do, I had better not see it again."

"Sir, I think perhaps you do." Kran's voice suddenly lost the familiar, iron-clad tones that turned recruits to jelly.

Witzko caught it at once and brought his faceplate up to Kran's. "You know something, Sergeant, something you forgot to tell me? You never forget to tell me things, but you forgot about this."

Kran let out a breath. "Under the circumstances, sir, the critical nature of the situtation here, I didn't, ah, feel the lieutenant needed any more hassle at the moment. Sir."

"I still don't, but I've got it. Now let's have it straight—how, when, and why."

"After that gambling thing, sir, with Chen? We kept an eye on them. As you suggested, sir. You recall that, sir."

"Yes. I certainly do. Don't stall, Sergeant."

Kran told him the whole story. How they'd caught Chen, Lee, and the t'sa—who had apparently quickly allied himself with Chen, after more or less spying on her for Kran—stealing drive engine parts during the cleanup after *Stormbird's* battle in space.

"Birds of a feather, sir," Kran put in.

He also told how the Unholy Three had used those parts to set up their own private gambling den in an empty storage room, a scheme that had lasted half a day before Sergeant Belier had accidentally—or so he reported—happened upon the operation.

Witzko could guess the rest. Court-martial action was called for, but Belier had a better idea: avoid the paper work. Send them down to Lieutenant Witzko. Let them mess up *his* life. Probably Belier had gotten an okay from Captain Savant. Savant would think it was a great idea.

"I appreciate you trying to protect me, Sergeant," Witzko said, "but don't do it again. I can handle bad news, even news as bad as this. Give them something to do, something unimportant, and something where I can't see them." Witzko paused. "Is there anything else, Sergeant, while we're at it?"

"No, sir. Nothing I can recall, sir."

"Good. Get them out of here. Let them guard a rock or something. If they want to steal the rock, fine."

"Sir!"

Platoon Sergeant Kran left as quickly as he could.

Witzko walked off in the other direction. He inspected the outposts he'd set up around the cavern entry, a task he'd finished only moments before. He spoke to Stosser and Rizzo, moved on to Kasuga, and told Atanza to keep a close eye on the Unholy Three.

"May I ask, sir, what they're doing here? I mean—"

"No, you may not," Witzko told her. "Just watch them. Make sure they don't disappear."

"Yes, sir," Atanza said and gave him a curious shrug as he turned away. Officers didn't have to answer questions—sometimes they would, though, and it never hurt to ask.

Witzko was halfway back to the command post when the comm blasted harshly in his ear:

"All hands! All hands! Battle Group Seymoyr! There is a ground combat situation in progress for Second Company in Red Ridge zone. Shots fired, marines down, heavy weapons detected. All hands! All hands!"

Witzko punched in Seymoyr at once. "Witzko here, sir. Any orders for us?"

"You have any action there, Lieutenant?"

"No, sir. We're just watching. About Red Ridge—"

"You can't do anything for Red Ridge. Sit tight."

"Colonel, I respectfully suggest we *don't* sit tight, especially considering the action at Red Ridge. If there's a fighting unit in this cavern, I don't much like the idea of sitting here waiting for them. Maybe they're engaged at Red Ridge at the other end of this hole. If they are, we're doing just what they'd like us to do."

"All right, Lieutenant."

"Sir?"

"I said yes, Witzko. It's a reasonable suggestion. I'm not talking about a major assault, I'm talking about a probe, textbook definition; minimal exposure, minimal risk. Get back to me."

"Sir—"

Seymoyr was gone. Witzko signaled a general comm alert. Kran came running. Witzko gave him quick commands, cut in his induction engine, and reached the lander in a fifty-meter leap. As he landed ankle-deep in the snow, the last of the lander's cargo slid down the ramp on to the snow. The pilot powered up, readying for takeoff. Witzko dashed up to the bow, waving down the pilot.

"I'm taking a dozen armored marines down in the canyon near the entry to the cavern," he said. "You drop us off, we'll come back on our own power."

The pilot nodded. "You want me to stick around out here, sir?"

"Negative. If we get in trouble in there, you won't be able to help."

The pilot thought about that. "I have an idea they'll jerk me out of here in a couple of minutes anyway. They'll either have us running up to *Stormbird* or hauling our tails down to Red Ridge."

"Good enough. Luck to you."

"Luck to you, sir."

Witzko turned to see Jobal Kran with his squad ready at the ramp. Witzko looked behind them. Chen, Lee, and the t'sa stood guarding a rock in the background.

"We've got a crew of weren back there, Lieutenant," Kran said. "They wanted me to, ah, respectfully remind the Worthy officer, with no offense or dishonor intended, that it was about time the marines decided to pay attention to the problems in the north. They say no one listens to them. They say—"

"Yeah, I can imagine what they say, Sergeant. They're probably right. Hop on, we'll talk to them when we get out of the hole." He glanced back at the squad, huddled in the lander, snow melting as fast as it struck their armor.

"Heads up, people. Everybody goes in, everybody comes back."

Chapter Twenty-Three

October 30, 2501

Advancing clouds formed a dark canopy over Red Ridge as the biting wind tossed fresh snow on the ground. By the time Lavon's section reached the center of the settlement, visibility was down to ten meters in all directions.

She had avoided Sergeant Belier as best she could, but Belier knew she was there. He waved and came up beside her as she halted to check her direction. Directly across the small square was a crudely made stone and ceramic building with lights strung haphazardly over the door.

"Looks like a back-alley bar I knew in Babel," Belier said. "What do you bet it's just the same inside? Dirty glasses filled with sour beer and some kind of local head mounted on the wall."

"I wouldn't know, Sergeant," Irina said with no expression at all. "I try to stay out of bars with dirty glasses. To each his own, I guess."

Belier laughed in her ear. "Hey, there's just the two of us on comm, Queenie. Try and be nice. You and me been marines a long time. No reason we can't act decent to each other."

Irina turned on him. "You can't think of anything? *I* certainly can, Sergeant."

"You mean that little incident with you and the lieutenant? Shoot, I don't care a thing about that. What you do is your business—"

"What I *don't* do is my business, too."

"Whatever. Anyway, you can forget about that. We get a little action, you write me up a nice hairy combat tale, just like we talked about. I get my Valor and ship out; you don't have to mess with me again."

"It would almost be worth it," Irina said darkly. "I am damned near tempted, Sergeant. That's how much you disgust me, but then I'd be rid of you, and I'd have to live with myself. I couldn't handle that."

"Listen, lady!" Belier's armored fist drove into her side.

It was futile blow against metal that would absorb nearly anything short of plasma fire. Still, Irina turned on him and gave him the blow right back. Belier staggered, righted himself, and tried to laugh it off.

"You just remember we got us a deal, baby. Don't go forgetting that."

"Don't hold your breath, Jacques *baby*. I'll see you in hell before I—"

She saw the grenade an instant it soared over them.

"*Down*!" she shouted into her comm, then dropped face down in the snow.

The silver object blurred, whined, and burst overhead. Death cries reached her ears, some cut mercifully short while others grew louder and wouldn't stop. She felt the tiny rattles on her armor.

Stay down and don't look up! Homing grenades usually came in pairs—the first burst in molten needles of fire, the second came three breaths later, catching you on your feet while you looked for a place to hide.

Irina risked a look. Charge guns erupted around her, targeting something she couldn't see from her vantage point. The second missile detonated off to the right. Incandescent metal sprayed the street. A third grenade followed the second, but a laser beam caught it and flung it in two pieces against the seedy bar. One piece licked at cold stone. The other skipped off the wall, struck a marine, and consumed him.

Irina stared in horror. He was wearing battle dress, not armor. One moment he was rising to a crouch, weapon at the ready. Next he was a black silhouette against white plasma flame. Heat seared the breath from his lungs before he could manage to scream.

Irina saw Belier moving, heading for a casualty to her right. She moved up quickly to another marine sprawled in the street nearby. The charge had scooped a pound of armor from his chest. A hundred needles had blunted themselves and fallen away. She plugged into the marine's helmet, looked down at his face.

"Is your trauma pack working? Are you okay?"

The marine nodded and tried to smile. "I'm okay, Sarge, but it's really hot in here."

"I'll bet," she grinned. "Hang on, we'll get you out of here."

His medic light was already on. Someone would pull him out. She stood then and found Captain McRae staring at a scorched patch of snow.

"Unless I miss my guess, those grenades were fired remote," she said. "We won't find anybody near the launcher, but there's a sniper out there who set it off. I want him alive and in shape to talk. Get a squad over to the Municipal Building. Just before we launched, word came in they had some weren prisoners there. Let's find out."

"Yes, ma'am," Irina said. "Deadly force?"

"Regular priorities. Any prisoners now have the same priorities as marines. I want those weren in one piece, hides and honors intact, walking, talking fur-heads, Sergeant."

"Yes, ma'am." Irina checked her weapon and loped off.

Two hundred marines had scattered quickly into tactical response. Two teams spread around the buildings where Ridgers had been watching the landers unload. Now there were no civilians in sight. As she ran to gather a squad, she looked back to see snow already softening the dark shapes of dead marines.

* * * * *

The pilot was good, and Witzko's lander moved toward the cavern entry at near stall speed, scarcely faster than a marine in an overland suit. No one talked. All passive sensors were open wide. Witzko looked back and saw a storm building up south and east. He knew it had to be approaching Red Ridge at that moment. If it didn't break up before it reached the canyon, both marine forces would have weather up to their necks. Arist had plenty of excuses for weather: magnetic fluxes from Platon, solar flares from Hammer's Star, and God only knew what from the thermal heat within the moon itself. It would be hard to kill a well-suited marine with such weather, but anyone could have nav trouble and wander off and get lost.

The lander touched down, and the marines filed out quietly. The last soldier had scarcely stepped off the ramp before the lander lifted off and disappeared over the canyon wall. Witzko got a communiqué from *Stormbird* and passed it on. Five marines lay dead at Red Ridge. The rest of Seymoyr's force was sliding down out of orbit *Priority Urgent*. For a heartbeat, Witzko thought of Irina Lavon but pushed the thought aside before it could take root and distract him from the business at hand.

Witzko stood in the center of the cavern. The floor was fine gravel, still churned up from the hundreds of boots that had recently passed by. The knowledge that a large force had been here recently and was very likely not far away was slightly unnerving. The sensors showed nothing, but that didn't mean a thing, only that no one was nearby.

Sweeping a bright beam around the walls, it was clear that this section of the cave was mostly natural, a lava tube burned smooth as glass by magma coursing up from the moon's living core. Only twenty meters in, the cavern branched out twice; one branch was narrow and clearly carved out by a machine, the other a natural extension of the area they stood in now.

"This is a wonderful experience, sir," said Sergeant Kran. "There could be anything in here. It's a real challenge, great training for the squad."

Witzko looked at him, but couldn't tell if Kran was being serious or sarcastic. "Take Atanza, Rizzo, and Stosser, two marines to a sensor. Go thirty meters up each branch, no more. Keep comms open all the time. Take a long-range reading and leave the sensor there. Whichever tunnel we take, I want to know who's biting me in the rear."

"Yes, sir," Kran said and set off with his crew.

Witzko waited. He wanted to check in with *Stormbird* to see what was happening at Red Ridge but didn't want to call from in the cavern itself. There were five casualties up there, maybe more. He didn't want to think who those five might be. Sergeant Lavon was there and Captain McRae. Who else? Barker, Lasanti, Sergeant Price—

"Lieutenant!"

Witzko turned. Kasuga was standing behind him with his rifle pointed toward the mouth of the cave. The other marines looked jumpy as well. They went into a combat crouch and followed Kasuga's move.

"Easy!" Witzko said. He moved away from the center of the cavern, drew his own rifle, and shouted, "Whoever the hell's there, call out if you want to stay in one piece."

"Do not fire, please!" a voice said. "We are marines as well."

Witzko's light and half a dozen others shone upon three figures as they came into the cavern. Gre-Ikwilisan's reptilian eyes glowed in the dark from behind his faceplate. Chen and Lee walked hesitantly behind.

Witzko felt the heat rise to his face. Killing them all seemed a sound idea, but there were regulations against that.

"You lunatics better have one hell of a good reason for being here," he said. "Right now, I can't think of one. Anyone like to start?"

The t'sa bowed. "I shall start, sir. We were clearly not included on this venture. It is easy for us to understand why. We have acted in a manner that is not acceptable in the Concord Marines—"

"What are you talking about? You're a civilian *advisor* or something. Don't you dare call yourself a marine." He glared at Chen and Lee. "You two can start calling yourself something else too, because your careers just went down the drain. Do the words *military prison* ring a bell?"

"I told you both this was a lousy idea," Chen said. "This isn't going to cut it, you guys."

Lee groaned and shook his head. The t'sa held up a hand.

"We are well aware of the shame of our acts and the penalties involved. This is why we decided on such a course of action. Our heads, as they say, are in the soup—"

"—on the block," Lee corrected.

"Yes. Quite right. That too. We are here because only our lives can possibly make amends. It is hoped our sacrifice will erase our dishonor. If we die in action, those who remain will remember that we—"

"Cut it," Kasuga said. "Begging your pardon, sir, but we know these clowns. They've cheated the whole platoon out of a year's pay, stolen everything they can get their hands on, and they're lying to you right now. Whatever they came in here for, Lieutenant, it was not to die in glory, not these bozos, sir."

Hurik Lee and Ajayla Chen glared at Kasuga, but Kasuga stood his ground. For once, the t'sa kept quiet.

"Thank you, Private. I am aware of the record of these three, and I quite agree. Now, it's against my better judgment, but I'm going to be the dumb guy and ask. What did you *really* come in here for, and what did you hope to gain?"

Gre-Ikwilisan showed him a typical, overexuberant t'sa grin.

"Truth is very close to a lie in this case, honored officer. We came, because we believe we can redeem ourselves and live as well. I regret it is not entirely true that we wish to die."

"I'm truly surprised to hear it," Witzko said.

"Indeed. When we learned—by listening to others on post outside this cavern—that entry might be involved, we immediately saw how we could be of service. We—"

"He takes forever, sir," Lee interrupted. "We stole a bunch of stuff up there, all right? Everyone knows that. One of the things we stole, Chen here said we might turn into a real good odds interrupter. It can read faint heat signatures on a cellular level and project a virtual holographic image of whatever it sees. If tuned properly, it can even read colors based upon the heat radiance."

"Is that not remarkable?" the t'sa said brightly. "She is a wonderful engineer, is Chen."

Chen rolled her eyes and pretended she was somewhere else.

"Anyway," Lee went on, "we'd planned to use it to read cards in a high stakes poker game, but it turns out this gizmo could also do a terrific job as an improvised IR scanner, better than anything you've got now." Lee smiled. "That's when we thought of you, sir."

Witzko frowned. "Let's see it."

"Here," Chen said. She slid out of her heavy-weapons pack and laid it on the ground. "We've managed to get rid of some the excess weight, sir. With Thumn's help, we think that we can rig your unit's standard gravometric scanners with our little IR snooper. This will give you fairly detailed map of the tunnels within a two kilometer radius. It will also be able to give you an eyeball, holo-look at anything within fifty meters of the scanner.

You'll not only know that something's coming, but you'll have a pretty good idea of what it is. You want to know what's happening underground? This is the instrument for you."

Witzko looked as if he'd tasted something bad. "Don't turn on your sparkling personality for me, Chen. You're a marine, not a used skycar salesman." He turned to Sergeant Kran. "Since you've been *protecting* me from these people, Kran, I'm turning them over to you. I don't have the time or the authority to shoot them. Get 'em up front, and point that machine somewhere. Don't let them in my sight again. Understood?"

"Understood, sir!"

"Good. We're wasting time. Kasuga, Rizzo, let's get this show on the road. We're standing on someone else's real estate. It makes me nervous, and that's against regulations in the Concord Marines. Oh, Chen—"

Chen and her friends stopped and turned. "Master Sergeant Belier sent you down here; I'm aware of that. Does he know about this, uh, device of yours?"

Chen looked surprised. "No, sir. I hope I'm not out of place, Lieutenant, but the sergeant would never have sent us here if he thought we could be helpful in any way."

* * * * *

The sounds of war shook the roof of Kuhudag's cell and sent dust and small stones rattling off the walls. He could even hear the screams of the dead and dying among the thunder of heavy vehicles rumbling across the frozen ground.

"I believe there is a great deal of combat taking place, Worthy," Grutok said, "just above us, I would say."

"You are most perceptive," Kuhudag said. "Do not feel obligated to tell me things I already know."

The guards looked alarmed. After the first tremor from above, the one tagged "Evans" came close to Kuhudag's cell.

"There is no reason for us to remain here," he said. "It is our duty to either fight or surrender, depending on the odds."

"A wise decision," Kuhudag said. "If you live, I would appreciate it if you would tell someone we are here."

"We will certainly do that," said the second guard. "If anyone asks, such as a Concord Marine, you might tell them you were not ill-treated."

"That is not entirely true," Grutok said darkly. "There were incidents of dishonor."

Kuhudag waved him off. "Go, and we wish you good fortune."

"To you as well."

The two guards vanished, closing the armored door behind them. Kuhudag and Grutok were left alone.

"They could have opened the cell. That would have been a courtesy."

"That would have been foolish on their part. We might have attacked and killed them."

"We wouldn't do that," Grutok said.

"I don't think they'd be certain of that. Our relations have not always been cordial. You, if anyone, should remember that."

"Still, it would have been an honorable act. Even if we *had* chosen to kill them after that."

Kuhudag cuffed him sharply on the head. "Sometimes you appall me, whelp. I shall not tell your honored mother you spoke in such a manner!"

"I was just saying I—"

"*Attention!*" the speaker blared from above. "*Attention! This is Master Sergeant Irina Lavon of the Galactic Concord Marines. In the name of the Concord, I declare this facility to be under Concord Peacekeeping Protection. Custody of all herein, citzens or detainees, is hereby under Concord authority. Please note that I am empowered to meet refusal of this command with deadly force.*"

"Well, it's good to hear someone finally take charge of things," Grutok said. "I look forward to meeting a marine."

"Lesson Four. Or is it Five or Six? At any rate, never look *forward* to a new event. You don't have the slightest idea what that event might bring."

"I am sorry, Worthy. I spoke too quickly."

"You always speak too quickly. *Think* quickly, listen attentively, and speak slowly." Kuhudag looked up sharply. "Now is the time to start, I think. You will get all the practice in honorable restraint you can handle, Grutok."

The armored doors sprang open. Six marines tramped in, swiftly melting snow dripping from their battle gear. At their head was a trooper nearly as tall as a weren, as pale as the snow outside, yet clearly a human female.

"Kuhudag," the hunter announced in his most formal voice, then pointed at his companion. "Grutok."

"Sergeant Irina Lavon, 26th Concord Marines," the woman warrior said. "Are you well?" She repeated both phrases in heavily accented Common Weren.

Kuhudag was pleasantly surprised.

"Grutok and I have suffered nothing that need shame

any human here," he said in Standard. "Some have not been as honorable as others, but their comrades protected us from them, and those persons have not been here for some while. I will say this now, because it must be said. The folk of Red Ridge owe the weren of West Lodge many explanations and perhaps a blood-price. That is a thing that must come to pass after council among the weren."

"Well, as you say, these are things that will perhaps come later," Irina said. "For now, you understand, this area is under the peacekeeping authority of the Concord."

"That is understood," Kuhudag said. "We greet you in peace and honor."

"Your honor is recognized and understood, Kuhudag. Continue to behave honorably, and you will be treated honorably."

She then turned to the nearest marine and ordered, "Let them out of there."

Kuhudag and Grutok walked out of their cell. They towered over most of the marines, who did their best to look as if they were in the company of large, fur-covered, tusked warriors every day.

"The detainees may go armed, if their customs require it," Lavon announced to everyone in the room, "and if they give an oath not to fight save in self-defense. As for an oath itself, let me suggest you give it to Captain McRae when she arrives."

"How long will that be?" Grutok asked.

"Eager to get out of here?" Lavon said, baring a splendid array of white teeth. A weren woman with such teeth would be considered a great beauty.

"That, and eager to learn if there is still hope for justice on Arist," Grutok said.

Irina raised a brow. "I would very much like to talk to both of you, if you will permit it," she said. "To be quite honest, there is much we don't understand about the conflict on Arist. As you can imagine, there are many opinions on the subject."

"Ours is the correct opinion," Grutok put in.

"Quiet," Kuhudag told him harshly. "You do us no honor with talk like that."

Kuhudag shook his head and gave Irina a courteous bow. "I agree with the young one, please understand that, but I am also aware that you have a duty to perform as a disinterested party. I will tell you all I know that does not compromise weren security."

"I would be grateful," Irina said.

"I can tell you nothing about the battle that has taken place above," Kuhudag said. "We took no part in the fighting at Red Ridge. Our battle took place far to the north. Humans may deny all they wish that their forces are there, but I can assure you they are. I have the battle scars to prove it. The whelp and I—"

Irina held up a hand, cutting him off. "To the north? You fought in the north?"

For a moment, her face seemed even paler than before. "We have recent reports that the trail of a large force has been spotted in the north. So far, our patrols have not actually *seen* this group. Is there anything you can tell me about it?"

"I can tell you what I have already told you," Kuhudag said, loud enough for everyone in the room to hear. "We fought these humans and killed them, as they killed some of us. I will also repeat that many of the humans here at Red Ridge will deny that these soldiers exist. They call them outcasts and wanderers, but as an experienced warrior, I can tell you they do not *fight* like outcasts. They fight like disciplined, well-armed soldiers!"

Irina let out a breath. Kuhudag was not the best judge of human temperments, but the woman sounded frustrated, annoyed, and more than a little scared.

"I'd like you to come with me, if you will," she said. "There are some people you need to talk to, Kuhudag."

Chapter Twenty-Four

October 30, 2501

Damion Witzko got the news from Sergeant Lavon's group at Red Ridge via Colonel Seymoyr aboard *Stormbird.* A weren named Kuhudag had clearly created quite a stir aboard the ship. From the colonel's message, Witzko imagined command as a bed of ants stirred with a stick. Now there was fairly reliable confirmation that there had, indeed, been a well-armed force in the north attacking weren settlements. As this Kuhudag said, members of the human colony were willing to swear a death-oath that there was no such force in existence. The more Concord Intel questioned them, the more they insisted—with great anger and indignation—that the weren were responsible for *all* dishonorable attacks that had taken place on Arist.

"I don't know what we'd expect them to say—or the weren either, for that matter," Colonel Seymoyr said. "We've got either one or both factions lying here, Lieutenant, but we do have those tracks you're onto, and the boot sizes are somewhat small for weren."

For a baby weren, Witzko added to himself.

"I'm leaving half the new troops in a holding pattern, Lieutenant. They'll be there if you need 'em. The rest are going to Red Ridge, and a smaller crew is headed out to some of the weren settlements. Watch yourself down there. Sound the alarm at once if you run into anything."

"Sir, there are only two answers to this business of the tracks. Either the Ridgers are lying and they *do* have a big force up here, one large enough to wipe out the entire population of weren, or these caverns lead to Red Ridge or some other settlement—"

"—and we're seeing humans come out of both ends. I know, Witzko. I am not happy about either proposition. Keep in touch with me."

Witzko did, but by the time his scouts stumbled upon the cache of arms, ammo, food, and power cells two kilometers down the tunnel, the storm over Arist had blanked out any chance of communications with *Stormbird.* Witzko sent a runner back to the entry at once to let the colonel know. Even then, he knew, a storm with lightning, horizontal hail, and winds up to three hundred kilometers per hour would likely bring everything to a stop topside.

"There's enough stuff here to keep a light infantry battalion in the field for a couple of weeks, Lieutenant." Sergeant Kran shook his head. He had just inspected a crate of rifles that were better than his own. Every crate they had opened so far was equipped for heavy winter wear as good as new. That equipment, Kran figured roughly, could have come from any of the stellar nations. These people had gone to market and filled their shopping bags with an alarming array of goodies.

Machines had worked the rock in this part of the cavern. The walls, ceiling, and floors were all spray-coated a bubbly white plastic that held the heat and gave sure footing. The area was almost antiseptically clean, cleaner than it needed to be, as far as Witzko was concerned. The whole thing brought a chill to the back of his neck. He knew the humans on Arist were mostly VoidCorp, and VoidCorp had a reputation for a total lack of interest in the well-being of those outside its own nest. If this cache was any indication of the size and strength of the forces holed up here, it was fairly clear what the humans on Arist had in mind for their neighbors: complete and total annihilation. Nothing less than that.

If we hadn't gotten the word, they would have pulled it off, and no one would ever really know for sure what had happened to the weren.

"Lieutenant?"

"Yes, what is it?" It was Gre-Ikwilisin, the t'sa. He bowed in the traditional manner, his large eyes gleaming like some creature under a thousand meters of water.

"We have set up the IR device, and Chen has calibrated it most perfectly. Would you care to inspect it?"

"I wouldn't," Witzko said, "but thanks for asking. Return to your duties, please."

The t'sa looked greatly disappointed. "I will do as you wish, honored officer. Still—"

"Just go, all right? Tell the others in your crew to watch out for booby traps. I'd be surprised if we didn't run into some down here."

"I am not a booby," Gre-Ikwilisan said, "or would you dispute that, sir?"

Witzko didn't try to explain. "Booby traps can catch more than boobies. Many of them are well hidden. Some of the deadliest traps react to only to organic life—heat signatures, sound, you get the idea. You fall into that category, I believe."

The t'sa looked thoughtful. "Yes, I believe I do." He looked quite pleased, then turned and walked away in the peculiar, hop-lope fashion of the t'sa that was accentuated by his modified armor. It made Witzko dizzy to watch him too long.

Witzko waited for his runner to return. When she did, she confirmed that the storm had, as expected, cut off all but rudimentary communications with anybody. Witzko felt distinctly uneasy without contact. It had happened at the worst possible time, when he and his platoon could well be in a precarious situation. It did little good to know he could call on Seymoyr's orbiting reinforcements if they couldn't hear him call.

Witzko refused to take a look at the Unholy Three's device until Sergeant Kran reported that it did, indeed, produce a nice holo of the caverns in a spherical display. When he saw what the trio had actually done, he was more than a little amazed and did all he could to keep from showing it. Chen, Lee, and the t'sa had all the overconfidence they needed without adding his own praise.

"Very nice," he said, with a glance. "Keep it working. See if you can extend the range."

"Oh, we will, sir," Hurik Lee assured him. "This is only a preliminary setting."

"Good, but this is not a preliminary situation. This is a *now* situation. Your gadget won't do me any good next week."

He knew he was being hard on the three, but he also knew the only way to get through to professional con artists was to challenge them to greater heights. "Getting even" was a far more effective goal to the three than praise for their efforts.

The thing *did* seem to work. The holodisplay, in

shades of green, showed a warren of twisting, spiraling caverns that looked remarkably like a cross section of an ant bed. It gave a good idea of depth, distance, and even a hint of rock composition. It showed an area roughly four kilometers in diameter, but the images grew fuzzy toward the edges. What it didn't do was show any trace of the small army that had clearly entered the cavern some time the day before. If they were in there, then where were they? Where had they gone?

Witzko did all he could, which was to extend his scouts farther into the several branches they'd covered and set the rest of their sensors. Lance Corporal Julie Travino and Private Stosser were keeping an eye on both the standard sensors and the Unholy Three's contraption. One thing the IR did do was show Witzko that his scouts were still out there and alive, and he was grateful for that.

*****

The storm began to let up two hours later and had nearly blown itself out by the time Witzko walked with Sergeant Kran to the mouth of the cavern. Scouts had been sent into the caverns, placing sensors that would relay information back to the platoon's main computer, which was manned by the Unholy Three. They now had a fairly accurate map of the caves for at least three kilometers in all directions, and they could detect heat and movement in the tunnels within the last half kilometer of the base camp. All scouts had been withdrawn, and every sensor was in place. Every display showed the cavern to be free of any forms of life that gave off heat.

A light snow was falling, but the main fury of the storm was gone, allowing them to re-establish contact with *Stormbird*.

"We still don't have anything," Witzko reported to Colonel Seymoyr after he'd informed the CO about the supply cache. "They've been here, but they're not here now."

"You've got support at your discretion."

"I don't have any legitimate reason to call on them, sir, but I'm glad to know they're there."

"I know what you're probably thinking," Seymoyr said. "It's what's bothering us up here, too. We can't just sit around and wait to see what runs out there. On the other hand, I've got a bunch of citizens up here right now, humans and weren both. They know about what they call the 'cavern intrusion.' They aren't real happy about it. The caverns are what they call 'sacrosanct,' which doesn't mean a damned thing if either of them violate that tradition."

"Considering you have weren confirmation of a human attack near my position," Witzko said, "I'd think the weren would want us to scour the place out, sir."

"The caverns are all interlocked, Lieutenant. I don't think *they* know which belongs to what. Besides, there are more holes down there than either of them have ever wandered into. It's a mess, Witzko. We're trying to untangle it up here. Meanwhile, I'm afraid I have to ask you to sit tight. I don't like the idea, but I don't want to rock the diplomatic boat right now. We're not seaworthy as it is."

"Got you, sir. We'll hang in."

"Hurry up and wait, sir," Kran said after the connection closed. He'd been standing back listening to the comm-talk with *Stormbird.* "That's the marine way, Lieutenant."

"I'd rather be down here than up there, Sarge. Sitting in a nest of mad Red Ridgers and outraged weren is not my idea of fun. Waiting for something to shoot at is a lot easier than keeping two contentious parties from starting the shooting. That's why colonels want to be lieutenants again."

"Sometimes they do, sir, but not too often," Kran replied.

* * * * *

Seymoyr sat at the head of the large, round table in the Tactical Center, contemplating his guests. No one had wanted to take the trip up to *Stormbird,* but the colonel had insisted, with the backing of Captain Myklebust. They both understood it was much more intimidating to have a peace parlay on a Concord starship than down on their home turf.

"Good afternoon," he said. "I appreciate you coming here. I know I speak for Captain Myklebust when I say it's a pleasure to have you aboard."

Captain Myklebust showed them all a frozen smile. It was not *her* pleasure to have them aboard, and they knew it.

Seymoyr whispered a command, and the holo blinked to life overhead. It showed a map of the inhabited area of Arist, with enlarged insets of Red Ridge, West Lodge, and other major human and weren settlements. The display was discreetly edited to omit current marine positions. The fact that it so accurately depicted every other rock on Arist brought a grumble from the gathered civilians.

"I'll try to be brief," Seymoyr said. "Hold your questions if you will."

True to his promise, Seymoyr gave a quick overview of the history of the conflict on Arist as it had emerged since the arrival of the Concord Marines. He included the interrogation of the weren and human detainees, and listed those still under "protection" of the marines. No one in the room liked that.

"Normally," Seymoyr said, "I would have declared this whole planet under martial law rather than Peacekeeping Protection. The death of marines gives me that power. We could still call such a declaration and bring in as many additional forces as we need. Should the need arise, I can carpet this moon with troops inside of five days."

"You're bringing in reinforcements?" a woman asked. "Where? From Spes?"

"You are . . .?"

"Port Director, Red Ridge. I'm Josephine Handerlast. We're already overcrowded at my facility. I can't handle any more traffic down there. You'll have to find somewhere else."

"I didn't say there would be reinforcements or where they might come from," Seymoyr said mildly. "If that should occur and it makes extra work for you, let me know, and I'll loan you some marine controllers."

"I don't need any extra help," Handerlast said sharply. "I don't want the hassle, that's all."

"Well, I don't think we need concern ourselves with something that hasn't happened, do we?"

He knew they were all curious about any future landings, and Seymoyr thought it was childish to imagine that he'd tell them. Spes had been on alert since the klick attack, and if more ships and marines were needed, they'd be there.

"The purpose of this particular meeting, you understand, is to fairly and equitably end the conflict between the two quarreling parties on Arist. I don't pretend that we can solve your differences today, but it won't hurt to begin talking about it. That's what we're all here for."

One of the weren stood, a large, silver-maned warrior with a splendid robe and heavily ringed tusks. "I am Burwab, chieftain of the Okabi weren. What *I* have come to talk about is compensation for the loss of life and property suffered by my people." He turned and shook an enormous, decorated staff at the human side of the table. "I call upon any humans here to meet me in challenge. If there is any courage among you, you will not back away from me! You will meet Burwab on a field of honor!"

The weren with Burwab roared. The humans sprang up at once, shaking their fists. A shout from a marine sergeant brought his men into action. Weapons slapped to port arms, and both sides of the table grumbled and took their seats.

"I'm sorry we've begun this way," Seymoyr said. "Let me be blunt with both of you. The Concord will resolve this situation whether you do or not. If that is the case, there will certainly be no *compensation* for anyone on Arist. Instead, we will build support facilities here and *stay*. It will be expensive for us, but we will get our money back in an added sense of security in the area."

A tall, red-bearded man came to his feet, his face clouded with rage. "I'm Paul Dimmock, leader of the VoidCorp construction workers here. You try a stunt like that, Colonel, and you'll have a breach of contract suit on your hands. A marine base here will put us all out of jobs!"

"Not necessarily." A gaunt, simply-dressed man at the end of the table stood. "I am Dr. Alexander Ohito, sir. I believe the Concord, the government of Arist, or even the weren could file a countersuit, charging your workers with armed harassment and acts of terrorism."

Dimmock exploded. "Damn you, Ohito. Don't forget you work for VoidCorp too. I'll see they hear about this!"

"You apparently forget, Paul, that I am VoidCorp's official executive on Arist. You work for *me*."

"Hah! You think so, do you? Get off it, Ohito. You know better than that."

Seymoyr decided there was clearly more here than met the eye. He knew about men like Dimmock; he was VoidCorp arrogant to the core. This Ohito, now, was something else—accusing Dimmock and taking up for the weren. It wasn't something Seymoyr could go into feet first now, but it was a start.

"I'm interested in getting to the truth of the matter, here, and I will," Seymoyr said bluntly. "I'll use whatever authority I have to to get the job done. Marines were killed today in Red Ridge with sophisticated weaponry. I don't know who killed them. I *will* know, I assure you. I don't know who started this conflict. Each of you blames the other. I hope I can discover what started this affair. At any rate, I *will* be the man who stops it."

He paused and let his gaze sweep both sides of the table. He wanted very much to tell them about the cavern in the north, with the tracks of hundreds of human boots leading in. *That* would certainly stir them all up, but it wouldn't help stop the war.

Instead, he said, "I would like to thank you for coming. Instead, I find I have little to thank you for. Talk to one another, people, here or down there. If you don't, we'll handle it our way. If either of your people has the killing of more of my marines in mind, you will have me to answer to. personally. I understand the storm has blown over on Arist. It's a clear day. Do something useful with it."

Chapter Twenty-Five

October 30, 2501

With a final snow flurry, the last slivers of daylight faded over Recon Base. Night on Arist came so abruptly that Witzko could swear he heard the tinkle and crash of shattering ice as the light vanished from the sky. Platon would not be up for hours, so the stars had the sky to themselves.

As Witzko watched, a dark shape slid over the camp, nearly silent and at least a thousand meters up. It was Unicorn Flight, patrolling Arist at midlevel, sending a hundred thousand holos and sensor readings back to *Stormbird's* computers with every nanosecond that passed.

Using his suit's sensors, Witzko checked his security perimeter at the entry to the cavern. Every marine was suited and armed. Every trooper was a fully operational sensor station, a transmitter, and a holo center. They were tired, and they were bored. If they were the men and women he thought they were, they would be wishing right now that this peacekeeping mission would turn into a more active situation. That's how they'd been trained to think, and that's what they were. Anyone foolish enough to take them on now would get a rude answer for trouble. At the moment, his people would cheerfully turn a large area of this frigid wilderness into steaming rock, knowing that somewhere in the ruins lay the killers of marines and provokers of a stupid, useless little war.

With a final scan of the perimeter, he headed for the newly assembled warming shelter, starting on his helmet locks as he went. You could conceivably sleep in a suit, but not well. It worked a lot better with your helmet off, lying down in a protected environment.

There were four off-duty marines already there. He couldn't see their faces in the dark. He thought about hot food, a hot shower, and a foam mattress for ten or twenty seconds, then he was out.

He dreamed about something; he wasn't sure what. It had to do with engines—great, rumbling engines, sky-cars, groundcars, all howling at once, racing out of the dark. That's what it was, then, a race. More racing cars than he had ever imagined, all roaring by him at blurring speeds, passing one another, fighting to win. All at once they veered and screeched across the track, metal scraping metal, all of them coming straight at him, all of them out of control—

Somebody screamed, someone close, someone far away. Witzko came awake fast, grabbing for his helmet. The walls of the shelter turned blinding white and then collapsed. He glanced at the others. Everyone had their helmets on; everyone was down flat.

The cluster warhead had come in over the horizon on a peak-skimming trajectory, exploding a thousand meters above the camp. From the vivid blossoms of green and red, Witzko knew it was a mixture of high-temp flares to baffle the sensors and killer arrays of needle frags.

"Casualty! Medic!" someone shouted on the comm, and Witzko, on the run, saw two marines racing for their buddy who was writhing on the ground.

Sergeant Kran spotted Witzko, started toward him, then looked up and shouted a warning. Witzko hit the dirt. Plasma rose up in a dirty white ball, turning the ridge behind him into slag. He knew marines were up there; he'd put them there himself. He glanced at the display in his suit. Everything was haywire. Radiation and magnetics had scrambled every sensor for five kilometers in every direction.

When Witzko got to Kran, the sergeant was already directing fire for friendlies, getting his people undercover, and cursing the sensors that crackled meaninglessly in his ears. Witzko grabbed a spare display and tried to unscramble the blips that were dancing everywhere. Something screeched in his ears and sent tremors through the frozen air.

"Unicorn!" Kran shouted.

The cutter sent three bright streaks through the lower atmosphere. All three hit. Something exploded in a blinding white sphere. The sphere flared for a second, them shrank and imploded, vanishing out of sight.

"Unicorn to Recon," a surprisingly calm voice came over the comms, "give us additional targets; we are here for support."

"We don't *have* any targets," Kran told them, "all we have is what you can see, Unicorn. We don't know where the hell they are!"

"Got a couple to your west, Recon. We'll keep looking. . . ."

Unicorn whined through the lower atmosphere, then streaked out of sight. A moment later, the ground lit up in two spots ten kilometers away.

". . . had something, Recon, but they slipped away from us fast. We'll keep on it."

"Thanks, Unicorn, hang around as long as you like." Witzko turned to Kran. "They're coming up out of holes somewhere, shelling us, then ducking out of sight. They're down there, Sarge, we just can't see 'em."

Kran looked grim. "They can sure as hell see us."

"All right," Witzko said, "pull 'em back. We're not going to sit here and take it. They know where we are."

Kran turned away and shouted quick orders. All across the blasted plain, marines rose out of the frozen ground and began to regroup away from the cavern entry.

Witzko called in to Seymoyr. Seymoyr confirmed his lieutenant's decision. Get out, regroup. Don't make easy targets.

Witzko called a lander in from orbit. The pilot said five minutes, but Witzko insisted on three.

As he stepped up to gather in the platoon, darkness turned to fierce daylight again. It came so fast that his helmet filters scarcely had time to save his eyes. Seconds later, three miniature suns blossomed to the west.

"Got that nest of baddies for you, Recon," Unicorn said. "My personal advice is it's time to look for another home."

"Got you, Unicorn. Home's coming at us now. You should have it on your display. Please give us cover going out."

"Will do, Recon. Luck to you—"

"Incoming!" several voices shouted at once.

Witzko looked up, and a chill touched the back of his neck. Eight marines on scout duty in the cavern had gone airborne to get out quick. All but two cut power, dropped to the ground, and went flat. A small white sun caught the two soldiers in the air at once. They vanished in a cloud of plasma light.

Somewhere above, Unicorn fought back. Witzko didn't take the time to look. The surviving marines came to their feet and ran toward the rest of the platoon. The last to stand were Chen, Lee, and the t'sa. They came to their feet, dragging a silvery device between them.

"All right, lander's on the way. Get up here, marines, now! Get your heavy weapons, leave everything else behi—"

Something slammed Witzko across the back of the helmet, flinging him forward so hard that his nose struck the faceplate. Built-in padding and restraints saved him, but his head was ringing like a bell. His helmet displays were either blank or scrambled. Kran helped him up and started unlocking his helmet. Witzko sucked in frigid, fresh air. The cold was so intense that he lost all feeling in his face almost immediately. In thirty seconds, Kran had a new helmet for him, slammed it on tight and ran off to help another marine.

Witzko shook his head and stood. The small missile had come in from nowhere. One marine was down but still alive. Witzko looked at his old helmet. A needle frag the size of a butcher knife had struck the armored metal, bent itself double, and bounced off onto the ground.

"Lieutenant?"

Jobal Kran was standing by Lance Corporal Julie Travino.

"Are you all right, sir?" Travino asked.

"Yeah, I'm fine. Someone bought it. A couple of marines were coming out of the cave—"

Witzko caught their expressions and stopped. "What is it? We lost more than two? Who? Who else got it?"

"It's the lander, Lieutenant," Kran said. "They got it, blew it to bits five hundred meters up."

Witzko felt something start to die inside. He thought about the pilot and co-pilot, whoever else had risked it all to bring them in.

"They'll send another lander," Kran said, "but it'll take a while."

"We'll have to wait," Witzko said. "Tell 'em we'll be here, but tell them not to try until they've got cover."

* * * * *

Kuhudag wondered how the sick were supposed to become healthy on hospital food. It was better than some of the rations he'd eaten in his travels but worse than meals he'd cooked on an open fire even when the meat was half-raw. This food, though, was for sick humans, not healthy weren hungry for their first decent meal since getting out of a cell.

There were several weren in the hospital. He recognized one, Burwab's cousin Fygora. He couldn't ask her about Burwab. She was being fed fluids, nutrients, and various regeneration accelerators through tubes injected into her arms.

Kuhudag and Grutok had the hospital dining room to themselves except for a few bandaged humans. The weren didn't speak to them, and the humans sat on the far side of the room.

"If one of them looks this way, I intend to challenge him," Grutok said. "This war may be over before I am able to earn adequate honor. My mother would be shamed if I came home without a kill."

"Your mother is a woman with good sense," Kuhudag said. "She will be pleased to see you have done nothing overly foolish while you have been away."

Grutok put down his fork and stared. "Worthy, am I to understand that you do not wish to fight? You fought well when we were attacked. You took many lives. What has changed since that time?"

"It is clear you have listened to none of my lessons," Kuhudag said. He jerked the fork from Grutok's claws and dropped it on the floor. "Honor does not come from killing or not killing but from knowing when bringing death is the only choice left to you. The true warrior knows the difference. If you do not pay attention to these things, only *dis*honor will come your way!"

"Worthy," Grutok hung his head, "I do not deserve your patience and understanding. If I do not improve at once, I hope you will beat me severely."

"Grutok, it is kind of you to remind me of that, but I assure you that you do not even have to ask. It is something that is always on my mind."

Grutok looked startled. Kuhudag growled low in his throat and turned away. Grutok took the opportunity to snap his tusks in the direction of the human's table. The humans there got up at once and left their meals.

"I saw that," Kuhudag snapped, "and you will pay for it, whelp, I vow that you will."

He looked past the young weren then and spotted Sergeant Lavon coming toward them across the room. Two other marines were with her, one carrying a business case under one arm.

Even with only her battledress and pistol, Kuhudag thought that Lavon looked magnificently warlike for a human. She was a really fine specimen, and one Kuhudag was sure that human males would covet.

"Worthy Kuhudag, Grutok," Irina Lavon said as she took a seat. The two marines with her continued standing. One opened the case and handed Lavon a handful of papers.

"These are printed copies of the statement you made when we first talked. If you would care to read the copy on the screen and verify that it matches the printouts, I would be grateful."

Grutok only glanced at the screen. He seemed less than enthusiastic about the proposition, though not yet hostile.

"Plague take you hairballs!" someone bellowed from the kitchen. "Why don't you eat outside where you belong?"

Out of courtesy to Sergeant Lavon, Kuhudag pretended that he didn't hear. Grutok, though, presented such a broad, toothy smile that the two marines behind Irina backed away. Grutok knew he had just received an insult worthy of a challenge, one he could lawfully accept.

"I will pay for your armor, if you wish to offer challenge," Grutok told the cook, who now stood glowering in the kitchen entryway, "and I will keep my claws retracted. As a further inducement, I will—"

"Oh, stop fussing and behave yourselves," Lavon said. "We don't have time for that."

Grutok looked hurt. Kuhudag had to grin. The sergeant sounded remarkably like Medlyna when anyone, male or female, tried to cross her. Kuhudag hoped he would greet her again soon, after the humans apologized and the weren were properly compensated.

"The paperwork was necessary," Lavon said, "but

that's not the reason I sought you out. What you told me about engaging humans in the north . . ." She looked strained now, the weariness beginning to show. "The humans are there, in the caverns. There are a great many of them. We haven't seen them, but they have attacked Concord Marines. We have losses."

"I said this, and it is so!" Kuhudag banged an enormous, clawed fist on the table, nearly cracking the plastic surface. "I share your sorrow. Your warriors are courageous. May I be selfish enough to ask if my people have been attacked as well?"

"Not that I know of," Irina said. She paused, then said, "That's why I'm here. The weren—as well as the humans on Arist—have the right to defend themselves against obvious aggression. The Concord will not prevent you from bearing arms for your protection. This is the law. If any weren or human from the Arist settlements wish to form armed units for protection, they may do so. Along with that privilege, of course, goes a vow of honor not to fight one another. Such behavior will not be tolerated in light of this greater threat."

"Do I hear you correctly?" Kuhudag was appalled. He almost stood, then gained control and eased himself back in his chair. "You have discovered the humans that I have already fought, and you are giving *other* humans arms to—what did you say?—protect themselves?" He raised his head, shaking his tusks in the air.

"Do you know what they will do, Sergeant? They will join these other humans and help them slaughter weren *and* marines. Do you not understand that the humans in Red Ridge and these others you have found are one and the same? They are all together in this. They are all dedicated to killing my people!"

Irina remained calm in the face of the weren's rage. It was not an easy task, for there was blood in the warrior's eye, and his fur stood up in ridges, making him look even larger than he was.

"I understand your concern," she told him. "I will tell you that the humans, when I announced this procedure to them, had the same feelings about the weren. The Concord does not take sides in these conflicts, as I'm sure you understand. So far nothing has been proven in either direction. Until it is, the arming of both races stands."

Irina paused again. "Now if you wish to participate, I offer you passage to the north where weren volunteers are gathering right now. Red Ridge volunteers are also on the way."

Kuhudag glared. "Not in the same vehicles, I trust."

Irina tried not to grin. "We are marines, Worthy Kuhudag. We are not perfect, but neither are we complete fools."

Chapter Twenty-Six

October 31, 2501

A tapping on his armored shoulder woke Witzko from a half-doze.

"Ten minutes, Lieutenant," said Private Atanza.

"Right," Witzko said.

He glanced at the time display. The five landers were flying on a northeast course at more than 500 kph. Four of them had joined Witzko's group after Lander Blue had battled its way in and pulled the battered remains of Recon out. They were now well on their way.

Activity trailed the five landers, staying well below the sensor horizon of anybody within fifty kilometers of the combat zone. Witzko watched the holodisplay of the action at the cavern. Cutters from *Activity* had been blasting the entryway relentlessly for over an hour. There was nothing to see now but a great smoldering hole in the ground, a molten pit bubbling with red-orange slag. In the sub-freezing temperature of Arist, the steaming slag cooled and turned black only moments after the shells found their mark. Just before the marines disembarked, the cutters would lay down a final curtain of fire.

"If they don't want to come out," Kran said, "we'll have to dig 'em out. That's what we get paid for."

"If there's any of 'em left," a marine yelled from the back of the lander.

"Uh-uh." Kran didn't know the man. He was from another company and had clearly not seen action before. "You go in with that kind of garbage in your head and you'll come back without it. I've never seen a thermonuclear device that cleaned out a hole for marines. There is *always* something for us down there. Don't you forget it, son."

The marine bit his lip and stared at Kran for a moment. He found something to do and didn't speak again.

Witzko walked forward between two files of armored marines, a hard core of Recon Platoon with no more doubts about their leader than he had about them. They'd done their job and didn't have to go back into action immediately. Colonel Seymoyr had told them that, but not one of them had taken his offer. They had all seen friends die in the fight, and whoever had killed them had to answer that.

Lieutenant Commander Dabur turned as Witzko entered the cockpit. Up to now, *Stormbird*'s senior lander pilot had been too busy to fly a mission himself. His white-toothed grin told Witzko the man welcomed the chance to get in the hot zone again.

"Eight minutes, fourteen seconds," Dabur said. "What the hell do you think is going on down there, Lieutenant? We still don't have any life signs. *Nobody's* coming out of that hole."

"That's why we're going down," Witzko said.

"Nasty job." Dabur shook his head.

Witzko didn't answer. The ribbons on Dabur's chest told him the lieutenant commander had been in the thick of it himself.

Witzko checked his time against the lander clock. The frozen landscape whipped past below. The sky today was gray, and wind had stripped the snow from the largest rocks on the plains. Now the surface of Arist was the same sullen color as the sky.

"Two minutes," Dabur announced. "Everybody up!"

The landers peeled off and swung wide, hovering for a few seconds, then arcing in for the drop.

"Thirty seconds . . ."

"Twenty seconds . . ."

The rear hatch opened, slipstream air boomed in Witzko's ear and then he was diving out into the sky as the lander whined and climbed away.

The two columns of marines came out no more than fifty meters apart. Power displays showed Witzko's suit straining to break his fall as the induction engines kicked in. Witzko's stomach seemed to be crawling up his throat as he decelerated, but he landed smoothly, his sensors straining to pick up anything and his weapon ready to fire.

Armored forms dotted the landscape. Witzko stood in the midst of a veritable swarm of marines. Whoever wanted a fight on Arist definitely had one coming their way.

Sergeants shouted orders through the comm as squads moved forward into position. Witzko saw Kran assembling a small squad. He nodded and took off to the right, heading the second squad.

From somewhere in the clutter of destruction where the cavern entry had stood before, a sharp *crack* broke the air and a plasma trail flashed white hot into a nearby marine. The soldier fell, picked himself up, and stared at his dented armor. He was scarcely on his feet before his squad mates returned a withering fire.

A squad surged forward and tossed a volley of grenades. Yellow bursts blossomed in the debris. A dark form twisted and fell.

"Retrieve?" Kran asked.

Witzko wanted to say no, but it was the first enemy they'd actually seen. Seymoyr would want the evidence.

"Wait until we can cover. Get it out of there fast."

"Sir. I'll send second sq—"

"Hey, is this where the action is, or is this a bunch of holiday shoppers?"

Witzko turned. No one could mistake the voice of Irina Lavon for anyone else. She had just jumped out of a nearby lander that had just sat down in the snow.

"How'd you get here?" Witzko asked. "I thought you were keeping the peace somewhere."

"I was, sir, until you guys kicked over the nest down here."

She turned, shouted a few terse orders, and Witzko saw some fifty-odd weren warriors begin to descend from the ramp in a loose formation. He knew they were volunteers from West Lodge and other nearby settlements.

"Is this your company, Master Sergeant?" Witzko asked. "Scary-looking crew."

Irina gave him a sour look. "You think these people are scary? You ought to meet the pair I brought with me."

"As long as they're all on the same side, I'm glad to have them."

Just behind the weren were nearly a hundred humans from Red Ridge. The two groups stayed well apart.

"It's been rough here, Lieutenant."

It wasn't a question. She didn't have to ask.

"We're losing marines, and we've only got one enemy body to show for it." He nodded at the civilians from Red Ridge. "I'm not worried about the weren; I know who they'll fight. These volunteers are going to be facing other humans. I could get a little nervous about that."

"Yeah, well, we'll just have to—" Irina stopped and looked to her left. "Those three!" She drew in a breath, gawking at Chen, Lee, and the t'sa, who had been stunned into an awkward silence by her reaction. "What in the flaming nine hells are they doing here? Would you kindly tell me what's going on, *sir*?"

"I wish I had the time, Sergeant," Witzko said. "Get your group moving and let's get out of here."

* * * * *

The marines went in to the cave as they'd been taught. The first squad sprinted in, dove behind whatever cover they could find, then provided cover for the second squad. The second squad moved in, sprinted past their comrades, then took cover as well. The ground around the ragged hole where the cavern entry had been was still hot. In the thin, frigid atmosphere, the rock gave off a hissing steam. Witzko couldn't feel it, but he could read the temperature gauges in his suit.

The heavy-weapons squad tossed grenades down the tunnel, waited for the rock fragments to pass and the tell tale tremors to cease, then jumped in themselves, spraying the area with bursts of rifle fire. The heavy infantry followed, weapons at the ready and tossing concussion grenades at every corner of the cavern. After the first bursts of fire had died away, the cavern was deathly quiet. The marines were wired up tight and ready to shoot at rocks or anything else that dared to move.

"Easy, easy," Kran said over the comm. "First squad, twenty meters. Hold it there. Third squad cover. Second, check out that tunnel on the right." He edged up close to Witzko, giving the signal for a closed comm.

"Where are they, Lieutenant? What is going on down here?"

Witzko studied the man through his frosty faceplate. If Platoon Sergeant Kran was getting itchy, the rest of the platoon was close to going ballistic.

"Nothing on the sensors?" He already knew the answer.

"Nothing. Not a peep. Do you want to take the time to have the Unholy Three reset their contraption?"

"Negative on that. They'd be little more than targets. Move first squad up another twenty meters, then hold 'em there."

Kran looked at him. "Yes, sir. Will do."

Irina Lavon moved up beside Witzko. "It seems that we've scared them all away, Lieutenant. They must have heard of the Concord Marines."

"I'll buy that story if they will, Sergeant."

"First squad on the move, sir," Kran reported. "I'm bringing second back in. That right-hand tunnel's a dead end."

Irina checked her weapon for the fifteenth time. "Why do I keep thinking they *want* us to get as many marines underground as we can? If they do, we're right on time."

"My thoughts exactly," Kran said. "You could have gone all day without saying it aloud."

"Sir?" came an all-too-familiar voice. "Most honored

officer, I would have a word with you, if it pleases the most honored lieutenant."

Witzko turned. The high-pitched, cheery voice of the t'sa was bad enough under normal circumstances. Down here, waiting for the planet to explode, it was more irritation than he could handle.

"Advisor, get back to wherever you're supposed to be. Do it now. I won't tell you twice."

"Sir, you may punish me severely, but you must come with me at once. It is extremely necessary that you do so! I fear that I must insist."

Witzko let out a breath. "Sergeant, come along," he said and followed the t'sa's dizzy path.

Chen and Lee were waiting in a small alcove. Their patched-together machine was nearby. It now bore a collection of scrapes and dents from the hasty evacuation, but it still seemed to be working. Witzko started to speak, then he caught the pure, undiluted fear in their eyes and didn't have to ask.

"How accurate are these readings?" he asked.

The t'sa looked to his two companions, then spoke, "The array of extra IR sensors we laid down were destroyed in the last assault. I would not count on them for anything beyond fifty to sixty meters. However, despite the beating it took in our hasty retreat, the gravometric unit seems to be functioning properly."

"Damn," Witzko said as he looked at the display again. "Damn, damn, damn!"

"There, Lieutenant. It's . . . it's—" Chen pointed a shaky finger at the flickering display.

Witzko looked. His stomach turned to lead. The holo still looked like the cross section of the world's largest ant bed. Now, though, every tunnel was swarming with tiny green blips, and each and every one was moving straight for the Concord Marines.

* * * * *

"Alert!" Witzko shouted, "Baddies in sight! All squads cover fire!"

Kran was already on his way. In a moment, he sent a dozen marines forward, each carrying a small bandoleer of AP grenades. The marines spread into four different tunnels. Each marine descended thirty to forty meters down each tunnel, set up an array of grenades with remote detonation devices, then raced back to their squad. Two more marines in each tunnel went down another ten meters and released a "sniffer" mine.

Witzko watched the action on the Unholy Three's holoscreen. The sniffers were red blips, hovering centimeters off the cavern floor. They were bio-sensitive robots that were programmed to find anything resembling a living being, "sniff" it out by detecting a heat signature, regular air fluctuations indicating movement, or even key organic compounds. They would then fly into the midst of the largest group and blow it to bits. The beauty of the mines was their ability to pass up the first group they approached if they sensed more targets ahead. They would find the largest group at the farthest stretch of their range, take them out, and let their buddies clean up behind.

Witzko watched the devastation. Only one group of the approaching enemies saw the sniffers before they struck. That group tried a hasty retreat, but to no avail. The red blips winked twice on the screen before disappearing, the cavern shook with a deafening roar, and the green blips died. The second wave, the third and the fourth, swallowed the enemy whole. The tunnel to the right of the platoon collapsed, spewing a cloud of grit and frost over the marines as the last rumbles faded to silence.

Lee, Chen, and the t'sa cheered until Witzko glared them down. There were plenty of dead, and one entrance was completely sealed, but the remaining forces didn't even hesitate. They came on as if nothing had happened at all.

"AP teams fire at discretion," Witzko ordered over the comms, and the three crewmen all acknowledged.

Witzko raced off, Irina coming up quickly behind.

He had not gone three steps when two sets of the AP grenades detonated, clouding the chamber with even more debris. A scarce two seconds later the third array exploded, and tunnel number one collapsed, killing everyone inside and leaving only two openings for potential targets.

Even through his suit's filters, Witzko could hear the deafening roar of gunfire as the marines met the first wave of the enemy force. He reached the main tunnel as a hail of death poured out of the darkness ahead. Witzko dove behind a pile of boulders and took his first good look at the enemy. Through the gloom and murk of battle he could see many shadowy forms—most carrying heavy charge rifles and an occasional laser, all covered in light combat armor—peeking out from the meager cover of the tunnels' entrances and doing their damnedest to kill every marine in sight.

Two marines went down. A trooper went to his knees and launched a small smart grenade from the end of his rifle. The tiny missile wobbled in flight, straightened, then tore into the enemy lines. Screams erupted from the tunnel and were immediately followed by withering fire from Kran's marines.

Witzko turned to see Lavon attending a wounded marine. The man had a ragged metal hole where his right arm used to be. Lavon was spraying the area with a foam that would harden and seal the area almost at once. Two medics crawled up, turned the wounded marine's induction unit to "low," and guided him back down the tunnel.

A cloud of smoke poured down the tunnel. Two marines charged into the murk and came out leading another. Witzko heard an unearthly roar through his audio and turned to see half a dozen weren charging through the marines, pushing the armored troopers aside as they ran blindly into the enemy lines, firing hand weapons and slashing with their heavy *chuurkhnas*. One of the weren went down and did not move again, but the others kept going, carving a terrible gap in the enemy's forward lines. The enemy held for an instant, then turned and fled, leaving their dead behind.

More explosions ripped the air far down the tunnel, as another array of released sniffer mines took their toll. Bits of rock fell from the ceiling, turning the marines into grim, dusty figures that moved in the half light of the tunnel.

Kran yelled an order, and four marines went to full induction power in the confines of the tunnel. They roared past the enemy dead and the weren, catching the stragglers from the rear. Bodies pulped as the armored troopers drove ahead. In moments they were back, their armor covered in a gory mud of dust, frost, and blood.

Witzko moved his troops forward, keeping his

advance a cautious ten meters at a time. Now he had a runner going back and forth to the Unholy Three, bringing reports on the enemy positions ahead. The enemy was taking terrible losses but still kept coming. They fought with terrible ferocity. No matter how obviously outnumbered or outgunned they were, many of them refused to lay down arms. The marines often had no choice but to kill or be killed.

Despite the best efforts of the platoon, they took no prisoners. The enemy fighters wore masks to protect them from the nonlethal gases. They apparently knew the tunnels backward and forward and would disappear in the maze, only to reemerge minutes later through another tunnel, killing marines as they did so. The two prisoners whom one squad had managed to capture died of their wounds before they could be brought back for medical attention.

Witzko knew Seymoyr would be livid over that. He wanted answers, and prisoners were the only way he could get them. He was baffled over the bodies of the enemy. They were ordinary humans, most of them in reasonably good armor. Who the hell were they, and who were they working for? Not Red Ridge, he knew that now. This group was too big, too well equipped, not too big a job for VoidCorp, though, if they wanted to clean up Arist, kill all the weren, and start some project here. It was hard to dismiss the thought. VoidCorp had a well-deserved reputation for showing little concern for other sentient forms of life—especially weren, many of whom had been held in bondage until the weren managed to flee to Arist.

Thuldans, maybe? The Empire was a likely candidate. Whatever they had, the Thuldans always wanted more. Who else could it be? The Austrins? The Hatire?

Witzko shrugged. It was no use guessing. They could be from any number of stellar nations, or they might even be nothing more than a well-trained force of renegade mercenaries. Witzko would be willing to bet a year's pay no one would find a trace of evidence to show who had paid the fare for this bunch.

"They're coming up," Kran shouted into Witzko's comm. "I need people over here!"

We need people everywhere, Witzko thought, and that means more dead marines.

* * * * *

"They're *not* our people," Paul Dimmock shouted at Seymoyr. "Damn it all, Colonel, you have no right to accuse VoidCorp of this madness! No right at all!"

"Sit down," Seymoyr told him. "I don't know who's behind this, but you're protesting too much, Mister. We'll find out who's responsible, and when we do, I'll take payment in kind for every dead marine."

Dimmock was startled. "You don't mean that. The Concord doesn't have the authority to—"

"What? Take revenge?" Seymoyr spread his hands. "You must have misunderstood me, Mr. Dimmock. How could you even imagine such a thing?"

Dimmock gave him a narrow look. He was about to say something else when Seymoyr stood, looked him straight in the eye, and rasped, "Let me make myself clear, Dimmock. If I have to bring in a Concord Administrator and spend the next ten years trying each and every one of those bastards, or if I'm have to line them up and shoot them myself, anyone who killed one of my men will answer for it *in kind*. Do I make myself clear, sir?"

Dimmock apparently had the wisdom not to push the matter further. He put his hands behind his back and walked to the end of the shelter. Seymoyr had put up a hasty HQ not three kilometers from the cavern entry. That wasn't close enough for Seymoyr, but it seemed much too close for the VoidCorp representative.

"I don't think the colonel is actually accusing Void-Corp," said Dr. Ohito. "though I regret mentioning it, I can't say that I blame him. He is Concord, and he must keep an open mind in this situation."

"Oh, fine." Dimmock gave him a nasty look. "That's helpful, Doctor. Is there anything else you'd care to say, such as you'd do most anything to get me off of Arist and out your hair? You can give the planet away to *them*." He gestured angrily toward the two weren in the room. "Let those *folk* run the show here."

"I take that as a direct challenge." Burwab came to his feet and extended his claws. "I call upon you to defend your honor!"

"Forget it," Dimmock said. "I'm a human, pal. I've got more sense than that."

"Please!" Seymoyr held up a restraining hand. Burwab's eyes blazed. The elder weren shook as he eased himself back into his oversized chair.

"We must talk to each other," Doctor Ohito's daughter said. "It doesn't matter what we may or may not feel. We must *talk* to one another, and we must stop all this!"

"I don't think talking's going to help much at this point," Seymoyr said. "We'll talk, and we'll keep talking until this nonsense is over. If you people want to do something constructive, go join your own groups of volunteers. I understand *both* races are taking casualties out there. They're fighting and dying for your world. My marines are fighting and dying too, and this *isn't* their world."

The room was silent for a long moment. The only sound was the distant, high-pitched crack of small arms and the deep, throaty rumble of heavy weapons.

Dimmock glared at Colonel Seymoyr. "If we all go out there and get killed, what's that going to prove? You're innocent if you die, guilty if you live? Is that Concord thinking, Colonel? If it is, I can understand why you're so *popular* around the system."

Seymoyr wanted to stand and smash the self-satisfied grin off Dimmock's face. Instead, he said nothing at all. Dimmock tried to hold his glance. Seymoyr refused to turn away. It was Dimmock, in the end, who found his heavy gear and stomped out of the shelter.

"I will fight, of course," Burwab said, nodding to the warrior at his side. "There was never any question. I hope you did not intend to imply otherwise, Colonel. I came to this meeting because you asked me. It was useless, as I knew it would be. It always is, when one deals with VoidCorp. The weren know what VoidCorp wants out of us. It is the same thing they have always wanted."

Burwab and his companion stood, bowed courteously to the others, and left.

"We have accomplished little," Doctor Ohito's daughter said. "I deeply regret this."

"So do I," said Colonel Seymoyr.

He had to agree with the weren. The meeting had been useless from the beginning, but it was his job to have meetings, to try to talk people into compromise before they started shooting one another. Meetings were possibly the worst part of command as far as he was concerned. They were certainly the most annoying and often the least productive.

* * * * *

Sergeant Kran joined Witzko and Irina Lavon. He had scorch marks on his armor and a fist-sized dent in his helmet. "They want to die," he said, "and that's what they're doing. If that gadget's right, we've wiped out about half their force. The trouble is, we've got to finish off the whole mess of them. No one's quit so far."

"Still no prisoners?" asked Witzko wearily.

"None," Kran replied. "They're too well prepared against our nonlethals, and they know these damned tunnels too damned well for us to corner them. Squad six thought they had a band of them cornered, but it turned out to be an ambush. Only three marines made it out alive, and two of them were wounded. Ramirez won't walk again until he sees major surgery."

"Damn," Witzko said. "We may have to begin sealing side tunnels just to protect our backs. Why aren't our gravometric sensors detecting them?"

Lavon broke in. "At least some of the enemy parties have managed to lay jamming equipment in a few tunnels. We're simply can't get an accurate reading until we find the jammer and take it out. Unfortunately, the last squad that found one also found out that it was rigged with heavy explosives. If the squad leader hadn't seen it, we'd be out one more squad right now."

Witzko thought a moment then said, "Spread the word. If anyone runs across any more of the jammers, they are to take them out. Don't waste time trying to disarm the damned things. Just blow them to hell."

"Still," Kran put in, "that's assuming that we find them all. Some have been quite well hidden. These guys obviously have been here for a long time. They're well supplied and have been preparing for this. They know the turf. We don't, and what we do know may or may not be accurate."

"Can either of you give me *any* good news?" It came out more harshly than Witzko had intended.

"Well," Kran offered, "they do seem to be backing up into one section. That should make it easier to put an end to them. Of course they'll have all their strength in one spot. If we can hit them hard there . . ."

Lavon gave a weary shrug. "Right. We'll lose more people, but we'll win. What's the point? They didn't gain anything. They just killed themselves and some of us."

"If there is a point, Sergeant, I certainly don't get it," Witzko said with a trace of bitterness in his voice. "Ask me something I can answer."

Kran nodded and looked away. "You're right. Absolutely, sir."

Witzko regretted his own tone and the sergeant's as well. Everyone was getting uptight, and for good reason, too. Once they mopped up the enemy, what would they have to show for it? Only a whole hell of a lot of dead bodies. There was no victory, nothing here to win.

* * * * *

At six hundred meters down, the marines struck an overabundant area of geothermal heat, rendering their IR scanners almost useless. The complex of tunnels, according the the Unholy Three's gravometric device, was getting deeper instead of spreading in lateral directions. The exception was one tunnel that led upward and sideways two hundred meters and ended in an enormous ice cave. Clearly there was some point where it had to broach the surface high above. The cavern couldn't have remained frozen otherwise with so much heat nearby. The cave seemed big enough to be a tourist attraction, Witzko thought, if any tourists were crazy enough to come to Arist.

A marine scout found the place and guided Witzko and Irina Lavon to it. The tunnel floor held a thin blanket of frost littered with boot prints. There were empty supply canisters scattered about.

In case any hostiles were still about, Witzko declared the spot as Recon Listening Post One. He assigned the Unholy Three to the place with their scanning device and left them there with a handful of marines. The spot was magnetically clear for a change, and Witzko contacted Colonel Seymoyr before he left.

"Any idea how many hostiles are left?" the colonel asked.

"Impossible to tell, sir," Witzko answered. "There have been no more skirmishes reported in the last half hour, and the last parties seen all seemed to be headed in the same general direction. It may mean that we've broken their main strength, or it may mean that they're all gathering in one place to get out or hit us again."

"You'll have to go in and root them out," Seymoyr told him, which was no big surprise to Witzko. "If you could toss a fair-sized nuke in there, I'd say do it and don't risk any more lives. What you'll likely do, though, is start a quake that'll shake the place up like rocks in a can. There are settlements all over the place, and we can't risk that."

"No, sir," Witzko said. "I don't think we can."

"I know you won't do it unless I order you, Lieutenant, but you don't have to keep Recon down there anymore."

"No, sir. I know that. Thank you, sir."

"Out," Seymoyr said.

Chapter Twenty-Seven

October 31, 2501

Kuhudag crouched at a bend in the tunnel and tightened the scope on his rifle. There were seven weren stationed there, waiting for a patrol to return with any news of enemy presence. The tunnel had been eerily quiet for nearly half an hour. Kuhudag had reported this at once. A marine messenger returned to tell him to keep his group alert and that most of the other tunnels had been just as quiet.

Kuhudag grunted to himself. Why did humans always tell you something you already knew? Of course his group was alert. They were weren, weren't they? Anyone could see that there was, indeed, "quiet" on the part of the enemy. Every time he thought he was beginning to see what humans were like, he realized that he didn't understand them at all. He smelled Burwab before he saw him.

"It is an honor to be in your presence again," Kuhudag said, whether he thought it was or not. "We have been concerned. Much has occurred since we spoke."

"I think it is safe to say that." The West Lodge chief squatted down beside Kuhudag and wiped a furry paw across his face as he spat on the ground.

"What in the name of the Greater Glories is that?" he said, staring at Kuhudag's weapon.

Kuhudag repressed a smile. A smile would be grossly impolite. Burwab loved weapons and coveted any he hadn't seen before. He was carrying a standard charge rifle as well as his old slug pistol, which was nearly as old as Burwab himself.

"This is a Goebel and Schatt Model 74," Kuhudag said. "It has a 15 mm bore with a ten-round magazine. It has an effective range of about two thousand meters with this sight. I liberated it from a dead enemy. They have many fine weapons. Even the marines are impressed, though they pretend not to be."

"*I* am impressed," Burwab said. "I am not ashamed to deny it. And the hand weapon, if I may ask?"

Kuhudag brought the dark, polished weapon from a holster at his side and handed it by the grip to Burwab. "It is an 11 mm charge pistol, a copy of a GW2 model, I am told. I have ten magazines for the rifle and five for the pistol."

He looked at Burwab and made a decision at once. "If you would not be offended, I would be grateful if you took the pistol as a gift. As a matter of fact, when I found it I said to myself, 'This is a fine pistol. Only a warrior such as Burwab would truly appreciate such a weapon.' "

Burwab looked at Kuhudag. A gift from a weren who opposed him was obviously the last thing he had expected.

"Truly, it is a fine gift, Kuhudag. You do me honor." The last word seemed hard to get out. "I accept and give you my thanks."

"They are graciously received."

Burwab paused, looking thoughtfully at his claws. "We have not always seen eye to eye, Kuhudag. In fact, we have often found ourselves at opposite poles. I feel it is time that such behavior came to an end. Not that we will likely ever agree on more than the weather, but I have come to understand that is of little importance in light of greater needs.

"I have just come from a meeting with the Concord colonel. A doctor and his daughter were there, two humans who seem amiable enough for their race. The thing is, though, Paul Dimmock was there as well."

Burwab saw Kuhudag begin to frown. "Yes, he is VoidCorp, as are the others, but Dimmock is a weren-hater. He insists his people know nothing of the enemy we face now. I cannot say if this is true or not. There is little such a being says that I would accept. Nevertheless, if and when this conflict is settled, we will have to deal with him again. The others, the doctor and his daughter, do not have the strength to fight him. This is why I have come to ask you to stand for election to the Council Chief's chair this autumn, or even sooner, if the price of a treaty with the humans is my stepping down. This is a task I feel you, of all the weren, can handle best."

Kuhudag's jaw dropped so far his tusks were pointing at Burwab's vitals, a mannerless gesture under other circumstances.

The chief smiled, which somewhat eased Kuhudag's suspicions. He could not recall when he had seen such an expression on Burwab's aged face.

"I am both stunned and honored," Kuhudag said, "but if this came to pass, would I be accepted by the humans?

They are used to dealing with you, and humans cannot stand change of any sort."

"Kuhudag," Burwab said angrily, "we cannot allow humans to say who will lead our folk on Arist. There can be no peace and no equality that way. Many humans—including too many on Arist—consider weren as barely sentient beings. That must *stop*. It is an attitude ingrained in these creatures, I fear. Whoever they meet who is not like them is a lower being. Our reluctance to face this attitude played a large part in leading our people to virtual slavery under VoidCorp. We cannot suffer VoidCorp here on this world. It cannot happen, Kuhudag. It *must* not!"

Burwab paused for a breath. "Besides, you have good in you, despite your insufferable pride. You have fought against the humans, but you have been their captive as well. You suffered but did not return suffering. There will be much to argue with the humans, and you are more likely than I am to refrain from slaying one of these beings on the spot in a moment of forgetfulness. I am uncertain that I could do that."

All of the chief's points made good sense to Kuhudag. Burwab had not lost his powers of persuasion. Still, Kuhudag wondered if the folk of West Lodge might not be better off with the chief they had than with a footloose hunter. It was much to consider.

"I will say this," he told Burwab. "This is an honor beyond any expectation I have ever had. I will sit in your chair at any time you wish it, or if you fall in battle. If I should fall first, of course, I would not ask for a leader's honors—only enough stones to cover what is left of me."

"That is what you will have," Burwab said, "and I thank you for the gift. It is truly the finest hand weapon

I have ever had the pleasure to hold. May it soon be put to good use."

* * * * *

Late that same afternoon, several squads ran into small pockets of resistance in the caverns. Seven more marines died in the fight, and the enemy continued its retreat deeper into the tunnels. The Unholy Three's device showed less than three dozen enemy troopers holed up in what appeared to be a dead-end tunnel whose entrance was heavily guarded by at least one quantum minigun and several well-armed snipers. The marines were preparing to go in for what they anticipated to be a grim, weary cleanup operation when the small green blips on the gravometric sensor began to trickle away.

"Damn!" Witzko swore. "I thought you said that tunnel was a dead end."

"No, sir," answered the t'sa defensively. "I said that the sensor detected no tunnel beyond thirty meters. I would postulate that yet another gravometric sensor is in operation farther down somewhere. Given enough time, we might be able to compensate for—"

"We have no more time." Witzko cut him off. "Can you at least tell me if the snipers are still guarding the tunnel?"

Before the t'sa could further irritate the lieutenant, Chen piped in. "Several shapes moved out with the others, but as Thumn said, the sensor is likely being jammed, sir. I wouldn't trust the reading, sir."

Witzko sighed. Everyone watched him intently. No matter what he decided, some of the faces of the platoon would likely never see sunlight again.

"All right, Sergeant. Gather a squad and take out the sniper post."

* * * * *

"Nothing," Sergeant Kran said when he reported in a half-hour later. "The tunnel narrows to little more than three meters across farther in. There was another jammer, but the explosives to which it was rigged carried enough charge to bring down the tunnel. It's been disarmed, but whoever was down there is long gone. I've still got patrols out, and they'll stay out until I decide to pull 'em back. If there's anything breathing out there for eight kilometers, Lieutenant, I'll be damned if I've run across it."

The corridor was safe enough, and Kran had taken off the helmet of his suit to wipe his face and remove some of the stench from himself. Witzko had done the same. Even the best environmental suit ever made—and the Harkamp *was* the best—did not contain enough recycling, cleansing, and deodorizing equipment to keep a fighting marine from becoming an undesirable person to be around.

"I'm not even going to think about body retrieval," Witzko said. "That's somebody else's department, and I don't mind letting 'em have it."

He turned to watch a squad of marines coming back from a far tunnel. They looked weary, drained, and sick—but none looked as bad as a group of volunteers from Red Ridge. Their faces were drained of color, and he was certain many of them had retched until they had nothing more to bring up. There was no shame in that, he knew. There wasn't a marine anywhere who hadn't reached that point in his combat career.

Irina Lavon came up with Captain McRae and PFC Atanza. All had their helmets off, and all were keeping a safe distance from the others. Everybody smelled bad, but your own odor was always better than the marine standing close by.

"I've talked to Colonel Seymoyr," McRae said. "He wants you on the comm when you can, but I'll give you the short version. We're going to do what we're already doing—making sure we're clean in here, keeping up full patrol, and leaving sensors everywhere. The colonel's got a lander coming down from *Stormbird* with every sensor anyone can find. We're going to spread them out like breadcrumbs. If anything moves, we go in and get it."

The captain sighed and ran a hand through her short blonde hair. "Is anybody sick of this mess? Can somebody tell me exactly what happened here?"

Kran shook his head. "Ma'am, if I knew where these spooks came from, I'd get a medal on the spot. I've been in a lot of firefights, but nothing like this. They're jamming all our sensors then ambushing squads in the narrow tunnels. Plain and simple: they've got home field advantage."

"Give as many of your people a break outside as you can," Witzko told Kran. "Let some of the new people get a tour of this place."

"Yes, sir," Kran said. "They'll be delighted, sir."

"Captain," Witzko said, "if you've got any company techs around somewhere, we could use a few up in the hot zones. We've sent enough bodies out for the med people to look at, but I think we ought to have a sample of every weapon that was in there to see if we can trace where it came from."

"We can do that," McRae said. "I'll get Sergeant Tragger on it. She knows more about weapons than a—"

The captain kept talking for a moment, but nobody heard her. A shrill, eardrum-piercing alarm echoed through the close cavern walls. Witzko, McRae, and the others stared at one another for a second and a half, then jammed their helmets on, activated their suits, and grabbed for their weapons.

"What the hell?" Kran muttered through his comm. "Who set that thing off?"

Marines began pouring out of the tunnels, running into one another, unsure where to go or what to do.

Witzko spotted Kasuga with his helmet off, his dark eyes wide, and his face drained of color.

"It's . . . it's klicks, sir," Kasuga blurted out. "*Klicks* are boiling out of the ground back there!"

Chapter Twenty-Eight

October 31, 2501

There was no time to think, no time to do anything but fight. Once more, Recon was in the thick of it along with assault platoons, Red Ridgers, and a small army of angry weren. Word was coming in too fast to act. Klicks were swarming up from below, boiling out of caverns that weren't on the map. It seemed that the klicks also had jamming devices to confound the gravometric sensors and whatever else was in use by the Concord Marines.

Some of them came on their own, suddenly breaking through into the lower tunnels. Many of them followed bizarre, clunky machines that bored through the rock with massively powered blacklasers.

One squad had sent back a holo. Witzko stared, scarcely able to believe what he saw. The klicks were more than simply alien; they looked all too terribly familiar. Nearly two meters tall, the creatures had six legs, each ending in prehensile, pincerlike claws. The pincers were clearly the instruments that had given the klicks their name. These razored claws clicked and clacked together constantly, moving so fast they seemed no more than a blur.

In the few seconds he had to look, Witzko could see that the seemingly fragile creatures were protected by a hard, thick exoskeleton that reflected little light.

Worst of all was the ending of the brief picture. The marines who met the creatures had been quickly overrun. They had been taken by surprise, and even their thick battle armor was little protection against the blacklasers at such close range. The image died as two of the klicks slashed out at the marine with the holocam. The holo went suddenly dark, but not before Witzko heard the fearful scream of the marines and the awful, whirring sound of the monsters that killed them.

"My God . . ." Witzko said and could say nothing more.

"They were there," Irina Lavon said at his side. "They were *down* there, and we didn't even know it." She stared at Witzko. "This is what they wanted, Lieutenant. They *wanted* us in the caverns. They wanted the place full of marines!"

Witzko left her with quick instructions to pass on to Kran. Racing down the stone corridor with the sound of gunfire behind him, Witzko searched for a spot where a comm could get through to *Stormbird*. Instead he found Colonel Seymoyr at the head of an entire company of heavily armed assault troops. Over a hundred marines carrying frag grenades, charge rifles, and a deadly plasma gun were marching in to join the fight.

The colonel, dressed in full armor, wasted no time with greetings. He waved the company on and drew Witzko into a side tunnel. "What have you got, Witzko? Tell me what you can. I saw the holo."

"We caught it out here, Colonel," Witzko replied with

a hasty salute. "Damn it, we've been hooked! Every step of the way, the klicks sucked us in—the attack in space, the whole thing. Unless I miss my guess, this so-called *war* down here is their doing, too. Human troopers harassed the weren. The weren thought the Red Ridgers were behind it and went after them. The Ridgers fought back. The klicks were smart enough to keep their attacks in the north so nobody could get together and compare notes. They got a war going and brought us in."

Seymoyr nodded. "That's pure conjecture, Lieutenant. You may or may not be right, but we can't confirm any of that. Those damned, sorry-excuse-for-humans may be nothing more than renegades. The klicks being in the same spot is likely nothing more than pure coincidence."

"It's a damned strange coincidence, sir."

"Granted, Lieutenant, but not half as strange as those damned spiders being allied with humans. As I said, you may be right, but we need proof."

"Yes, sir," Witzko said.

The last of the company was passing by. The colonel seemed in a hurry to be gone.

"I've been in touch with *Stormbird*," Seymoyr said. "We're sending down everything we've got. Captain Myklebust and I agree that the klicks will likely hit us up there, too. Spes has been on standby, but they're on the way now." He squinted at Witzko. "We're in the soup, son, up to our necks. Keep in touch."

Seymoyr sprinted off to catch up with his company. Witzko heard the far-off scream of landers as reinforcements and supplies arrived outside. They expect us to do that, too, he thought. Everything we do, they know we're going to do it.

* * * * *

While he was gathering support for the marines already in the tunnels, another assault team came in on three waves of landers—the rest of Recon platoon, 4th Company, 2nd Company, and a support echelon of medics, ammo, and supplies. Moments later, 3rd Company arrived, sweeping down from orbit with its own fire support and supply echelons.

Recon, he knew, would go straight down the lower tunnels where more klicks might appear, then they'd pull back when the other two 3rd Battalion companies arrived. The orbital group formed a cordon of a hundred and fifty armored marines. They'd hold the perimeter and go in when needed.

Witzko managed to find most of his Recon group and bring them out for ordnance checks and a quick meal in their suits. It wasn't much, but it was more than they'd had in over twenty-four hours on Arist.

Platoon Sergeant Jobal Kran was waiting when Witzko's Recon people returned. Witzko had ordered him out with the others, but Kran had respectfully disobeyed orders on the grounds that not all of the platoon was present. As long as he was platoon sergeant, he would stay back and find them.

"With all respect, sir," he added.

Witzko didn't say anything. There were times when an NCO should get a chewing out and other times when he should get a medal. Witzko gave Kran a brief nod as he led the platoon back in—just enough of a nod to let the sergeant know where he stood.

* * * * *

Sergeant Lavon led a patrol down the steeply sloping tunnel to an area now designated as Low-Boy Five. If anyone had an answer as to how the klicks had avoided detection, Irina hadn't been informed. The best guess was the one everyone had thought of first—they were simply using jammers to confound the gravometric waves.

Lavon had led her patrol no more than two hundred meters when Stosser, riding point, suddenly went still and held up an armored hand. The platoon halted. Stosser backed off, stopping beside Irina.

"Something," she said, keeping the comm line direct. "I don't know . . ."

"You got a reading on something?"

"Nothing, Sergeant. I've got an itch, that's all. All I'm saying is that I don't like it. I feel so tired all of a sudden, like a—"

The wall in front of the platoon suddenly exploded. An incandescent black beam spat out fiery death, stitching the floor and the walls. Lavon yelled a warning, but it was too late. The top half of Stosser went down, her body sliced in half, armor and all.

A swarm of chattering klicks poured out of the broken wall. Irina, Rizzo, and Phelan were in the front line. A sudden fatigue hit Lavon, and her head began throbbing with intense pain. The marines backed off, spraying their charge rifles at the klicks. The creatures howled, jerking their multiple limbs as they died. Their exoskeletons took an amazing amount of damage before the monsters finally fell down. Irina shot low, Phelan shot high, and the klicks' tough frames cracked and shattered under the heavy fire.

Rizzo caught a fragment of debris and staggered, nearly falling. Two marines behind pulled him back, and two others took his place. The klicks kept coming, firing their blacklasers that melted solid stone. When the black rays hit, they turned armor into boiling mush. The platoon retreated down the corridor, cover fire coming from the rear to the front. Lavon felt stunned all of a sudden, as if someone had given her several good bashes to the head.

Someone shouted in her comm.

"Coming through! Big Daddy coming through!"

An assault team forced their way past Irina's platoon. The awesome "Big Daddies" went to work. White beams of plasma tore into the klicks. The klicks didn't fall or back off. They simply disappeared in white, molten fire. In seconds, there was nothing in the tunnel but dripping slag. Even the body parts were gone.

Irina leaned against the wall, exhausted. Stosser was dead. Rizzo and Oshima were badly hurt. Two other marines had lost half the circuits in their suits. One of them had ripped his helmet off and was decorating the cave floor with vomit.

She looked at the assault sergeant who had led the way in. The heavy, ominous plasma gun was slung across his shoulder now.

"I know you, right?" she said. "Tremont, 3rd Company, 2nd Battalion?"

"You got it, Sarge. You're Lavon."

"I think so, but I'm not sure anymore. Didn't your mother ever tell you not to shoot that thing in the house?"

"No, ma'am," he smiled, "she never did."

"Good for her. Thanks for showing up."

"No problem. Termites, ants, klicks, whatever you got."

The assault platoon checked out the hole where the klicks had come through. Someone tossed enough frag grenades down to annihilate anything within a hundred meters or so.

Irina led her crew back, and medics met them on the way. Two took Rizzo and Oshima back. Two more took a collapsible grav-induced stretcher up to retrieve what was left of Stosser.

Irina took off her helmet. It was against regulations this close to the hot zone, but she didn't much care. What could they do? Send her back home? She tried not to think about Stosser, but the picture wouldn't go away. The pictures never did. They stayed there, new chapters in the continuing nightmare of a combat marine. The trouble was, she thought, they never came back as nice, filmy spirits. They came just like they'd been, the moment they caught it.

If I ever get it, she told herself, I hope I have the courtesy to stay dead and not bother anyone else. You'd think people would have a little consideration for the buddies they left behind.

"Hey, Queenie, what are you doing here?"

Irina looked up, startled. Master Sergeant Jacques Belier was standing above her, a big grin spreading across his ugly features. He wasn't wearing armor, just a regular CM camo outfit that looked ridiculous in the cavern.

"I work here, Sergeant," Irina said grimly. "It's called 'combat marines.' Right now I'm on a peacekeeping mission, and it isn't going all that well. What the hell are *you* doing here? Headquarters taking the day off?"

Belier shook his head. "You just will not let us be friends, will you, Queenie? No matter how hard I try."

"Don't knock yourself out. What do you want, Belier? I haven't got the time."

The two medics came back up the tunnel, leading a stretcher covered in a thick tarp.

Belier shrugged and dropped his voice to a near whisper. "I don't want a thing, Sarge. I just saw you and thought I'd stop and say hello, and I wanted to remind you of our little deal in case it slipped your mind."

Irina bristled. "We haven't *got* any deal. I haven't done anything and neither has the lieutenant. You know that as well as I do. If I *had* done anything, do you truly think I'd crawl down to your level and beg? My God, I can't believe you."

"I'd sure like that medal when I'm sitting in my rocking chair, Queenie." Belier speared her with a look that had melted a thousand raw marines. "Wouldn't be all that much trouble to you, and I *don't* think you want to go through all that court-martial mess. You've seen 'em before. Nobody gets out clean, no matter what. Everybody gets dirty. That's just the way it is."

Irina stood. "Get out of here, Jacques. Get out of my sight. Now."

Belier grinned and scratched his balding head. "Yeah, well, you give it some thought. I'll be around you want to talk abou—"

It came out of nowhere, falling in a low, hissing arc—a dark missile the size of small fist. Irina saw it. She watched it coming all the way. She saw it bounce with a muted clang on the cavern floor, then she watched in slow motion horror as she slammed her induction engine on full and yelled out a warning.

She hit the far wall hard, nearly knocking herself out, even with the padding and insulation in the suit. The grenade exploded just as she hit. The blast was a quick, blinding flash of cobalt blue. A concussion right after that deafened anyone within earshot. Irina pulled herself up. Three marines were down. Nothing too bad, they were wearing good armor, and the blast merely knocked them to the ground.

Everyone else came slowly to their feet. Irina looked where she'd been standing. Belier lay there, blood pouring out of his mouth and ears. One wickedly sharp frag had slammed into his lower chest. Another had gone through his thigh.

She ran to him quickly, jerking out a trauma kit. His vital sign readings were dropping fast. She slapped the trauma kit in place, watching the displays.

Belier opened his eyes and looked up. "Hey, Queenie, what the hell hit me?"

"Jacques, take it easy. You'll be okay."

"Hey, I know that."

"Hang on. Just hang on a minute, we'll get some help here."

The display straight-lined. Belier kept looking at her, a curious frown on his face as if he'd seen something puzzling and couldn't figure it out at all.

An assault squad was searching the corridor walls, trying to find the spot where the missile had come from. She loathed Jacques Belier, despised everything he stood for, hated him for the way he'd disgraced the uniform she loved. He had lied, stolen, and cheated his way through a lazy, worthless career. There was nothing good about the man, nothing he'd ever done for anyone but Master Sergeant Jacques Belier.

Irina stumbled down the tunnel until she was alone. She turned off her comm and began to shake. The tears came and wouldn't stop. She let them come and didn't even try to make them go away.

Chapter Twenty-Nine

October 31, 2501

Not for the first time, Colonel Seymoyr regretted his rank. It was no act of cowardice to return to *Stormbird*, and no one would have ever accused him of such. Still, he felt he was deserting his post. Though duty and logic dictated otherwise, he still felt that he ought to be there with his marines instead of heading back to the ship to meet with Captain Myklebust. An "emergency strategy session" was what it was, and there was no question that they were in one hell of an emergency situation. Still, a council of war aboard *Stormbird* wouldn't mean much to marines dying down on Arist. They wouldn't understand why their officers were up drinking coffee somewhere while they were fighting hordes of klicks.

"*Alert! Alert! Enemy craft to port!*"

Seymoyr sat up straight. The cutter veered off sharply to starboard as a missile streaked by and exploded half a kilometer away.

"Hang on!" the pilot called out. "We've got some trouble here, Colonel!"

Seymoyr didn't have to be told. He could see them on the holodisplay: fiery streaks in the sky, half a dozen of them, increasing the magnification, he could see them clearly—squat, ugly craft with black-green hides, definitely klicks. Their hulls sprouted what he could only assume were pods, turrets, and sensor arrays—all in strange disorder, nothing at all like a ship from anywhere else. The minds behind a thing like that—how could you begin to understand what they were like?

As he watched, the klicks launched a second salvo. Colonel Seymoyr felt his throat constrict. The targets had to be marines who were dropping down out of orbit to join the battle in the caverns.

"Damn you," he said aloud, pounding his fists against the seat, "Damn you all!"

He felt absolutely helpless, strapped into a cutter, blasting through the darkness of space with no way to fight back. He could hear the garbled talk from several different comms.

"Recon Five-Anna, watch it! You're—"

". . . on Lander Blue! Get out of there!"

". . . no clear shot on the . . ."

"Heavy klick skyfire in drop area. Ground alert! Ground alert! Get everyone out of there, now!"

Seymoyr watched in horror. The klicks had been clever. They had a clear field of fire above and below. The marines in the sky couldn't shoot without hitting ground troops. The troops below had the same problem. If they fired, they'd hit the landers.

A lander exploded in a brilliant, rolling ball of fire and smoke. The initial light from the blast was so bright that the holo blanked out. When it came on again, nothing was there. Missiles brightened the ground, a hundred kilometers below.

"We're going in now," the pilot's voice crackled in Seymoyr's ears. "*Stormbird* dead ahead."

Seymoyr didn't answer. He hadn't been close enough to see it, but he saw it in his mind's eye anyway: dead marines, charred bodies plummeting out of the sky.

* * * * *

From *Stormbird's* Tactical Command Center, action in space and on the ground had a way of looking unreal. Klick ships were red; Concord ships were white. On the ground, various colored blips represented machines, troops, supply dumps, medical units, and landing areas. Nothing on the read-out showed who was alive or dead. That information came on another screen whose digital numbers kept blinking and growing at a frightening rate. The figures here were rough estimates only, but they gave a fair idea of how the fight was going.

Seymoyr watched in growing rage as his marines fought and died on that worthless chunk of ice and rock. Orbital drop 3rd Company, Fifth Marines had lost nearly a quarter of its strength before they got it all together. Evasive action, return fire, and decoys turned the tide. Three klick fighters vanished in balls of flame before the others turned away. Two landers had been destroyed in the air. Another was forced down with casualties. The battle in the caverns was one-sided, with klicks taking a beating simply because the marines outnumbered them. It seemed that the klicks didn't seem to care about individual losses.

Seymoyr's restraints nearly snapped as *Stormbird* went into violent evasive action. The NCO next to Seymoyr wasn't so lucky. He flew out of his chair and smashed his face on one of the displays. Seymoyr called for help, and Star Force medics scurried in a few seconds later to take the man away.

"Suicide pass," said Captain Myklebust. "We got him, but he took a slice out of us."

He looked up to see her behind him, grasping the back of his chair. She was good at what she did. Her ship had been hit, and her face betrayed nothing at all.

"Any projections," Seymoyr asked, "as far as klick space action's concerned?"

The captain took a seat beside him. She pretended not to notice the NCO's blood on the smashed display before her.

"I've got all kinds of projections," she said, "from 'disaster' on up. The ones I believe in show that we win."

"Good. So do mine. No offense, Captain, but if our respective staffs have all they need from us, I'd like to get back down where I belong."

The captain looked straight ahead. "It might be best if you ran the show from up here. No offense, Colonel."

Colonel Seymoyr respected the captain, but he wasn't sure that he liked her. This definitely didn't improve his opinion of her at the moment. "I believe you stay on your bridge during the action, ma'am. That's where I'd be if I were in your place. Where would you be in mine?"

"I haven't changed my mind. I told you what I think."

"I appreciate it, Captain. Now, if you'll excuse me, I'll get back to my people, ma'am."

* * * * *

Kuhudag believed only somewhat in omens. Nonetheless, as he emerged from the tunnel back into the frigid Arist, he thought it was probably a good omen that seventeen of his twenty West Lodge Militia had come through their recent encounter with the klicks. Two of the other three were dead, and one could not walk without aid. All of the troops, both weren and human, were exhausted. Anyone who had been in close proximity with the klicks suffered either from nausea, fatigue, intense headaches, or various combinations of the three. No one could prove it at this point, but everyone was beginning to suspect that the strange fatigue was somehow a direct result of getting too close to the klicks.

Colonel Seymoyr and Burwab had arrived in time to catch the last phase of the fight as the klicks came down the corridor making their hellish sounds. Kuhudag, Grutok, and his weren had given them back some sounds they'd probably never heard before—full-throated weren war cries that seemed to distract the insectoids, if nothing else.

"There are likely more of them in there," Kuhudag told Seymoyr and Burwab. "These tunnels seem to have no ending, though I am sure that isn't so."

He turned to Seymoyr. "If it is of interest, sir, I would pass along what I have seen of these creatures. They rush in great hordes as if they are of one mind. I have not sensed a leader in any encounter. They count on strength and on the mass overwhelming their opponents."

Seymoyr nodded. "Very insightful, Worthy. Our people have been noting similar behavior."

"A swarm," Burwab put in, "is most successful in numbers, assuming that it is only a small force to be overcome, and if one has no sense of the loss of an individual."

"Such behavior is without honor," Gruotk put in, but one glance from Kuhudag and his chieftain reminded him of his place.

Seymoyr was no longer in armor, nor were the marines with him. He wore only battledress and a helmet thrown back over his shoulders, but he carried a charge rifle and pistol, several grenades, and comm gear. He had earned both Kuhudag's and Burwab's respect. They knew when a being was playing soldier and when he was truly a warrior like themselves.

"One of our cutters ate some debris from a klick ship," Seymoyr said. "I've got several dead back there. We had to leave 'em to get out of the air-fire."

"Our scouts will stand by your wounded until marines come," Burwab said.

Kuhudag nodded. "Of course. It will be done at once."

Seymoyr wasn't listening. He tilted his head, and Kuhudag saw that the helmet had wires running to the officer's ears and throat.

"That's a roger. Bearing 060 from you, 1500 meters."

"Are enemies approaching?" Kuhudag asked.

"One level down." Seymoyr twisted his lips as if he'd tasted something bad. "Exactly where we cleaned them out two hours ago. They're back again."

The colonel loped off toward the entry tunnel down. His heavily armed marines were already there. Kuhudag and Burwab pushed their way through the troops until they were at Seymoyr's side.

* * * * *

They waited in silence, but not for long. Their sensors suddenly went dead, showing only a scintillating cloud of static interference. In a moment, the all-too-familiar sounds began to rise from the ground. The marines were growing used to it, but it was always an eerie feeling to hear the buzzing and chittering of the aliens' jaws, the dry, rustling sound of their mandibles rubbing together as they crawled, hopped, and wriggled their way up through the dark tunnels.

Kuhudag wondered if the sounds were all body noises, or if the klicks had some way of talking to one another. There had to be some way, of course, but it might be through the senses of the mind—something similar to the talents of the mindwalkers. At any rate, it was nothing Kuhudag really wanted to know, nothing he cared to fully understand.

They waited. Kuhudag could hear the slow, almost imperceptible hiss of air from the marine's armor. One marine checked his weapon too loudly and earned a withering rebuke from the colonel. A sudden fatigue seized Kuhudag, lulling his senses. The enemy was near.

There! Kuhudag thought. The marines didn't yet see them in the dark recesses at the bottom of the rise. The marines' eyesight obviously did not approach the acuity of the weren hunter's eye.

A thin, jointed leg rose from behind a rock. Kuhudag aimed in one swift movement, his finger closing on the trigger. The bullet shattered the air with a sharp, clean crack. Before the creature could launch what it gripped in its claw-like limb, Kuhudag's slug sliced off the joint and sent it flying. The creature shrieked, the stump of its leg thrashing frantically about.

The marines flooded the tunnel with bright light and joined in at once, covering the bottom of the rise with a blinding flare of light. Rock, steam, and wet fragments of shattered klick bodies rose into the air as plasma trails and lasers shrieked down the tunnel.

There was a slight lull in the barrage as several marines had to reload. In that instant when only a few rifles were still firing, a dozen klicks broke through, firing their deadly blacklasers as they leapt and scuttled up the tunnel. Three marines went down. One writhed screaming on the floor, and the other two didn't move at all.

Kuhudag held his ground, dropped the rifle to his waist, and methodically did his best to blow the aliens apart. Grutok was beside him, firing in tandem with an armored marine. For what seemed like an eternity the klicks boiled up from the shadows of the tunnels below. The marines' weapons turned red with the heat of firing. A cloud of ammo smoke, steam, and scorched corpses filled the cavern, then, as quickly as it had started, it was done. There was nothing there but the lingering smoke and the enemy's ghastly funeral pyre.

"Keep a post here, Sergeant," Seymoyr said wearily to his top. "See if anything pops up. I want half the group with me." He turned and spoke into his comm again. "I'm going to meet Lieutenant Witzko on Low Niner. Worthy Kuhudag, Chief Burwab, come with me if you like or keep your unit on patrol in this area. I can't tell you where the bugs are going to pop up next. Thanks for the help."

"Honored Sir," Kuhudag said as he bowed. Burwab and Grutok repeated the gesture.

"He is a leader," Kuhudag said simply, giving the human the finest compliment he could.

"He is that," Burwab said. "In the meeting with the other humans, he showed no bias, only respect."

"I would like to have that pistol of his," Grutok said. "Did you see it? It was a copy of a Second Galactic War

Special, the one with the modified—"

"If you want to handle weapons, you may carry mine and Chief Burwab's for a while," Kuhudag said. "then you can pretend you are a heavily armed Concord Marine."

"I do not *want* to be a Concord Marine," Grutok protested. "My only wish is to be a weren warrior!"

"My point exactly," Kuhudag said.

Chapter Thirty

October 31, 2501

Seymoyr arrived at Witzko's point only moments after the lieutenant's scouts returned from the depths of Low Niner. The scouts looked grim, harried, and utterly exhausted. One of them was covered in nasty shreds of klick debris. There was no way to hose him down, and his comrades kept their distance. He might be a hero, but he was not a hero you cared to be around just yet.

The cavern was crowded. Seymoyr had taken a good look at the crude maps the lieutenant's men had managed to put together and decided that they were not perfect, but so far they presented the best overview available of the known "bug holes." On the strength of these maps, Seymoyr had cautiously called in assault forces from every unit in the caverns. Now the area was crowded with marines. They stood, sat, and leaned against the cold walls for fifty meters up three tunnelways. They were here because Colonel Seymoyr intended to bring the bugs up and exterminate them, all of them.

"They're not going to run any reinforcements in on you," Seymoyr assured Witzko and his other officers and NCOs. "Star Force and the help from Spes is keeping the klicks busy upstairs. We're taking bruises, but Captain Myklebust thinks we've got their number. We don't understand their tactics, but so far we've been able to overwhelm them simply by sheer force of numbers."

Witzko stood aside as Seymoyr passed out his assignments—who'd go when and where, with what kind of weapons, and how many. Witzko had Sergeant Kran, Master Sergeant Lavon, Captain McRae, plus the veterans of Recon Platoon and two more platoons attached from other units—one heavy weapons, one light assault.

After a final word with Seymoyr, Witzko led his own group off to the left, down a narrow, twisting lava tube that split from the main branch of Low Niner.

"Sergeant Kran goes with me," he told his crew. "We're Echo Two. We hit Low Twelve where it branches off. Captain McRae, with Sergeant Lavon, is Echo One. She'll take half the heavies and cut down parallel to us on Low Fourteen."

Witzko studied his troops. They all had maps. Everyone hoped that if their group and Seymoyr's other groups did everything just right, if the maps were perfect and the klicks were where they were supposed to be—and were willing to at least partially cooperate in their total extermination—the Concord Marines would come through this venture with flying colors. Still, there were too damned many variables and what-ifs for anyone's comfort.

Right, Witzko thought. A classic textbook assault, only no one could remember an assault where the textbooks had been involved. Somehow everything you learned turned upside down once you were actually in the hot zone. Marines who came through their first battle learned this lesson fast. Those who didn't learn this came home in body bags, assuming that their buddies could find enough parts to make the search worthwhile.

Irina Lavon had told Witzko and Kran about Belier's death. Both Witzko and the platoon sergeant muttered something appropriate but didn't discuss the matter. What was there to say that they hadn't said before? Kran spread the word to the rest of Recon, and they reacted much the same. No one liked Master Sergeant Jacques Belier—in fact, many of them hated him—but he was a marine. He was one of *theirs,* and he was dead. After that thought came the realization that said: if it happened to him, it could sure as hell happen to anyone. That was the thought everyone tried to put aside. It was one of the many thoughts that drew your attention from what might spring up in your path and make your grim prophecy come true.

Stosser was dead. Rizzo and some others had been wounded. Witzko tried to remember what Stosser had looked like. No image came to mind. It was a frightening thing when that happened, but it had happened before and it would likely happen again.

Witzko found himself wishing the Unholy Three were present with their contraption. The only problem was that neither their machine or the marines' gravometric sensors worked on the lower levels. The klicks had effectively hidden so many jamming devices and hidden them so well that no one even knew where the enemy was until they showed themselves. He supposed Chen, Lee, and the t'sa were crestfallen over the failure. He had an idea what they'd be thinking: now that they were no longer useful, the Concord Marines might forget that they *had* been helpful before. They had probably hoped their volunteer efforts would help their case when there was time to think about court-martials again.

Witzko wished *that* particular thought hadn't popped into his head. He and Irina Lavon weren't exactly in the clear, either. He couldn't help feeling a slight sense of relief when he learned Belier was dead. It didn't do a great deal of good, since the sergeant had already testified once. Captain Savant was still around, and he wasn't likely to let the whole thing go.

* * * * *

"I think I have something," Kran whispered, "not too close, but sound carries down here."

"Yeah," Witzko replied as he brought the platoon to a halt, "it does. Send out two pointers. Take the sensors we've got. Maybe we can tell where they're coming through."

Kran nodded. "Stephens, Milet, take point."

He signaled them down the tunnel. Witzko raised a hand to signal the rest of the group into position. Silence. Nothing, and this time, no warning at all—no chittering mandibles, no buzzes or whirs. There was the briefest instant—half a heartbeat only—of sudden fatigue and an intense pressure in his temple.

Witzko had time to yell out, "Down! They're here!"

Klicks dropped through the ceiling, countless numbers of them burning or blasting their way through solid rock. The tunnel was plunged into chaos, marines and klicks firing weapons, clinging to armor, clawing, scraping, everyone trying to kill the enemy without killing their friends.

In a moment it was over. This time the group was

lucky. Only four marines were dead. Several marines had cracked or shattered faceplates, exposing them to the nauseating stench of dead klicks and weapons smoke.

Witzko bent over his map. A chill crept up the back of his neck as he traced his finger from one tunnel to the next. Kran saw it at once.

"If they came from above us, they're bound to have a way straight on parallel to ours," Witzko said. "We didn't map them above us, but they are." He looked up at Kran. "If they keep going, they run right into Captain McRae and Lavon."

Kran jabbed a finger at the map. "Yeah, and they run into Seymoyr's bunch here. Hell, Lieutenant, we're not trapping them, they're luring us in for the kill."

Witzko let out a breath. There was no way to comm through the heavy rock and jamming signals. Even if they could, the klicks would probably sense it. They may have looked like bugs, but there was nothing wrong with their technical abilities.

"Get a couple of runners going," Witzko said. "Let's see if we can track down McRae and Seymoyr. We're going to have to do this the old-fashioned way."

Kran nodded. He pointed out two marines and sent them on their way.

Witzko motioned to Lance Corporal Julie Travino. "Make sure every sensor's in action. So far they haven't done a bit of good, but it's everything we've got."

"Yes, sir. If I may suggest, sir, maybe we can't hear them, but I think we can see them." She unclipped her light and flicked it toward the ceiling. "There's still dust falling around the breakthrough. Maybe we should keep someone on point with strong beam?"

"Good idea. Do it." Witzko glanced at his suit watch. "Kran, we're not going to wait. We've lost seven minutes already. I want to beat the other crews to the intercept point. If our runners don't get through, we'll have to beat McRae and Seymoyr's bunch. If the klicks have set us up, the captain and the colonel won't know what they're getting into—"

"What are you talking about, Lieutenant? What the hell do you think you're doing?"

Witzko's heart skipped a beat. Savant! He knew that voice before he turned around. He whipped the captain a salute, and Savant gave him a lazy return.

"Sir. I didn't know you were in the zone. I heard you were at Red Ridge."

Savant's scarred cheeks drew his mouth wide into its perpetual grin. "I was, Lieutenant Witzko. I got myself out of there. All that headquarters mess is not for me." He shook his head, squinting at the cavern floor that was covered with dead klicks.

"Nasty business, Lieutenant." He sniffed. "All right, what's the situation here?"

Captain Savant crossed his arms and leaned against the side of the cavern wall. Witzko could feel the seconds fleeing. He glanced at his watch and saw another half minute had gone by.

"Captain, excuse me, but we've got a situation here. If we don't get to our rendezvous point before the other groups arrive, we're going to lose some lives, sir. It's—"

"At ease, Lieutenant." Savant came close and almost touched helmets with Witzko. "Just give me the situation, Witzko. Think you can do that?"

Witzko gave it to him. Fast. Savant frowned, rubbed

one hand across his mouth, and squinted down the darkened corridor as he listened.

"The colonel's outfit and Captain McRae's. Who's the NCO with Seymoyr? Who's with McRae?"

Witzko looked straight ahead. "Master Sergeant Lavon, sir."

"Is that so?" The terrible grin seemed to grow until it threatened to split. "Your *friend.* Right, Lieutenant? We haven't had time to finish that business. You two make it out of here, and we will."

"Sir, time is—"

"Lieutenant Witzko!" Savant's face flushed red. "By God, boy, you would, wouldn't you? You'd risk every one of these marines to charge in and save your pretty little playmate! No, we won't, Witzko. That won't do. I will *not* put good soldiers on the line so you can play the hero."

He turned away from Witzko. "Sergeant Kran!"

"Sir!" Kran snapped to attention.

"I'll take command here, Sergeant. Lieutenant Witzko is relieved. The situation's clear. If this map is any damned good at all, we're walking right into a swarm of klicks. Am I reading this right or not? You tell me, Kran."

Kran swallowed hard. "The situation, sir—"

"Can you answer a question, soldier?"

"Sir. Yes, sir. There will likely be klicks up there. But the plan was—"

"At ease, Kran. Thank you. That's what I need to know. Now get these men deployed. I want it double-time back to command. If Seymoyr and McRae are in danger, the best thing we can do is get *real* help to them. Strength. Those runners I passed—"

"Were sent back to try and find the colonel and the captain, sir," Witzko said.

"Good. They'll do their job, and there'll be no problem."

"Sir. Did Colonel Seymoyr relieve me of my command?"

Savant scowled. "You're impertinent, Lieutenant. You've been in the service long enough to know better. I am company commander, in case you've forgotten, and I have *not* been relieved of that position, Witzko."

Savant turned to Kran. "Sergeant, lead these people back out of here. Now."

"Sir!" a strained woman's voice said behind them.

Savant jerked around. "What? Who the hell are you, soldier?"

"Lance Corporal Julie Travino, sir." Her voice was trembling, strained like Witzko had never heard it. Her hands were trembling. "I'd like to turn myself in for medical treatment, sir."

Savant blinked. "You what?"

"I think I'm-I'm . . . psyched out, sir." She blinked twice, shaking her head and swallowing. "I'm goin' nuts, sir. I just can't take this anymore! My finger's stuck on this trigger, and I can't get it off. I don't have any control of myself anymore, I just feel like something awful's going to happen any minute, sir."

Savant blanched. The bore of Travino's charge rifle was pointed roughly at his midsection. Travino's eyes seemed to roll behind her faceplate, and her body shook all over.

"Just take it easy," the captain said, sounding distinctly uneasy himself. "Let's put that weapon down, Corporal."

"Can't, sir. It's getting worse. I think I'm beginning to hallucinate, sir. You're not lookin' right to me. You're looking like one of those damned *bugs*!" She ended with a very convincing shriek.

Someone swallowed a laugh in the rear ranks. It was then that Witzko saw Savant realize what was happening. The captain glared at Kran, then at Witzko. "I will court-martial every one of you. I have all your names. *You*! You will wish you'd never been born, Witzko!"

"I wouldn't argue with you, sir. Right now, though, we've got work to do. Travino, lay off; you've made your point. Sergeant Kran, ask the captain politely if he'd care to give up his arms. If he does not, please take them from him. All right, double-time, double-time! Let's go!"

Chapter Thirty-One

OCTOBER 31, 2501

Irina Lavon stared at the carnage about her. Five marines were dead. One of them was Captain McRae. There was nothing left that even resembled a human being, just mangled remannts of scorched armor covered in blood and gore. They hadn't even seen the klick; the grenade had come whining out of the dark on its own power. Captain McRae had probably seen it, Irina thought—for half a second, maybe, before it exploded a centimeter from her chest. The captain had gone up front to talk to the point, Private Hangler. The rest of the group had been twenty meters back. Even then, the blast had thrown shrapnel at every suit. Hangler and the three marines who had been behind him were also dead. Two more had minor suit damage.

This time Lavon didn't cry. She was too hollow, too empty. There was nothing inside.

The tunnel groaned alarmingly, spilling a shower of rock from the ceiling.

"Move out, double-time!" she whispered harshly over her external speakers. "Romanov, take point!"

Even their internal comms were useless, meaning that there was at least one jamming device nearby.

Straining to see every shadow and peering down every side tunnel they passed, the marines left the bodies of their comrades and moved on.

She was certain they were fairly near the intercept point. They hadn't lost a lot of time. The deaths of the captain and the point hadn't really taken any time at all.

"Get two people back," she told Corporal Grammet, "thirty meters. They might try again from any angle."

Grammet gave her a peculiar look. Irina knew what she was thinking. She was right. If there were two marines far enough back, maybe the next flying grenade would take them out before it could hit the others. What do you want us to do, she wanted to tell the corporal, get up close and hold hands?

Trying to read the map in her head, she thought Colonel Seymoyr's group should be about thirty degrees left and fifty meters down. Lieutenant Witzko would be nearly straight ahead, coming at her from the left at an almost perfect ninety-degree angle. If she was right, all three units would meet at the intercept point, and they'd head down a tunnel that should be there, a tunnel that would lead them into a major horde of klicks. If all went as planned, they could hope to catch the bugs completely by surprise. Given the recent attack, however, Lavon was no longer counting on that.

The point marine ahead began to stumble, then she fell and rolled to her feet, racing back to the group with no care for stealth or silence. The ground began to tremble violently, bringing more rock down from the ceiling. Romanov had just made it back to the group when the floor of the tunnel ten meters in front of them erupted in a shower of molten rock.

Lavon motioned everyone back into a defensive

formation thirty meters down the tunnel, placing heavy weapons toward the front. The klick borer broached the surface in a cloud of fumes. It was an enormous, ugly machine that barely reflected the light from the marines' lamps. The device's blacklaser-tipped cutting element was four meters across. As Irina and her crew watched, it rose completely out of the hole until it began to bore into the ceiling. When it had completely blocked the tunnel, it stopped.

A hatch slid open, and klicks swarmed out of the vehicle. A seemingly endless tangling mass of jerking limbs and bulbous heads spewed from the hatch and charged straight for the marines. Blacklasers hissed across the cavern, lashing against the walls and the floor. Even though the klicks didn't bother to aim, simply spraying their deadly beams in every direction, two more marines went down almost immediately.

Just as the platoon was about the return fire, a blinding explosion rocked the borer from the inside. Stone and pieces of the machine shot through the cavern. Every marine was thrown to the ground. Many didn't move again, but Lavon suddenly realized that her comm was active again and was screaming in her ear.

"McRae, this is Seymoyr! McRae! You reading me, Captain?"

"I read you, sir!" Lavon shouted as she got to her feet and took cover behind a new pile of rubble. Half of an armored leg protruded from the rock. What she was seeing just registered in her mind when the platoon, not awaiting orders, returned fire on the klicks. She didn't stop them. It was hard to think. She felt so tired all of a sudden, and her head was pounding.

Her rifle was gone. She couldn't see it through all the

smoke and rubble. Deciding not to waste time looking for it, she drew her pistol as she struggled to make sense of Seymoyr's words.

"Lavon? Is that you? Where is the . . . the captain?"

"This is Lavon, sir," she replied. "Captain McRae's dead. We're up here with a bunch of klicks and a borer. They act like they've lost it. They're jerking around, shooting at everything in sight, and I'm afraid this whole damned tunnel is about to fall on us!"

Lavon thought she heard Seymoyr mutter something to himself. "Sorry about the captain, she was a—" static cut off his last words. A second later his voice came back in. ". . . those bugs aren't nuts, they're running from us. We're down a level, coming up on the tail of that borer and knocking 'em off before they can crawl up the hole. Witzko's to your right. We caught 'em, but . . . the way we figured. They're awake, alert, and mad as hell. You see any human types coming out of the woodwork, Sarge, it's us."

Lavon flinched as a stray blacklaser beam slagged off the wall a few centimeters above her head. "Sir, you and the lieutenant see any *marine* types up here with the bugs, we'd appreciate the same courtesy, sir!"

"You got it, Lavon. Take cover, if you've got it. Otherwise, keep down. Out."

Nice, she thought. Keep down? We might be buried under several tons of rock any second, and he says, "Keep down."

My God, Irina thought, I'm not here, I'm dreaming this. I'm in some demented soul's awful nightmare.

"Either that," she said aloud, "or I'm in the marines."

She rolled around the pile of rubble, aimed her pistol, and joined the fray.

* * * * *

Lieutenant Witzko's attack was purely unintentional. Seymoyr's voice suddenly blasted through the silence, and Witzko took his crew on a hard left turn, going exactly the wrong way according to plan. They were suddenly standing in front of more klicks than he'd ever imagined there could be, a horrible tangle of slashing limbs, the flash of compound eyes, the shriek of whirring mouths. Every one of the hideous beasts was clawing to get out of the tunnel ahead, climbing over one another in a twisted ladder of their own bodies, reaching for the hole in the cavern overhead. The hole was small, no larger than two of the klicks' own bodies. All of them wanted to go through at once, and more than one was crushed and tumbled back to the ground.

As Witzko watched, a giant borer clanked into sight from the shadows. The klicks were all over it at once; the borer reared up on its massive, spiked wheels and began to grind its way through the ceiling above. Rock shattered, tearing and shredding klick bodies too near the whirring head. The borer seemed to grip the edge of the hole it had enlarged and pull itself through. The klicks swarmed up its sides in countless numbers, clawing for the upper level in an attempt to get through the hole.

Witzko heard a roar that could not have come from the throats of the klick warriors. Seymoyr's forces exploded into the cavern just behind the fleeing klicks. Now it was clear why the klicks wanted out of there fast. Seymoyr's marines were firing point blank into the horde, lashing them with streams of white fire. The terrible weapons roared and the klicks blossomed into flame, their bodies bursting as their limbs melting away.

Witzko's marines didn't need the command to fire. They rushed the fleeing klicks, loosing every weapon they had. Still the klicks climbed, reaching for the haven above. The big bugs returned fire, killing many marines, but they were vastly outnumbered. The tunnel floor became a blackened, bubbling mass of organic matter.

A runner from Seymoyr's group ran up with instructions from the colonel. Witzko listened, then followed Seymoyr through a shadowy corner of the cavern and up a steep, narrow lava tube. A cleanup patrol was left behind, but the greater part of Seymoyr's group and Witzko's command hurried up to the next level.

They could hear the klicks before they reached the top. The heavy fatigue that had become a tell tale sign that the klicks were near seized upon all of them. The klicks who had survived were gathered about the borer, firing down the hole and shooting randomly about the cavern.

"Sergeant Lavon's back to your left," Seymoyr said through the comms. "Keep . . . fire out of there. McRae's dead. I . . . who else."

Witzko closed his eyes at the news, trying not to think about having drinks he'd shared with McRae, watching her laugh.

Witzko went to his knees beside Seymoyr, raised his weapon, and fired. Klicks fell away and died. Private Atanza suddenly appeared, firing her charge rifle as quickly as she could pull the trigger. The klicks were so thick in the tunnel that no one really had to aim. The heavy charge rounds ripped a klick open in four places just as it let fly with its blacklaser. The creature fell writhing to the floor, and its shot went high.

"Where's Kran? Have you seen him?" Witzko yelled. "What about the rest of our people?"

"That way." Atanza shouted, nodding down the tunnel but continuing to fire. Behind her faceplate, Atanza's eyes were red, and her armor looked as if she'd fallen down a cliff.

"Stay here," Witzko said. "I need to see him."

"Aye, sir." Atanza showed him a weary smile.

Witzko turned away. He felt the concussion on his back a nanosecond before he was slammed against the wall. When he turned, most of Atanza's right side was gone. Colonel Seymoyr blasted away at the klicks, but it seemed to be taking at least four hits from each charge weapon to finally put the bugs down. Two marines ran from cover and dragged Atanza's remains to safety.

The klicks kept coming, climbing over one another with desperate strength and fury, chattering and shrieking as they came, but fewer and fewer came as the cleanup marines in the tunnel below finished off the stragglers. The klicks kept coming until there were no more standing, until the last whirring mouth clacked shut. There weren't that many marines left, but their firepower was awesome.

* * * * *

Witzko stood, swaying on his feet and his head throbbing. He knew his ears would ring for days. His suit had a damaged joint. He punched his knee with an armored hand, watched the diagnostics show the damage, then gave it up and decided that a limp was fine for now.

He bent over a marine, reading the man's vital signs. The display described internal bleeding, several broken bones, and a punctured lung. The trauma pack in the marine's suit had done all it could. Witzko unclipped his own kit and punched in the command for massive doses of painkiller. The trooper could at least go out in peace.

When he stood, he found himself facing Jobal Kran.

"You're alive, huh?"

"I guess, Lieutenant, though I sure don't feel like it right now."

"You look like hell, Sergeant."

"Begging your pardon, you look worse, sir."

"That could be," Witzko said. He looked past the sergeant. "What about the others?"

"Twenty-nine dead, forty wounded, and four of those critical. That's as near as I can tell right now. I haven't gotten to Lavon's bunch yet."

Witzko nodded. He felt as if his head might fall off. "Get me what you can. The CO will want to know."

He walked toward Seymoyr's group, nodding toward his own marines, the remains of Recon Platoon. Some looked up, but some were asleep on their feet. He didn't see Captain Savant anywhere. No use worrying about that—trouble would come when it was ready, and there was no use hurrying it along.

For a long moment, he looked up toward the dark end of the tunnel at the group of marines gathered there. He knew who he was looking for. He wanted to see Irina Lavon, to know she was there, and to know she was all right, but the smoke from the firefight made the light from their lamps uncertain and deceptive. It was nearly impossible to see anything beyond a few meters. Everyone was a blur, an indistinct spectre. In his fatigued state, he feared that some of those spectres might be all too real.

"Lieutenant Witzko, over here." Witzko turned as Colonel Seymoyr spoke. Seymoyr was talking to an engineering sergeant from a company that he didn't know.

"Sergeant Rackler here's come up with something I think we ought to see," Seymoyr said. He glanced over his shoulder. "You seem to be the only other officer in the vicinity, so it'll just be us for now, Lieutenant. From what the sergeant tells me, I'd like to keep it that way for now."

* * * * *

Much later, Damion Witzko tried to remember exactly what he saw down there in the depths of Arist. The chamber itself was huge, at least a hundred meters long and half that tall. Strange, obviously alien machinery lay in shattered, often molten, heaps about the room, then there were the bodies.

Many were human—probably all that was left of the raiders who had been stirring up trouble among the weren and Red Ridgers. Some were weren, then there were the all-too-familiar corpses of the klicks littering the cavern floor. Aside from Witzko, Seymoyr, and Rackler, everything in the room was dead.

He'd seen enough death and dealt it out himself many times over during the past several hours that seeing more shouldn't have been a shock, but then there were the other bodies.

"The platoon that took this chamber found them," Rackler said in a rasping voice. "The damned things used some sort of dark plasma weapons that literally obliterated our armor. Nine marines died taking down these four bastards."

The things looked about two meters tall and were covered in what seemed to be armor but could have been part of the creature itself. Veins—or perhaps tubes—ran across the entire thing. Many of them had broken and leaked an acidic, green fluid that was beginning to corrode the surrounding rock. Bony plates and slightly serrated spikes covered the creatures' bodies, and their hands ended in sharp, bladelike claws, but none of this was what truly frightened and repulsed Witzko.

One of the things' helmets had been partially sheared away, probably by a marine's plasma gun. The same puslike gel eked from the broken cavity onto the floor. Rackler shone his light directly into the broken headpiece.

"What the flaming hell do you make of that, Colonel?" asked Rackler.

Staring out from the shattered helmet was a human, a man. His gaunt, starved features were frozen forever in a rictus of pain and terror. The sunken eyes and fiercely grinning lips made the corpse appear little more than a rotting skeleton covered in papery skin.

"Who else knows about this?" The Colonel sounded old and worn.

Rackler ran off a list of names that Witzko didn't hear. He could only stare in dumbfounded silence at the *thing* that lay before him. He couldn't imagine anything doing such a thing to another being.

"Witzko!" Seymoyr's sudden shout brought the lieutenant back to attention.

"Sir!"

"What do you make of this?"

"I—I don't know, sir. It's obviously no klick. I've never seen anything like it. I don't know *what* to think about it."

"That's good." Seymoyr looked Witzko directly in the eye. "You just keep it that way, Lieutenant. The same goes for you, Sergeant Rackler. If either of you breathe one word of this to anyone, I'll hang both your asses out an airlock just as soon as we make the next starfall. Am I clear?"

"Sir?" Witzko asked. Rackler stood wide-eyed, too stunned to speak.

"You heard me, Lieutenant. As of this moment, what you saw in here is something you never saw."

"Yes, sir," Witzko said after a moment of hesitation. "I understand."

"I'm having this chamber sealed until Intel can get here. I want four armed guards at the head of the entrace tunnel. They are to be given strict orders *not* to enter this chamber for any reason. They stay at the head of the tunnel and allow no one in. Anyone disobeying that order will go for a nice jog on the ice as soon as the sun is down. You both have your orders. See to it!"

Witzko walked back to his platoon alone. Seymoyr walked away with Rackler, who was speaking to the colonel in harsh whispers. He assigned the guards as ordered and wandered aimlessly through the carnage.

For the first time in several days—days that almost seemed like centuries, Damion Witzko had nothing to do, no one to lead, and no one to fight. It was the way it happened after a combat action. You were tired, hurt, beaten to a pulp, and too strung out to even think about getting anything but rest. He couldn't rest yet, so he walked, just to keep himself moving.

Don't even try to lie down or sleep, he told himself. You don't have the authority to make that decision. The Concord Marines would tell you when to stop.

Chapter Thirty-Two

October 31, 2501

It was a grim walk, even for warriors used to the sight and smell of death. Kuhudag walked with Colonel Seymoyr through the large cavern near the ruined entryway. The cavern was lit with large lamps, evenly placed in rows and dimmed to settings low enough to reflect the somber nature of the place.

Bodies were lined neatly in rows. Weren, Concord Marines, and Red Ridge volunteers were there together, one next to the other. There were no quarrels, no differences between them now. Kuhudag wondered if this was the only way such a thing could have ever been accomplished. It seemed it had always been the only solution between beings who were different from one another. Would it always be this way? He knew beings wiser than himself had long sought the answer to that. They were welcome to keep searching. For now Kuhudag was willing to accept the situation as it was.

One of the bodies was that of Paul Dimmock. No one could say where he had fought or where he had fallen. He didn't look like an enemy now. Kuhudag could find no hatred for the man in his heart nor any more understanding for this human than when he was alive.

It was Medlyna and Grutok who found him and took him to Burwab. Medlyna touched his arm gently. Grutok fought back tears and kept his back straight and his hands locked behind him in the proper warrior's stance for the honored dead. Kuhudag was proud. Grutok would be a fine warrior one day.

Kuhudag knelt and laid his hand on each of Burwab's tusks. It was a touch no warrior would have allowed this side of death. Now it was a gesture of the highest respect.

"He had much honor," Kuhudag said. "He was a good chief."

"It was my privilege to know him for a short while," Colonel Seymoyr said. "I share in your loss. I share your pride in your chief."

Kuhudag hid his surprise. Instead he leaned down and laid his fists on the marine's shoulders and said, "I fold my claws before a friend."

"You have honored me greatly," Seymoyr replied in common Weren, making only the smallest error in grammar.

* * * * *

Alexander Ohito and his daughter were waiting outside the cavern. The wind had picked up, and they both looked small—even for humans—as they huddled in their heavy wraps.

Christine Ohito cried openly when Kuhudag appeared, the cold breeze freezing the tears on her cheeks. Kuhudag and Grutok touched them both gently. Medlyna, who didn't know her but knew who she was, stepped up and put an arm around the doctor's shoulders, holding it lightly so the woman would not sag under the weight.

"I shall never forget your kindness and honor," Kuhudag told the young woman and her father. "I gain hope from your feelings. I will tell you what I have never said before, a thought that has never entered my mind until now: I no longer think there is entirely no chance of sharing Arist with humankind—not if there are others like yourselves."

"You will find that there are," Alexander said.

"You will see this," his daughter said. "You will see it, because I will show it to you."

"I believe you have begun to do that already," Kuhudag said.

"You have my thanks as well, Worthy Human," Grutok said. "If I am hunting near Red Ridge, would I be permitted to stop and speak to you?"

Kuhudag jabbed him in the ribs. "You forget yourself," he said. "You are not *supposed* to be hunting near Red Ridge, whelp."

Grutok looked pained. "No, Worthy, I believe I forgot."

"If you were," the young woman smiled, "it would be easily forgiven."

"Not by me," Kuhudag growled. "Honor is to be followed. That is our way."

"Come," Medlyna said, taking both Kuhudag and her son firmly by their arms. "These people are not weren. They are getting cold. Show courtesy by letting them go."

"This is true," Kuhudag said. "You are not weren, but you do not act entirely human, either."

"Why, thank you." Christine Ohito smiled. "What a nice thing to say."

"Yes, it is," Kuhudag said.

Medlyna rolled her eyes. "Come on, Kuhudag, I am not going to ask you again."

Chapter Thirty-Three

November 03, 2501

The sky over Arist was the same dreary gray as the stones of the cairns. Kuhudag smelled snow in the wind and knew the day would bring a major storm from the east. Both the human and weren dead had been given the appropriate rites two days before. Search parties would likely find more bodies in the days to come, but that was always the way. It was necessary for the living to honor the dead, but it was equally important to put the dead aside and go on with the business of living.

The names of newly discovered warriors could be honored and added to the plaques by the cairns. The weren of West Lodge and the humans of Red Ridge would see to that, and Kuhudag thought, after enough years, if the cold, howling winds of Arist don't wear the names away, those who came by will not be able to tell who was weren and who was human. If such a time came, then the dead would have even more honor to their names.

Shubud and two human priests were finishing their rituals of consecration. Earlier Alexander Ohito and his daughter had been there, and Kuhudag had spoken to them again. He was pleased to see them there. Many among both weren and human were already saying that Kuhudag and Alexander Ohito were the two most powerful civilians on Arist. Even the small garrison of Concord Marines that Colonel Seymoyr had left on the planet recognized them both by sight and respected their authority.

Kuhudag kicked a stray stone aside and ducked his head inside his hood. The wind had a bite to it that he could not remember feeling in many days.

Much had occurred. No matter what happened now, the life he'd lived before was gone. If the weren of West Lodge did not recover from their madness and carried through with their threat of making him Council Chief, he would be something that he had never dreamed of before. He would have real power and a real need to be friends with Ohito. Only a few days before he could not have imagined that he would actually welcome the chance for such a relationship. Ohito and his daughter might still be the servants of VoidCorp, but their feeling for other beings was a far cry from that of Paul Dimmock and his kind.

Kuhudag knew he would miss Colonel Seymoyr. The man was human, but he was a warrior as well. The other, the female Master Sergeant, Lavon—now there was a person of great honor, one any weren would be proud to have by his side in battle.

As the sky began to lighten, his thoughts turned again to the battle he had fought deep within the caverns below Arist. He had never mentioned the fight to Colonel Seymoyr, and he had sworn the weren warriors with him to silence. It was a thing of honor they had done, but it was not a thing to share with a human. Even though they had fought together against the klick creatures, Kuhudag knew that humans—even those such as Seymoyr and Ohito—still looked upon the weren as alien. Alien, even to a well-meaning human, still meant *not human*. To be fair, his own folk felt much the same. Others, outsiders, were *not weren*. That was simply the way things were.

Kuhudag saw a long road before him, but it was no longer one without hope.

* * * * *

Several hours later, the light of Hammer's Star was a cold and ashen sphere behind the oncoming storm. Kuhudag faced the wind, letting the icy pellets sting his face. On a hill behind the cairns, waiting for him, were Medlyna and Grutok. He had become greatly attached to the young whelp, though he vowed he would never let that affection get out of hand, for it would spoil the young weren rotten. Give the lad a pace, and he would surely stretch it into a kilometer.

Medlyna was another matter entirely. She had made it clear through her bold—but always mannerly—ways that a deeper, more intimate relationship was not only possible but would be welcomed on her part. That, Kuhudag thought, would be a desirable path to pursue. Of course, such an affiliation would surely be good for Grutok, and Kuhudag felt obliged to do all he could for the welfare of such a fine and promising youth.

A sonic boom rolled across the cold plains of Arist. Though Kuhudag could not see past the dark barrier of clouds, he turned his face to the sky. The Concord Marines had been lifting off the planet all morning, and this was likely the last of their landers. When he was certain no one was watching, he lifted his great arm in a reasonable imitation of the marine salute. Even if someone saw him, he reasoned, they would likely think he was merely scratching his head. There could be no harm in that.

Chapter Thirty-Four

NOVEMBER 03, 2501

"With all due respect, Colonel Seymoyr, I must assert my right to make this charge. I refer to Article Nineteen of the Rules and Regulations of the Galactic Concord Marines, which states—"

"Captain Savant, with all due respect, don't quote marine regulations to *me*. I know them backward and forward, sir, and I am well aware of the fact that you have the right to make additional charges against Lieutenant Witzko."

Colonel Seymoyr took a calming breath. It was important to choose your words carefully in such a situation. In a court-martial, anyone had the right to throw your words back in your face. If those words were even marginally prejudicial . . .

"What I am trying to say, Captain, is that it is highly unusual for a company commander to bring charges against an entire platoon. It is not simply disobedience and threatening behavior you note here—specifically against First Lieutenant Damion Witzko and Lance Corporal Julie Travino—but the *entire roster* of the marines present at this event."

"Yes, sir." Savant nodded smugly. "That's exactly

what I am doing, sir. They are all guilty, and they are all charged. Not all of them took an active part in the mutiny led by Lieutenant Witzko, but neither did any of them rise to object to the lieutenant's and the corporal's criminal actions. That comes under the regulations too. Anyone who does not attempt to thwart an illegal—"

"Yes, I know, I know."

Seymoyr waved him off and pretended to study the file before him. It was hard to look at Captain Savant for very long. The man couldn't help it, but that wound that had curled the captain's lips into a permanent smile was damned distracting. Why the man hadn't had the wound surgically corrected was beyond Seymoyr.

"You are aware, Captain, that differing opinions of the incident in the cavern have been submitted. Members of the platoon—*all* of them, incidentally—feel that your decision to change Lieutenant Witzko's orders and not proceed to the rendezvous point were not in the best interests of the service."

"That is their opinion," blurted Captain Savant, "and the opinion of a *renegade* officer who is, I remind you, also up on charges of gross immorality. The testimony is tainted. *Tainted*, sir!"

Seymoyr was startled by Savant's outburst. The man was shaking all over, and his face was flushed red. He looked, with his terrible smile, like a demon from some nightmare.

"As you say," Seymoyr replied calmly, "you have every right to make these charges. It's going to affect—and likely ruin, I might add—the careers of quite a few NCOs and enlisted personnel."

"And Lieutenant Witzko's."

"Yes, of course, and Lieutenant Witzko's."

Seymoyr was getting a splitting headache, but he knew there was no way out of this mess. In his own mind, he knew Savant had made the wrong decision in the cavern. He also knew that the platoon had, without a doubt, mutinied to a man and that Lieutenant Witzko had let it happen. Witzko had done the right thing as far as duty was concerned, but a court-martial could hardly condone his behavior or that of any of his platoon. They were all going to come out of this smeared. If the morals charge didn't bring Witzko down, the mutiny case would. He might be able to stay in the marines, but he'd never gain rank with a record like that.

"This is only a suggestion, Captain," Seymoyr said, knowing as he spoke that he was on dangerous ground, "as I say, only something for you to consider. The mutiny charge is strong enough, I'm sure you know that. With the morals charge on top of it . . ."

Savant straightened. He stared at the colonel through narrowed eyes. "What are you suggesting, sir? I'm afraid I don't understand."

"I'm not suggesting anything. I'm giving you something to think about. The morals charge is something that is bad for the overall morale of the Corps, as I see it. I think you know what I mean, Captain."

"Sir, I *don't* think I see at all."

"Well, then listen, Captain, and maybe you will."

Seymoyr tried to swallow his irritation, but it was not an easy task. Damn, the man was stubborn. He was determined to have his way, no matter who it brought down, including Seymoyr thought, me. I hate to be selfish about it, but all this mess isn't going to do much for my career, either.

"Are you suggesting, sir—"

"Yes, Captain Savant, if you want it on the table, I am. The charge of immorality between the lieutenant and his sergeant is based on testimony given by Master Sergeant Jacques Belier, the *late* Sergeant Belier, as a matter of fact."

"Whose testimony against these two is already a matter of record. I have taken the liberty of looking it up, sir. The sworn testimony of a deceased complainant has the same strength as that of a living witness, sir."

"I know that, Captain—"

"Then, sir, if you will not take offense, may I say I am wasting your valuable time, sir? I stand by my charges, *both* of them. I will see justice done, Colonel. I will see the guilty punished. If I may say so, sir, you are new to this command. What has happened is no reflection on your actions. I will only say, sir, if there was more discipline in this battalion, more—"

"Captain Savant!" Seymoyr stood and slammed his hands on his desk. "That will be *all*. Your actions will be filed as you have requested. As *you* say, I believe you are wasting *my* time. You are dismissed, Captain!"

"Sir!" Savant saluted smartly, turned on his heel, and marched out the door.

Seymoyr sat back. He closed his eyes and practiced the breathing exercises he had learned as a cadet. He was suddenly very tired. He had won a victory of sorts, stopped a small war, and driven off a horde of klicks. He had also lost marines, weren warriors, and the Red Ridgers who had fought by their side. None of it had been easy. They had defeated the klicks only because there had been more marines than bugs. For every klick killed, the number-crunchers were estimating that three marines had died.

Now Seymoyr had this: the very probable ruination of a number of careers. He couldn't say Witzko had been right in his relationship with Sergeant Lavon, but he had sure as hell had been right in doing what he thought best for his platoon and the other units he had been ordered to meet. That, no matter what anybody said, was the correct and courageous thing to do. Seymoyr also knew that he could no more stop what was going to happen to Lieutenant Witzko, Sergeant Lavon, and the rest of the platoon than he could flap his wings and fly. This thing was going to happen, and—

"Sir?"

Seymoyr sat up straight. Platoon Sergeant Jobal Kran was standing at attention at his door.

"Yes, Sergeant, is this important? I'm a little busy right now."

"Yes, sir. I believe it is, sir."

"Well?"

Kran took three steps forward and came to attention. With his right hand he whipped out a white envelope from under his jacket and handed it to the colonel.

"It's addressed to you, sir. It's from Master Sergeant Jacques Belier. I found it while gathering up the last of the sergeant's personal belongings."

"Oh? I guess I'd better have a look at it, then." Colonel Seymoyr took the envelope and drew out a single sheet of paper. It began:

Sir:

In the event that something should happen to me on this combat mission . . .

* * * * *

"Come in," Witzko said. "It's open." He set down the cup of bad coffee he was drinking and didn't bother to look up.

"I hope you'll excuse the intrusion, sir. I know it's quite improper for an NCO to enter officer country without a valid reason, but I thought I'd take the chance."

Witzko stared at Irina Lavon. As ever, she looked fine in her newly pressed dress blues, but her broad smile was more than irritating. As far as Witzko was concerned, there was very little aboard *Stormbird* to smile about. He wondered if she'd been drinking. If she had, he wouldn't blame her, but he saw no reason for her to share her cheery self in here.

"I'm always glad to see you, Sergeant, but you're right. Under the circumstances, this is not a good idea."

"Oh, it really is, though, Lieutenant, under the circumstances."

Witzko frowned. "Maybe you'd better—"

"All right, sir, I will. I just came from meeting with Sergeant Kran, who seems to know everything that I don't. He knows the Unholy Three aren't going to hang—or at least anytime soon. They're being transferred to the Concord Investigative Bureau as soon as we get home."

"Why does that not surprise me?" Witzko asked wearily.

"Yes, sir. Anyway, Kran also told me that we're all having steak tonight, and you and I are off the hook. Did I forget that? It seems Master Sergeant Belier had a little more conscience than we gave him credit for. Frankly, I'm not sure conscience had anything to do with it. I think he decided that he'd gotten in way over his head and that he couldn't trust Captain Savant all that much. Good thinking on his part. If he'd made it back from

Arist, he'd have the dated letter to show the colonel—"

"Letter?" Witzko cut her off. "What letter?"

"Well, sir," she said with a rather mischievious grin, "it seems that Belier's heart was in the right place after all. In the letter he completely retracted all accusations against us and said that Captain Savant had forced him into lying about us. You've got to give the old guy credit: he never stopped thinking, right to the last."

"My God." Witzko slid back onto his bunk. "Dropping all this on me at once, Sergeant . . . I don't know if I can handle it."

Irina stepped into the room, shut and locked the door behind her, and looked Witzko straight in the eye. "Well, see if you can handle this, Lieutenant, and I'm going to get it out before I lose my nerve." Was there a slight tremble in her voice? "You and I are innocent as charged. We are not immoral. Nothing ever happened between us. If it did, we'd both be in a lot of trouble, wouldn't we?"

"Yes, Sergeant, we would."

"An awful lot of trouble. A lieutenant and his master sergeant. It would be one hell of a mess."

Witzko looked at her. "I've thought about what a mess it would be, Sergeant. Many times."

Irina grinned. "You have, sir? Imagine that."

"What do you think we should do, Sergeant?"

"You're the platoon leader, sir. What do you think?"

"I think we are definitely in trouble, Sergeant."

"Is that a promise, sir?"

Witzko frowned. "I'm a little surprised at you, Irina Lavon. How can you doubt an officer's word?"

Epilogue

November 03, 2501

It wasn't that Seymoyr *couldn't* tell anyone. He had to do that. The bigger question was, *who*? Secrets, even secrets like this, had a way of getting out, no matter how careful you tried to be. He'd thought he'd sufficiently scared anyone who knew about the situation into a frightened silence. Concord Intelligence was taking care of the rest. Maybe that's why Seymoyr had chosen to take Witzko into his confidence. The colonel was Concord all the way, but he wasn't so stupid that he trusted everyone in Intelligence. It never hurt to cover your ass.

These weren't exactly ordinary secrets. These were secrets that could stir up a nest of hornets and spread panic through the entire Concord.

Stability and balance, Seymoyr knew, were the factors that held the worlds together. Take that away, and everything went haywire. It had happened before. Chaos came in through the door, twice, and they had named that chaos Galactic Wars I and II.

Now beside the concern over externals such as the klicks, it looked as if there was a new baddie out there waiting to bite the Concord on the ass. Something from somewhere had left its mark in that cavern under Arist, and whoever they were and wherever they'd come from, they were far more alien than anyone had imagined, or were they? Whoever—or whatever—had been in that damned suit certainly had looked human.

There was the matter of the little container that they'd picked up farther out in the system. The Star Force engineers had finally managed to crack the thing. All they'd found inside were what appeared to be data crystals of some sort, but from an obviously external technology. The Star Forcers hadn't been able to make head nor tail of the stuff, but as soon as Intelligence had gotten wind of it, they had swarmed in and confiscated everything. That in itself was enough to make Seymoyr nervous, but Myklebust had told him something more. Along with the data crystals had been several holographic star and system charts—detailed charts of not only Hammer's Star, but of several other Verge systems and what appeared to be a rough map of the Stellar Ring.

That little matter was very likely as chilling as what he'd discovered under Arist. Sergeant Rackler—a CIB operative, though only Seymoyr knew this—had taken a bio-sample from one of those corpses. DNA analysis had confirmed that at least one of the bodies inside those pus-filled suits was not only human, but a clone. Clones were common among the Borealins, and the Borealins had established several colonies on Spes, colonies like Silver Bell.

What would the Concord do with this one once it dropped into their laps? How long, Seymoyr wondered, would it stay a secret after that?

The End

Glossary

Aegis - A G2 yellow star. The metropolitan center of the Verge.

Alaagh - A weren hunter of West Lodge.

AP grenade - short for "armor-piercing" grenade. An explosive device that creates a shaped-charge blast on contact.

Arist - The third and largest of Platon's moons. Despite its frigid temperature and thin atmosphere, it is the only habitable world of the Hammer's Star system other than Spes.

Atanza, Nadya - A private first class of the Concord Marines.

AU - short for astronomical unit. 150 million km.

Austrin-Ontis Unlimited - A corporate stellar nation that is best known as the strongest arms dealer in the Stellar Ring. Most Austrin-Ontis citizens view themselves as strong individualists with a deep sense of altruism.

astronomical unit - 150 million km.

Babel - The capital and urban center of the Tendril system.

Barker, John - A corporal of the Concord Marines.

Belier, Jacques - A master sergeant of the Concord Marines.

Biggert - A Concord Marine.

Bluefall - Capital Planet of the Aegis system. Ruled by the Regency of Bluefall government.

Borealis Republic - A stellar nation whose citizens best educated in known space.

Burwab - Chief of the Okabi weren at West Lodge.

CDC - Concord Defense Corps.

cerametal - An extremely strong alloy made from laminated ceramics and lightweight metals.

charge weapon - A firearm in which an electric firing pin ignites a chemical explosive into a white-hot plasma propellant, thus expelling a cerametallic slug at extremely high velocity.

Chen, Ajayla - A sergeant of the Concord Marines.

chuurkhna - A deadly melee weapon of ancient weren design. It looks like a huge, four-pronged battle axe with a haft about a meter and a half long. Its blade is large and heavy, intended for chopping rather than thrusting.

CIB - short for the Concord Investigative Bureau.

CM - short for cerametal.

Concord, the - see "Galactic Concord."

Concord Defense Corps - The principal branch of the Concord military.

Concord Invesitgative Bureau - The intelligence-gathering arm of the Galactic Concord, often called "the Silent Bureau" because of its many clandestine activities.

cutter - A small, lightly armed military patrol craft.

Dabur, Kyle - A lieutenant commander of Star Force.

damool - A carniverous mammal native to Arist.

darut-eg iermarkhta - A weren phrase meaning, "Where is the honor in such a criminal?"

Deihudt - A Concord Marine.

Deirta - A guard at the Red Ridge prison facility.

Dimmock, Paul - Leader of the VoidCorp construction workers on Arist.

Diomedes - A Thuldan cruiser currently assigned to the Aegis system.

dreadnought - A large space vessel designed for strictly military purposes. Most are about 500 to 1,000 meters long and carry 1,000 to 2,000 crew members.

driveship - Any space vessel that is equipped with a stardrive.

drivespace - The dimension into which starships enter through use of the stardrive. In this dimension gravity works on a quantum level, thus enabling movement of a ship from one point in space to another in 121 hours.

durasteel - Steel that has been strengthened at the molecular level.

flapper - A derogatory term for sesheyans.

Fortinbras - A class of starship designed by StarMech.

Fygora - A weren of West Lodge.

Galactic Concord - The thirteenth stellar nation. Formed by the Treaty of Concord, the Concord is seen as the arbiter of affairs for the stellar nations and has a substantial presence in the Verge.

Goodson - A Concord Marine.

Grammet - A lance corporal of the Concord Marines.

gravity induction - A process whereby a cyclotron accelerates particles to near-light speeds, thereby creating gravitons between the particle and the surrounding mass. This process can be adjusted and redirected, thus allowing the force of gravity to be overcome. Most starships use a gravity induction engine for inner system travel.

gravometric - of or relating to the force of gravity.

Grecko - A Concord Marine.

Grusin - A Concord Marine.

Grutok - A weren of West Lodge; son of Medlyna.

Gumad Mountains - A mountain range of Arist.

Guthru - A mountain near West Lodge.

Hale, Christopher - Commander-in-chief of the Regency government on Bluefall.

Hale Regency - The militocratic government of Bluefall headed by Christopher Hale.

Hammel - A lieutenant commander of Star Force.

Hammer's Star - A yellow G5 star. The outermost Concord outpost in the Verge.

Handerlast - Director of the Red Ridge Port Authority.

Hangler - A private first class of the Concord Marines.

Hardy - A Concord Marine.

Hatire Community - A theocratic stellar nation. Also the name of the anti-technology religion.

Hatire Faith - A religion that worships the Cosimir, an alien deity that the Hatire have adopted as their own. Hatire have a passionate dislike of advanced technology, especially the alteration of the human body through cybernetic implants.

holocam - A camera that records and reproduces holographic images.

holocomm - A holographic communication.

holodisplay - The display of a holocomm that can be viewed either one, two, or three dimensionally.

Hootak - The first and greatest Orlamu philosopher among the weren.

Hrenich - A VOIDCORP construction worker on Arist.

IF-3 11 mm charge rifle - A light, rugged, and long-ranged charge rifle. The standard infantry weapon of the Concord Defense Corps and the Concord Marines.

Ikido - A lieutenant commander of Star Force.

infrared scanner - Any sensor device designed to pick up and analyze heat signatures.

IR - short for infrared

Iron Oath - A binding oath among traditional weren.

Karlo - A Concord Marine.

Kasuga - A private first class of the Concord Marines.

Killberry tea - A tea brewed from the killberry plant. Often used as a mild pain reliever.

klick - A large, hostile, arachnid-like external species of uknown origins. Few facts are known about the klicks, though they are the prime suspects for the destruction of the Silver Bell colony.

Kran, Jobal - A platoon sergeant of the Concord Marines.

Kuhudag - A weren of Arist; chief hunter and scout of West Lodge.

lanth cell - The standard lanthanide battery used to power most small electronic equipment and firearms.

Lasanti - A Concord Marine.

Lavon, Irina - A master sergeant of the Concord Marines.

Lee, Hurik - A corporal of the Concord Marines.

Leeman - A Concord Marine.

Long Silence - The period of time from 2375 to 2496 when the stellar nations lost contact with the Verge due to the Second Galactic War.

Lucennes - A corporal of the Concord Marines.

MacKenzie, Barbara - A corporal of the Concord Marines.

Magtan - A weren warrior of West Lodge.

mass weapon - A weapon that fires a ripple of intense gravity waves, striking its target like a massive physical blow.

mass reactor - The primary power source of a stardrive. The reactor collects, stores, and processes dark matter, thus producing massive amounts of energy.

McRae, Kira - A captain of the Concord Marines.

MedCorps - The medical section of the Concord Marines.

Medlyna - A female weren of West Lodge.

Milet - A Concord Marine.

mindwalker - A term used to describe any being proficient with psionic powers.

Moore's shark - A carniverous fish measuring 2 to 3 meters long that is native to Bluefall. Although it is not sentient and only marginally intelligent, the Moore's shark possesses innate psionic abilites to locate and subdue its prey, making it one of the most feared creatures in the ocean.

Morrek - A Concord Marine.

Morton - A Concord Marine.

Myklebust, Ela - A captain of Star Force. Commanding Officer of *Stormbird*.

mythleaf - A brand of Borealin tea.

Ogata - A Concord Marine.

Ohito, Alexander - One of the VoidCorp leaders in Red Ridge.

Ohito, Christine - A doctor in Red Ridge.

Okabi - The ruling weren tribe at West Lodge.

Olafson - A Concord Marine.

Opaaz - A famed prince of weren folklore.

Orlamism - A religion based upon the belief that drivespace is true reality, or as the Orlamu call it, "the Divine Unconscious." Orlamu believe that Ultimate Truth will be received by communing with the Divine Unconscious.

Orlamu - A follower of Orlamism.

Orlamu Theocracy - A theocratic stellar nation founded upon the principles of the Orlamu faith.

Oshima - A Concord Marine.

Pelletin - A major of the Concord Marines.

Phelan - A Concord Marine.

Planke - A corporal of the Concord Marines.

Platon - An inhospitable gas giant of the Hammer's Star system.

Price - A sergeant of the Concord Marines.

quantum minigun - Also known as a particle or neutron gun, this weapon produces beams of heavy, fast-moving subatomic particles that slag anything they hit.

raasha - A large fish native to Arist.

Raastad, Adrianus - Vice Admiral of Star Force.

Rackler - A sergeant of the Concord Marines.

Rakke - An large asteroid in the Vicek Belt. The site of an intense battle between Concord forces and klicks in February 2501.

Ramirez, Martin - A Concord Marine.

Red Ridge - A large human settlement on Arist.

Reekmon - A Concord Marine.

Reeman - A sergeant of the Concord Marines.

Regency - see “Hale Regency.”

remote-piloted vehicle - Any small vehicle with a grav induction engine. They are generally equipped with various sensors and used for aerial surveillance by the Concord military.

Revealer - A Concord dreadnought.

Revik - The innermost asteroid belt of the Hammer’s Star system.

Rewall - A private first class of the Concord Marines.

Romanov - A private first class of the Concord Marines.

RPV - short for remote-piloted vehicle.

Russel - A Concord Marine.

sabot weapon - A firearm that uses electromagnetic pulses to accelerate a discarding-rocket slug at hypersonic speeds.

Savant, Woodlaw - A captain of the Concord Marines.

sesheyan - A species native to Sheya that has been subjugated by VOIDCORP. However, a substantial population of "free sesheyans" lives on Grith in the Corrivale system. Most sesheyans are about 1.7 meters tall and have two leathery wings that span between 2.5-4 meters. Sesheyans are bipedal sentients with a long, bulbous head, large ears, and eight light-sensitive eyes.

Seymoyr, Wilm - A lieutenant colonel of the Concord Marines.

Shubud - The senior Orlamu priest at West Lodge.

Silence, the - see the Long Silence.

Sill - A major of the Concord Marines.

Silver Bell - A Borealin colony on Spes that was completely annihilated by unknown forces in 2489 but has since been partially rebuilt.

Skaminine 92 - A mild soporific often used to treat drivespace sickness.

Skorbo - An admiral of Star Force.

"sniffer" mine - Bio-sensitive robots programmed to detect a heat signature, air fluctuations indicating movement, or key organic compunds. The "sniffer" homes in on its target and delivers a large-yield explosive.

spaceship - Any craft intended for in-system or planetary travel.

spider leech - A small, venomous leech native to Bluefall.

Spes - The innermost planet of the Hammer's Star system. Aside from Arist, it is the only habitable planet in the system and currently boasts a population of over 300,000 sentients.

stardrive - The standard starship engine that combines a gravity induction coil and a mass reactor to open a temporary singularity in space and thus allow interstellar travel. All stardrive jumps take 121 hours, no matter the distance.

starfall - The term used to describe a ship entering drivespace.

Star Force - The naval branch of the Concord military.

StarMech Collective - A stellar nation famed for its high technology.

starrise - The term used to describe a ship leaving drivespace.

starship - Any craft with a stardrive intended for interstellar travel.

stellar nation - Any of the thirteen independent nations of the Stellar Ring. They are: Austrin-Ontis Unlimited, the Borealis Republic, the Hatire Community, Insight, the Nariac Domain, the Orion League, the Orlamu Theocracy, the Rigunmor Star Consortium, the StarMech Collective, the Thuldan Empire, the Union of Sol, VoidCorp, and the Galactic Concord.

Stellar Ring - The systems that make up the thirteen stellar nations, the center of which is Sol.

Stephens - A Concord Marine.

Sternwitz - A Concord Marine.

Stormbird - A *Fortinbras* class heavy transport cruiser that has been refit for service in Star Force.

Stosser - A Concord Marine.

Tendril - An F1 blue star.

Thuldan Empire - A militaristic, fiercely patriotic stellar nation that considers the unity of humanity under the Thuldan banner to be its manifest destiny.

Toorhat One Tusk - A weren warrior of West Lodge.

Tragger, Linda - A sergeant of the Concord Marines.

Travino, Julie - A lance corporal of the Concord Marines.

Treaty of Concord, the - The Treaty that ended the Second Galactic War and formed the Galactic Concord.

Treece - A VoidCorp construction worker on Arist.

Treko - A sergeant of the Concord Marines.

Tremont, Shawn - A Concord Marine.

Triman - A Concord Marine.

t'sa - A sentient species native to the T'sa Cluster in the Stellar Ring. Most t'sa stand about 1.4 meters tall. Covered in thick, interlocking scales and possessing a bony head-ridge, t'sa look similar to a large, bipedal Solar reptile.

Ulaak - A great hunter of weren folklore.

Verge, the - The frontier region of space originally colonized by the stellar nations.

Vicek - The outermost asteroid belt of the Hammer's Star system.

Vigor - A cutter assigned to *Stormbird.*

VoidCorp - A corporate stellar nation. Citizens are referred to as Employees, and all have an assigned number.

weren - A sentient species native to the planet Kurg. Most weren stand well over 2 meters, are covered in thick fur, and have sharp claws. Male weren have large tusks protruding from the bottom jaw.

West Lodge - A weren settlement on Arist.

Witzko, Damion Lee - A first lieutenant of the Concord Marines.

yellowknife tree - A tree native to Bluefall. The leaves possess large, very sharp leaves of a brilliant yellow-gold hue.

On the Verge

Roland J. Green

Danger and intrigue explode in the Verge as Arist, a frozen world on the borders of known space, erupts into a war between weren and human colonists. When Concord Marines charge in to prevent the conflict from escalating off-world, but they soon discover that even darker forces are at work on Arist.

Starfall

Edited by Martin H. Greenberg

Contributors include Diane Duane, Kristine Katherine Rusch, Robert Silverberg and Karen Haber, Dean Wesley Smith, and Michael A. Stackpole. A collection of short stories detailing the adventure, the mystery, and the unending wonder in the Verge!

Available April 1999.

Zero Point

Richard Baker

Peter Sokolov, a bounty hunter and cybernetic killer for hire, is caught up in a deadly struggle for power and supremacy in the black abyss between the stars.

Available June 1999.